Timeless Wisdom

Timeless Wisdom

Maulana Wahiduddin Khan

Compiled and edited by
Raamish Siddiqui

PRABHAT
PRAKASHAN

Published by
PRABHAT PRAKASHAN PVT. LTD.
4/19 Asaf Ali Road,
New Delhi-110 002 (INDIA)
e-mail: prabhatbooks@gmail.com

ISBN 978-93-5322-415-8
TIMELESS WISDOM
by Maulana Wahiduddin Khan

Edition
2025

Price
₹ 500.00 (Rupees Five Hundred only)

Printed at
Yash Printographics, Noida

Introduction

Modern world is bestowed with boundless possibilities to turn a sea of potential opportunities into a reality! The world for the first time in the last century became truly global and human civilisation made such unprecedented progress that had never been witnessed by the human race before!

The advent of ideals like peace, democracy, freedom, liberty, technology, communication and industrialisation became the harbinger of renaissance. History, on the shoulders of these ideals embarked on a never-before-like journey to usher in modern civilisation. This progress came about in the last two hundred years. But during this time, there is one community that has seen a significant downturn in its situation and has failed to constructively create a future for themselves, and that is, *Muslims*.

Worldwide, *Muslims* succumbed to negative sentiments and developed a psyche of being victimised. This paranoia was further fuelled by the misinterpretation of *Islamic* texts by the so-called clerics. The rapid spread of this erroneous interpretation amongst masses rendered them incapable of developing a constructive mindset.

The self-proclaimed Muslim leaders not only lacked knowledge about *Islam*, but also their lack of vision alienated the Muslim community from the modern world.

Machines come with an operating manual but there exists no such manual for leading a human life. Therefore having right guidance in life is of paramount importance. A mentor ensures that one reflects, course corrects and continues the journey on the right path.

The choice of a guide or a mentor should not be determined by an individual's popularity or the material stature. A guide is one who is like a beacon of light in darkness. Guidance begins from our formative years and the first guide in a child's life is parents. Parents instil values, morality and a sense of good and evil in their children. They become the first role models for their children. The second stage of guidance is received from our teachers. A true teacher is one who is able to harness the potential of the child and encourage him/her to realise it.

In the same way, guidance is required by any community for it to develop and flourish. Unfortunately, *Muslims*, as a result of being misguided have derailed and become inimical towards their neighbouring societies. The present-day Muslim youth has either become disillusioned or have succumbed to the misinterpretation of Islam. They have not been able to find the right path to self-discovery and realisation.

My case was no different. Having finished my studies, I too was at crossroads, disillusioned by questionable events, the myriad of interpretations and the jungle of misconceptions that surrounded me.

I saw the so-called co-religionists perpetrating killings and violence around the world. These events left me disenchanted and filled my mind with a lot of questions. And thus began my quest to know more about Islam and why it was being hailed as a radical religion.

My journey made me delve deep in the study of religion to find answers to looming questions like Does Islam permit violence? Does it seek political supremacy? Why do men call themselves as "jihadis" and take the lives of others?

My questions took me to scholars, intellectuals and several religious leaders. I remained dissatisfied with the answers I was given. The more I learnt about them, the more appalled I was to see how some of these so-called faith leaders changed the interpretation to suit their vested interests. *While making the judgement 'to err is human', casting a veil upon truth and contorting it for one's worldly benefits, is a sin!*

Scholars play a crucial role in shaping the future of any society. They pave way for the next generation to develop ideologically.

I discovered such a scholar in my grandfather, Maulana Wahiduddin Khan. My relentless search found repose in his writings through which I discovered the true face of Islam.

Through his writings, I realised that real Islam lays greatest emphasis on peace and holds it to be *summum bonum*, that which is the most essential prerequisite for any human society.

The teachings by Maulana are based on the *Quran and Hadith*, the original Islamic sources, which encourages a believer to contemplate and reflect. As per him, ideology is a product of deep discovery and realisation.

It is the lack of self-discovery and misinterpretation of religions that has become the key cause of radicalization among Muslim youth. The radicalisation was excessively fuelled by terrorist outfits to suit their ill-intent.

I studied Quran, Hadith and life of the Prophet Muhammad to better comprehend the Quranic view on peace and non-violence. In the aftermath of 9/11, Ms. Karen Armstrong, a renowned British Author and commentator wrote an article for the TIME Magazine.

The title of the article was, "The True, Peaceful Face of Islam" (dated September 23, 2011). An excerpt from the article is given below,

The very word Islam, which means 'surrender,' is related to the Arabic *salam*, or peace...he (the Prophet Muhammad) devoted his attention to building up a peaceful coalition of tribes and achieved victory by an ingenious and inspiring campaign of nonviolence. When he died in 632, he had almost single-handedly brought peace to war-torn Arabia...It would be as grave a mistake to see Osama bin Laden as an authentic representative of Islam.

The above passage from the article is sufficient to illustrate the unbiased learning spirit of Orientalists as a result of which they could discover Islam as a peaceful tradition. Whereas,*Muslims* have failed to re-discover the religion of Islam.

A study of the history of Islam is adequate to convey that while pre-Islamic Arabia was caught up in a vicious cycle of tribal warfare, in which tribes fought with one another in the pattern of revenge and counter revenge. But despite the backdrop of such rivalry and violence, the Prophet *Muhammad's* entire life is a living example of striving for peace in the utmost manner.

The policies of the Prophet were aimed at garnering peace. There are numerous examples in his life where the *Prophet Muhammad* managed to avoid confrontation and opted for a peaceful course of action.

It was the strenuous and unilateral efforts of the *Prophet Muhammad* towards peace-building and harmony that ushered in a bloodless revolution when the *Prophet* along with thousands of companions undertook the *Meccan March*. Unlike the victors of cities who destroyed the city and plundered its inhabitants, the *Prophet* announced an unequivocal amnesty for all the inhabitants of *Mecca*, including the direst of his opponents.

Today, we live in the era of the United Nations but fourteen hundred years ago, at the time of *Prophet Muhammad*, nothing of this sort existed. There were no organisations to mediate peace, human rights or freedom of speech and religion. The religion of the king was the religion of his subjects and any deviation from this 'law' called for religious persecution.

It was in such an era that *Prophet Muhammad*, through his policies tirelessly and unilaterally strived to establish peace. In his book, '*The 100*', Dr. Michael Hart has placed *Prophet Muhammad* as the "Number One most influential figure in human history". In the words of Dr. Hart, "he (*Prophet Muhammad*) was the only man in history who was supremely successful on both the religious and secular levels."

The curious question that arises is how a religion led by one of the most peaceful and successful man in history, has come to be known as "a religion that sanctions violence"?

When a deep study of Islam is undertaken, two distinct models become prominent— *Islam* and the Muslim community. At this point, A student of *Islam* will have to differentiate between Islam and *Muslims* to ensure that he comprehends the principles of *Islam* as they are intended to be.

Islam is an ideology which is based on the *Quran*, a revealed book. So, the yardstick for assessing the social aspects of Islam will be the *Quran* and not the actions of the community that calls itself as its proponents.

The Maulana says that a religion starts as an ideology and over a period of time it is reduced to a culture. It means that once degeneration sets in, the ideology begins to fade away. As a result, those who follow the ideology come under the influence of their society and become conditioned minds. Under such circumstances, one has to, very objectively and in words of the Maulana 'mercilessly decondition' oneself. A person who will successfully decondition himself will be able to reach the kernel of his true nature.

In the modern world, several negative phenomena are associated with *Muslims*. These phenomena must be assessed by the yardstick of 'Islam as an ideology' and not in the context of '*Muslims* as a community.'

We must differentiate between the ideology of Islam on the one hand and the history of Islam on the other. The ideology is the real part of *Islam*, while the socio-cultural history of Muslims is not entirely a part of Islam. For instance, one of these phenomena is violence. The battles with *Byzantine* and *Sassanid* empires in the past of *Islam* are part of the history of *Islam* and not part of the ideology of *Islam*. If we do not differentiate between these two aspects, we would not be able to have a correct picture of *Islam*.

Peace is the greatest good in Islam. The *Quran* calls its way, 'the way of peace' (5:16). Islam does not ascribe any prerequisite or condition for attainment of peace. Rather, Islam believes in peace for the sake of peace only. The Prophet Muhammad's entire life is an illustration of this principle. He always took peaceful circumstances as an opportunity to work for justice and did not attempt to derive justice directly from peace; the treaty of *Hudaybbiyya*, between the *Prophet* and his opponents, is an example of this. The conditions proposed by the opponents for agreeing to a ten-year war pact were quite against justice. But the Prophet accepted this treaty, not because it was giving them justice, but because it was paving the way to work for justice by providing a war-free zone and a peaceful environment.

It is no exaggeration to say that Islam and violence are contradictory to each other. The concept of Islamic violence is so obviously unfounded that, *prima facie* it stands rejected. The fact that violence is not sustainable in the present world is enough to convince one that violence, as a principle, is quite alien to the scheme of things in *Islam*. *Islam* claims to be an eternal religion and such a religion cannot afford a principle in its scheme which will not be sustainable in later periods of human history. An attempt to bracket violence with *Islam* amounts to casting doubts upon the very eternity of the Islamic religion. The *Prophet Muhammad* so earnestly used to pray to God in his daily prayer:

"O God, You are the original source of Peace; from You is all Peace, and to You returns all Peace. So, make us live with Peace; and let us enter paradise: the House of Peace. Blessed be You, our Lord, to whom belongs all Majesty and Honour!"

A deep study of the Maulana's literature allows us to appreciate the importance that Islam accords to peace. It becomes clear that those who express Islam as a religion of warfare are simply misleading the Muslims.

The only benchmark in *Islam* is the life of the *Prophet Muhammad.* The Prophet was born in *Mecca* in 570 A.D in an era of religious persecution. His life was a manifestation of adopting the principle of peace in the complete sense of the word. It demonstrates how a believer daws courage from his conviction in God Almighty. Even in the face of extreme oppression, the Prophet did not resort to arms. Instead, the Prophet simply changed his area of work and migrated to Medina leaving behind his hometown of Mecca.

Another example from the life of the Prophet Muhammad is in the '*Treaty of Hudaibiyyah*':

Prophet Muhammad and his followers set out from *Medina* to perform a completely peaceful *Umrah* (short pilgrimage at *Kaaba*) in Mecca. But when they reached *Hudaibbiyyah* near Mecca, the Quraysh (the leaders of *Mecca*) stopped them. At this point, the *Prophet* and his Companions did not engage in any violent protests to be allowed entry into their homeland. Instead, the *Prophet* commenced talks with the *Meccan* leaders to strive for a possibility of establishing peace in the region. Eventually, after long negotiations, the two sides concluded what was called as the *Hudaibiyyah* Pact. This was a 10-year no-war pact, signed between Prophet Muhammad and the people of Mecca. It was a unilateral treaty favouring *Meccans* and even included a clause which said that the Prophet would not enter Mecca and will immediately return to Medina from *Hudaibbiyyah*. The conditions the Prophet had agreed to were apparently disadvantageous, but in reality it provided the much sought after peace in the region which paved the way for constructive activities and exchange.

The *Prophet* was an unwavering advocate of peace and non-confrontation. It is pertinent to note that setting such a high benchmark for making peace prevail is possible only when we are devoid of even a trace of negativity and consider every person to be a potential friend. This is the essence of Islamic teachings.

Islam upholds peace above all; this idea was so striking that it compelled me to put together the current set of compilation of Maulana Wahiduddin Khan's writings. The central idea of the book is to share the Quranic interpretation of *Islam* and remove that veil of misinterpretation.

The very survival of our race depends on peaceful co-existence. The plurality of cultures, religions and ethnicities enrich the human world.

We live in a beautiful world, we only need the eyes to see it and appreciate it! Lastly, I would say that life is a precious gift which we must cherish, and pass on to the succeeding generations so that they learn from it and make the best of their experience!

Hope you all enjoy reading this book as much as I enjoyed compiling it!

—Raamish Siddiqui

Contents

1

How to Achieve Peace in Kashmir?

I have been writing about Kashmir since 1968. At the very outset, I have been of the firm view that unrealistic politics has played havoc with Kashmir, but now through realistic politics, we can once again lead Kashmir to progress and development. Kashmiri Muslims have today become disillusioned. They are living in an atmosphere of mistrust.

It is indeed possible for the Kashmiris to start a new life at any given time, but for this, two conditions must be met. First, they must hold themselves responsible for the unpleasant situation they are faced with today. As long as they continue to hold others responsible for it, it will be almost impossible for them to make a new start.

Secondly, they must come out of their dream world and learn to live in the world of practical realities. They must abandon the wishful thinking their incompetent leaders have fed them on. For their growth and advancement to take place, they must carve out a new plan of adjustment with the present situation.

Admitting the existing realities, the Kashmiri Muslims must arrive at the brave decision – willingly and not out of compulsion – that destiny has decreed that they should be a part of India. They have no option but to willingly accept this verdict of destiny.

Furthermore, this is not an evil. It is certainly, in every respect, good for them. India is a big country. It has freedom and democracy. Here reside more than two hundred million people of their faith. Almost all the big Islamic institutions of the sub-continent are located in India. All across India is imprinted a thousand-year history of the Muslims, which should give them courage and inspiration.

Moreover, India provides great opportunities to Muslims in the footsteps of the Sufis to follow and spread the peaceful message of Islam – a task that, according to a hadith, can earn them salvation in the hereafter.

Once, on a short visit to Karachi, I met a Muslim industrialist, who told me that the Indian Muslims were in a far better position than they were. When I asked him why, he answered, "Pakistan is a small country. So, we have a limited market for the products we manufacture. In contrast, India is a vast country. If you produce a product in India, you have a huge market to sell it in."

What this Pakistani industrialist told me has now become a fact of life. In the twenty-first century, the Muslims of India have emerged as the most developed Muslim community in the whole of the subcontinent.

This is in no way an exaggeration. And a comparative survey of any city can establish the validity of this statement. For example, today the richest Muslim, of not only the subcontinent but of the whole Muslim world, is an Indian: Azim Hashim Premji of Bengaluru.

If the Muslims of Kashmir whole-heartedly were to become a part of India, then great opportunities for all kinds of development would open up to them. The prospects of progress here in the fields of education, economics and other fields are not in evidence anywhere else.

Furthermore, in the sphere of politics, there exist great opportunities for them. Sometime ago, I published an article in Hindi, Urdu and English newspapers, in which I urged the Kashmiri Muslims to abandon the policy of confrontation and whole-heartedly become a part of India. Then the first Muslim Prime Minister of democratic India could very well be a Kashmiri Muslim and I have no doubts about this.

I have been thinking of the issue of Kashmir since its beginning. By the grace of God, the view I initially formed on this issue appears correct to me even today. I have never felt the need to change it. I have been writing about Kashmir since 1968. My first article was published in the Urdu Weekly, *Al-Jamiat*, the official urdu weekly of the Jamiat-ul-Ulema-i-Hind. I quote here from *Al-Jamiat*.

"The time for receiving one's rights is when the decision is in one's own hands. But our leaders have realized this fact only when their case has become a moral one. I have read the speeches of the Kashmiri leader, Shaikh Abdullah, who is very bold and has made sacrifices which have earned him the title *Sher-e-Kashmir*. But his present Kashmiri campaign has nothing to do with reality.

"In 1947, he was in a position – had he opted for a realistic policy – to make a decision on the issue of Kashmir according to his own will. But, owing to his unrealistic dreams, he let the moment of decision pass him by. Now, when the time for decision-making has slipped from his hands, he is making a hue and cry. But now his clamor, a crying out for justice, on moral grounds, has no value in the world of today."

"Once upon a time one young man opened a shop. He had set foot in life's struggle for the first time. He had no idea of the safeguards needed in life when you initiate such a task.

"So, he used an ordinary lock for his shop. One day, he returned from the shop looking very downcast. An elderly acquaintance asked him what the matter was and why he was looking so sad. He replied, 'Thieves broke in my shop. The lock I used was an ordinary one and someone broke open the lock at night and stole all the goods.' The old man pointed out that this had been his own fault. The young man said, 'Yes. Now with this experience, I have learnt that I must use an extra strong lock on my shop door.' Then the old man asked, 'Is this something to be learnt after having such an experience? When you started out as a shopkeeper, you should have known from day one that a strong lock is needed to be used.'

"As far as a shop break-in or other similar personal matter is concerned, there is the possibility that one may make amends after such an experience. But, in the case of a national decision, the issue is totally different. In personal matters, even after incurring a loss, there is a possibility of being successful once again with further effort. But, in national matters, when the time for decision has slipped from one's hands, the problem becomes much more complicated and difficult to resolve.

"National leadership is only for those who can envision the future in the present. Those who can see only the present and the past cannot lead the nation.

"However, by their unwise steps, they can surely complicate matters." (*Al-Jamiat Weekly*, New Delhi, June 14, 1968, pg. 4).

Since then, I have been writing on the Kashmir issue over the years. If my writings for the last 35 years were to be collected, they would form a voluminous book. By God's grace, my writings have benefited a great number of Kashmiris, who, in consequence, have abandoned the path of militancy in favor of education and progress. I constantly receive letters and phone calls from Kashmiris telling me of the change in their thinking.

A 'movement' implies a movement of the masses but, in fact, it is instigated by leaders who mobilize the masses through their fiery speeches and writings.

Then, in the name of the masses they earn all the distinction that goes with leadership. This state of affairs increases the responsibility of the leader to a very great degree. That being so, only that person should enter the field who has made the preparations necessary for the performance of the task.

Those who enter this field without the necessary preparations are grave wrong-doers in the eyes of God, irrespective of how popular they are among the ignorant masses. The final hour has now come for the Kashmiris to rise above their leaders and to view the whole matter afresh – not in the light of the pronouncements of their leaders, but in the light of practical realities. In doing so, they must chart the course of their lives anew. There is simply no other way for them to succeed.

❒

2

How to Live in a Multi-Faith Society?

India is a multi-religious society. Muti-religious society is one where people have to live with differences. Now, difference is not simply a part of religion. In fact, it is an essential part of nature. It is a part of God's creation plan itself. So, we have no option other than to live with differences.

To deal with this problem, we need a formula for difference management rather than a formula for eliminating these differences.

I have studied almost all major religions. I found that every religion including Islam provides the art of difference management. Every religion tells us how to live in a multi-religious society with peace and harmony. We find this formula in the famous words of Jesus Christ: "Love your enemy."[1]

Love your enemy means: to manage the problem of enmity by the power of love.

The same principle is given in the *Qur'an* in these words:

"Do good deed in return for bad deed and you will find that your enemy has become your dearest friend." (*Qur'an* 41:34)

There is nothing mysterious about it. It is a well-known law of nature. It means that everyone is your potential friend. We have only to turn this potential into actual.

This Islamic principle was best represented by the Muslim Sufis in India. One Sufi poet has described this principle in this line in Persian: We don't know the stories of Kings and Generals. We know only the stories of love and compassion.

1. Matthew 5:44.

Muslim Sufis devoted themselves in spreading this universal message of love and compassion for centuries. Due to these peaceful efforts on the part of the Sufis and saints, this spirit of love and compassion was so deeply embedded in our society that it became part and parcel of our value system.

The social integration we find today in India owes greatly to the efforts made by our Sufis and saints.

In every field of life in India, people of different faiths are working together in a peaceful atmosphere. This owes to a large extent due to the religious and spiritual spirit the Sufis and saints inculcated among the Indian people.

It is true that there were some unpleasant events in India like the demolition of Babri Mosque in 1992. But it should be seen as an exception rather than rule. It is interesting to know in this regard that although one mosque was demolished by an unruly mob at Ayodhya, at the same time, there are more than half a million mosques throughout India. All are intact and functioning smoothly.

According to the Indian experience, multi-religious or multicultural society is not an evil. Rather it is a blessing. For, trying to eliminate differences destroys the very fabric of our own interests. So, we have no way other than adjusting with differences.

It means that multi-religious society leads us to necessary adjustment. Consciously or unconsciously, this principle has been adopted on a large scale by the Indian people. We can see its effects all around us.

According to Indian experience, the issue of peace and harmony is not simply an issue of administration. It also requires active involvement of non-governmental agencies. Non-governmental agencies have to educate people in this regard. They have to inculcate the spirit of patience and tolerance. To establish peace and harmony in a society, we need 50 per cent involvement of the administration, and 50 per cent of the non-governmental agencies.

Tension is unavoidable in a society. It is not possible to make a society free from tension. What is needed; that at the time of tension-building in a group or a community, senior members of the society should rush at the spot to pacify people and defuse the tensed environment.

In India, we have so many non-governmental groups of this kind. Even I am engaged in this social task. We have organized a peace-keeping group in different parts of the country. They always watch the situation and try to defuse the tension before it reaches to its break-down stage.

There are so many successful stories in this regard. For example, few years ago, in a town in Andhra Pradesh, there was tension between two groups. Tension and conflict were likely to lead to violence. At this critical juncture, one medical doctor, known to the people of the area, reached the spot. He met the leaders. And he succeeded in pacifying them. Then he advised them that instead of throwing stones, they must present flowers to the rival group.

They accepted his advice. They purchased some flowers from the market. When the crucial time came, they appeared with flowers holding in their hands. They presented these flowers to the leaders of the rival group by saying: We welcome you.

This gesture worked. The tension defused and the whole matter was settled within minutes.

We have a great lesson in India's experience in this regard. As we know, Indian subcontinent was divided into two parts in 1947 – India and Pakistan. After the Partition, the two countries adopted two different systems. Pakistan chose religious political system, that is, theocratic state, while India opted for non-religious system, that is, secular state.

Now after passing of more than half a century, we are in a position to judge both the systems on merit. It is an unavoidable fact that India is progressing very fast, while Pakistan is lagging behind in every field of life.

This difference in result gives a very important lesson. India's successful experiment shows that secular system is a better choice for a multi-religious society, while theocratic system results in fundamentalism, extremism, and sometimes even in violence, whereas secular system always brings about peace, tolerance and harmony.

❑

3

Islam and Hinduism

Islam and Hinduism both represent two great traditions. Both have been living together in India for more than one thousand years. It is very important to understand the relationship between the two religions.

At present, there are two divergent views on this subject. One group tries to establish that both traditions are very similar to each other. Once I happened to meet a Hindu scholar, who, with great enthusiasm, said: "I don't find any difference between the two religions. When I read the *Qur'an*, I feel that I am reading the *Gita* and when I read the *Gita*, I feel like I am reading the *Qur'an*." But this is an over-simplification of the issue. I don't think that this kind of notion will pass the academic test.

Contrary to this, the second group claims that Islam and Hinduism are both quite different from each other and that their only meeting point is in heated debates. This concept flourished during the British rule and reached its height at that time.

I think that these two concepts seem to be quite different from each other and that this kind of comparative discussion cannot yield any positive results.

There is the greatest need to assess the merits of the two religions in the context of intellectual development. Such development can come about only as a result of social interaction and intellectual exchanges. I am a great believer in such exchanges and experience has taught me that we can only benefit from the study of the two religions: and will show that their respective traditions have great values for each other.

To illustrate this point, let me cite some historical examples. Jawaharlal Nehru, in his famous work *'The Discovery of India'*, has observed: "When the Arabs came, they brought a brilliant culture to India. History testifies to this statement".[2]

The Arabs came to India in the 7th and 8th centuries. At that time, India was dominated by superstition, with the majority of Indians indulging in what is called nature worship. It was believed that everything, from stars to planets, rivers and trees, was divine in nature.

Here I would like to give an interesting reference. During the British period, John Beverley Nicholas (d. 1983), an English writer, wrote a book titled *'Verdict on India'* (1944), in which he depicted the Hindus as nature worshippers. He observed that in the west, the formula is: Government of the people, by the people, for the people, whereas in India, the formula is: Government of the *Peepal*, by the *Peepal*, for the *Peepal*. (The *Peepal* is a tree and is treated as sacred in India).

The advent of Islam proved to be a kind of 'future shock' for India.

According to Islamic belief, God is the Creator and the whole of nature is His creation. This ideology was highly revolutionary at that time. It brought about a trial change in the Indian mind in that it introduced scientific thinking into Indian society. After the introduction of this ideology, the Indian people tried to explore nature, exploiting it instead of worshipping it and treating it as God.

The second impact of the advent of Islam in India was to introduce the concept of universal brotherhood. At that time, the whole of Indian society was dominated by the caste system. The Islamic concept of equality changed this system to a great extent. Details of this Islamic contribution can be seen in Dr. Tara Chand's book *'The Influence of Islam on Indian Culture'*. This book was published in the year 1936.

From these examples, one can understand the positive influence and the healthy effect of Islam on the Indian society.

Now let us take some examples from the other side, that is, the contribution of Hinduism to the Muslims of India.

Not allowing oneself to be provoked, in spite of provocation, is an important teaching of Islam. I have found a beautiful illustration

---

2. *Discovery of India* by Jawaharlal Nehru, 1946

of this teaching in the life of Swami Vivekananda, a great soul of India. Once, one of his Christian friends wanted to put him through a test. So, he invited Swamiji to his home. When Swamiji reached there, he was asked to sit in a room beside a table on which the sacred books of different religions had been placed, one on top of the other. The *Bhagavad Gita*, the sacred book of Hinduism, was placed at the bottom. Other religious books were placed above it, and the *Bible* was placed right on top. Then he asked Swamiji what he had to say about this.

This was obviously meant to humiliate Swamiji but, instead of being provoked, he simply smiled and said: "The foundation is really good." This incident is a beautiful illustration of the fact that if an individual simply refuses to be provoked, he becomes so strong that he can turn his negatives into positives; he can turn his minuses into pluses.

Then there is a *hadith* in *Sahih Al Bukhari* and *Sahih Al-Muslim*. This *hadith* tells us the general policy of the Prophet of Islam. Aisha, the Prophet's wife, says: "Whenever the Prophet faced any such situation and he had to choose between two courses of action, he always opted for the easier than the harder, course."[3]

A successful example of this principle can be seen in the life of Mahatma Gandhi. In the pre-1947 period, India was struggling for her freedom against the British rule. At that time, there were two options before Indian leaders – violent activism and peaceful activism. Gandhiji avoided violent confrontation with the British regime and opted for a peaceful struggle. He was able to achieve great success without any bloodshed.

This example set by Mahatma Gandhi is a very good illustration of Islamic principles.

In my experience, differences in religion are not an evil but a blessing. The only condition is to accept these differences with a positive mind; to learn from each other and live as partners rather than as rivals. Life is all about cooperation and co-existence, and the relationship between different religions must be based on acceptance of this principle.

March 24, 2007

❒

3. Fath al-Bari, 6/654.

4

Islam and Politics

The Prophet of Islam has said: "Perform your prayer as you see me performing it." The same he said about *Hajj*. He said: "Learn the method of *Hajj* from my practice." It means that there is an example in the Prophetic life for prayer and *Hajj*. So, Muslims must imitate this Prophetic example forever. But it is significant that the Prophet of Islam never gave any advice about politics. Although he was the head of the Medina State, he never said to make your political system by seeing my political practices.

This difference between *ibadah* (worship) and politics is very important. It means that as far as the *ibadah* is concerned, there is a set example of it. And people are required to imitate this example forever. But when it comes to the political system, there is no such set pattern of politics in Islam.

From this difference, we can draw a very important principle and that is in contrast to the form of *ibadah*. Political system is based on social condition of a given time. In every society, we have to see the real social situation and we have to adopt Islamic politic accordingly.

From this difference, it is very clear that Islamic *ibadah* has a set pattern forever but Islamic politics has no such eternal norms. Islamic politics can be termed a kind of situational politics that is based on social realities.

This is the practical concept of politics. The Prophet of Islam has said: "As you will be, so will be your rulers." It means that Islamic politics is subject to people than to some fixed norms. In other words, the Islamic government is a people's government rather than any kind of theocratic government.

By seeing the Prophet's life, one can say that there are three forms of an Islamic government: the first form can be said as the secular government. Second form can be said to be a mixed government. And the third form can be called an Islamic government. And the examples of all these three forms can be traced in the life of the Prophet.

Prophet's Meccan period was the example of the first type of government. At that time, Muslims were a tiny minority in Mecca and the majority of the citizens were non-believers. Prophet accepted their rule, which was established under their tribal Parliament, that is, *Dar al-Nadwa*. Once the Prophet was offered to be appointed as the ruler of Mecca, but he refused because the society of *Mecca* was not prepared to accept a Muslim rule. So, in this first period, the Prophet accepted what may be called a secular government in Mecca. When the Prophet migrated from Mecca to Medina and settled over there for ten years, this period is divided into two phases. In the first phase, Muslims and non-Muslims in Medina were almost equal in number, so it was a mixed society. He accepted a mixed type of politics. At that time, there were two centers of power. One was the Prophet himself, the second was a Jewish leader Kab-bin-Ashraf. So, it was a bi-polar state. The Prophet accepted it as it is, without trying to bring a change in the political status quo of Medina. Then in the second phase of the Medina period, the whole city was Islamized. Medina became completely a Muslim society. At that time, the Prophet of Islam implemented Islamic *Shar'iah* in Medina.

Due to this nature of politics in Islam, there is no political structure in the Islamic system; for example, in the early period there were six heads of the political system – the Prophet himself, Abu Bakr, Omar-bin-Khatab, Uthman, Ali, and Umar-bin-Abdul Aziz. All these six were heads of the state in the early period of Islamic history, but every one of them was appointed political head in a different manner. There was no common method of their appointment.

This kind of political concept is a great contribution of Islam towards mankind. The political history shows that people always have some fixed political norms and they want to establish this norm. This kind of ideology is bound to create a conflict and lastly fighting. Islam gave a very practical formula in this regard. This formula is based on two points: one, in your personal life, follow your religion. Second, when it comes to the social life, accept the status-quo, establish a democratic government based on free and fair election. It is this formula that can save all kinds of political confrontations and wars. It is this political ideology that can certainly ensure peace in every situation.

❒

5

Modern-Day Sufism

Sufism (*tasawwuf*) ought to be just as important today as it has ever been throughout its long history. Being a way of purifying the soul – a necessity for each new generation – its role should never diminish with changing times and circumstances. Paradoxically, although it still has millions of adherents, as a form of religion, it is definitely in a state of decline.

This is because the traditional form of *tasawwuf*, which has been shaped by many historical accretions, has no great appeal for the modern educated mind. For instance, *tasawwuf*, as we now know it, is embroidered by tales of miracles and mysticism, and to find support for its ideology, it relies upon doubtful analogies. But the scientific mind is skeptical of analogies and is impatient with mysticism.

There is also the question of Sufism being heart-based, the heart in ancient times being regarded as the seat of thought and emotion. But now modern science has shown the heart to be nothing but an organ that controls the circulation of blood and it has been conceded that it is the mind that is the center of both thought and emotion. This being so, *tasawwuf* should now be developed as a mind-based philosophy. It will, thus, have a much stronger attraction for educated minds.

The need of the hour, therefore, is to modernize Sufism, couching it in the contemporary idiom, and explaining its ideology in a way that should address the present-day individual, whose major concern is as much with intellectual development as it is with purification of the soul. That is why, *tasawwuf* should necessarily be linked with real events and its objectives expressed in a scientific manner. Its attraction will, thus, reach far beyond the poor, the distressed, the under-educated and the downtrodden, who at present make up the bulk of its following. Even in a modern country like Egypt, the adherents of Sufism largely fall into the category of the underprivileged.

One constituent of present-day Sufism, which may appeal to the modern mind, is the practice of meditation. But it should be borne in mind that meditation, which began to be favored by the Sufis under the influence of local yogic practices, should be discounted for the simple reason that it fails to awaken the human mind. In any case, meditation is practised more to relieve stress and promote relaxation than to attain great spiritual heights. Likewise, the practice of inducing a state of ecstasy by means of special exercises is not a part of authentic Sufism, because it has nothing to do with that spiritual development, which is the actual aim of Sufism.

Formerly, people used to go to Sufis in order to learn the spiritual aspects of their religion and to be trained in spirituality. But now the situation has changed. One reason for this is that, at present, there are very few genuine Sufis in *khanqahs*. This has led to *tasawwuf* existing today in a degenerated form. For example, nowadays people do visit *dargahs*, supposedly to satisfy their spiritual feelings. But, in actuality, all that they accomplish is to meet Sufi *pirs* in order to ask for their blessings and then go and prostrate themselves at Sufi graves. All this represents Sufism in a diluted, if not distorted, form. In ancient times, a Sufi was revered on account of his great spiritual achievements. But, now *gaddis* have been formed in the name of past Sufis and anyone who acquires such a seat, mostly as a matter of heredity, is acknowledged as a Sufi. These Sufis, who have acquired *gaddis* in this way, carry out no new research and produce no new books, for no rethinking or soul-searching is allowed. How then can *tasawwuf* develop and face other disciplines of the modern age? Whereas, in ancient times, *tasawwuf* was a living discipline, now it is largely ritual-based and, as such, has become stagnant. This, more than anything else, has led to the erosion of true *tasawwuf*.

However, we do find some reform and development in certain Sufi organisations which, to a great extent, eliminate miracles and ecstasy as parts of Sufism and which look with disfavor upon "shrine worship". Fazl-ur-Rahman in his well-known book, *Islam*, has called this orientation towards reform 'neo-Sufism'. Reform in Sufism has actually been long overdue, for it had adopted so many indigenous rituals and practices that it had lost its original character altogether. For example, in the Indian context, it had adopted various yogic practices, including the inducement of ecstasy through loud music and song. All this went against the spirit of Islam. This ecstasy element has taken another form in Turkey, where its practitioners are called 'whirling dervishes'. They go on dancing in circular movements until they enter a trance-like state. According to Islam, we have come into this world for the purpose of God-realisation, not for self-realisation. Since the basis of Aryan religions was self-realisation. This concept crept into Sufi thought. The Sufis started different kinds of yoga practices in the form of exercises which were believed to aid self-realisation. This, according to them, amounted to God-realisation.

In this way, a number of Sufi orders had diverged a long way from the path of the *Shar'iah*. Ultimately, there arose a strong movement in different parts of the world to bring Sufism closer to the *Shar'iah*, the *Naqshbandiyas* being foremost among its promoters.

These new orders were also more organised than their predecessors. One reason for the revival of these Sufi orders in the twentieth century was colonialism, under which the Muslims suffered from an identity crisis. For the majority of Muslims, interaction with the West during the colonial period was too great a cultural shock to bear. Political power, their greatest support, had gone. Now they needed something to pin their hopes on. In this state of helplessness, *khanqahs, zawiyas* came to their rescue. In the hope of finding solace in spirituality, they thronged to these shrines and Sufi *pirs*. The *pirs* gave them incantations to recite on a rosary; and this was supposed to solve all of their problems.

Doubtless, not all of these Sufis were genuine, but they gave Muslims some hope of getting out of the morass they were floundering in after losing political power. This trading on false hopes worked and Sufism was again revived in a new garb. Some of the shrines have now amassed so much wealth that they are running their own TV channels, one of these being Q TV from Pakistan, where Sufi shrines abound.

People believed that they would bring about a spiritual revolution, but no such thing happened. No such revolution can be brought about by just reviving certain rituals. Spiritual revival can be effected only through a re-awakening of the spirit by means of intellectual development.

One reason for attaching importance to these Sufi orders was that the people associated with them engaged in missionary activities and they also played a role in bringing about puritanical reforms or spiritual revival, albeit more in form than in spirit. Their organisations served as a base for reformers to make efforts to purify religious practices in order to revive the faith. Most revivalists have Sufi affiliations. To cite one example, the great *jihad* at the beginning of the 19th century in northern Nigeria was led by Usman dan Fodio, who was a *Qadri*. In many other areas, Sufi orders were associated with reform movements and *jihad* campaigns against colonialists.

In the 19th and the 20th centuries, a number of Sufi traditions were directly or indirectly involved in shaping Muslim responses to the west. Thus they provided the organisational framework and the intellectual inspiration for Muslim responses to modern challenges to Islam. In most cases, they provided support to the movements of resistance to foreign rule, especially in the 19th century. Many major wars against expanding European powers were fought by Muslim organisations that had Sufi origins.

Sufi orders were also important in shaping the responses to the challenge to Islam in the modern age. In the 19th century, their participation was limited to providing organisational bases for opposition to European expansion and, at times, fighting in the battlefield. But, by the 20th century, these Sufi orders began responding to various needs of the community. In some countries, they even went to the extent of providing an organisational basis for political parties. In Sudan, for example, the *Khatmiya* provided the foundation for the National Unionist party. In Senegal, the *Murdiya* provided an organisation for the development of cash crops and played an important role in modernizing the agricultural sector of the Senegalese economy. Recently, in the war in Afghanistan after the Soviet occupation in 1979, the *Qadiriyas* and *Naqshbandiyas* played a great part in organising *mujahiddin* groups. Thus, in many countries, the organisational traditions of the Sufi orders provided important bases for responding to specific challenges.

Another major Islamic activist movement, the Muslim Brotherhood in Sudan, had many prominent leaders and were associated with *Tariqas* (Sufi orders) in Sudan. Hasan Turabi, the well-known leader, was one of them. Turabi emphasised the role of Ijtihaad, which meant making an effort to apply Islamic teachings to changing situations in order to update Islam. Turabi's revolution was, in fact, a reaffirmation of the ancient Sufi ethic, with its emphasis on the spirit rather than the letter of Islam. The Sufi organisational traditions provided direct means for meeting challenges in modern situations.

The Sufi orders, having withstood many reformist attempts to abolish them (notably Ataturk's initiatives in the 1920s and 1930s in the new republic of Turkey) continue to have special strengths. With their emphasis on individual devotion and small-group experience, they project the Muslim identity in a way that promotes peaceful co-existence with religious pluralism and even modern secularism. They have, moreover, become important vehicles for Islamic expansion in modern western societies, where the open inclusiveness and the aesthetic dimensions of the great Sufi philosophies have considerable appeal.

❐

6

Non-Violence

A study of the *Qur'an* and *Sunnah* (Sayings and Doings of the Prophet) tells us that Islam is a religion that teaches non-violence. According to the *Qur'an*, God does not love violence (*fasad*). We learn from the *Qur'an* that *fasad* is that action which results in disruption of the social system, causing losses in terms of lives and property. This shows that God loves non-violence.

He abhors violent activity being indulged in human society, as a result of which, people have to pay the price with their possessions and lives. This is supported by other statements in the *Qur'an*, for instance, that Peace is one of God's names (*Qur'an* 59:23). Those who seek to please God are assured by verse five of the sixteenth chapter that they will be guided by Him to 'the paths of peace'. Paradise, which is the final destination of the society of God's choice, is referred to in the *Qur'an* as 'the home of peace' (*Qur'an* 89:30), etc.

The entire spirit of the *Qur'an* is in consonance with this concept. For instance, the *Qur'an* attaches great importance to patience. In fact, patience is set above all other Islamic virtues — with the exceptional promise of reward beyond measure. (*Qur'an* 39:10)

Patience implies a peaceful response or reaction, whereas impatience implies a violent response. The word *sabr* exactly expresses the notion of non-violence as it is understood in modern times. That patient action is non-violent action has been clearly expressed in the *Qur'an*. According to one tradition, the Prophet Muhammad observed: God grants to *rifq* (gentleness) what he does not grant to *unf* (violence).[4]

4. Abu Dawud, *Sunan*, 4/255.

The word *rifq* has been used in this *hadith* as an antithesis to *unf*. These terms convey exactly what is meant by violence and non-violence in present times. This *hadith* clearly indicates the superiority of the non-violent method.

God grants to non-violence what He does not grant to violence. This has very wide and deep implications, embodying an eternal law of nature. By the very law of nature, all bad things are associated with violence, while all good things are associated with non-violence.

Violent activities breed hatred in society, while non-violent activities elicit love. Violence is the way of destruction while non-violence is the way of construction. In an atmosphere of violence, it is enmity that flourishes, while in an atmosphere of non-violence, it is friendship that flourishes. The method of violence gives way to negative values while the method of non-violence is marked by positive values. The method of violence embroils people in problems, while the method of non-violence leads people to the exploiting of opportunities. In short, violence is death, non-violence is life.

Both the *Qur'an* and the *Hadith* have attached great importance to *jihad*. *Jihad* means 'struggle', i.e., to make the greatest possible effort. This word is used in the *Qur'an* and *Hadith* for non-violent struggle as opposed to violent struggle. The *Qur'an* (25:52) says: Perform *jihad* with this (i.e., the words of the *Qur'an*) most strenuously.

The *Qur'an* is not a sword or a gun. It is a book of ideology. In such a case, performing *jihad* with the *Qur'an* would mean an ideological struggle to convey the peaceful message of Islam to people.

In the light of this verse of the *Qur'an*, *jihad* in actual fact is another name for peaceful activism or non-violent activism. Where *qital* is violent activism, *jihad* is non-violent activism.

The Prophet Muhammad followed the principle of peaceful activism throughout his life. He always adopted non-violent methods in preference to violent methods. It is this policy that was referred to by Aishah, the Prophet's wife, in these words:

"Whenever the Prophet had to opt for one of two ways, he almost always opted for the easier one."[5]

1. According to the *Qur'an*, there are two faculties in every human being which are mutually antipathetic. One is the ego, and the other is conscience, called respectively *nafs ammara* and *nafs lawwama* (*Qur'an*, 12:53; 75:26). What the violent method invariably does is to awaken the ego, which necessarily results in a breakdown of social equilibrium. On the other hand, non-violent activism awakens conscience. From this results an awakening in people of introspection and self-appraisal. And according to the *Qur'an*, the miraculous outcome of this is that 'he who is your enemy will become your dearest friend'. (*Quran* 41:34)

2. A great advantage of the non-violent method is that by following it, no part of one's time is wasted. The opportunities available in any given situation may then be exploited to the fullest extent – as happened after the no-war pact of *Hudaybiyah*. This peace treaty enabled the energies of the believers to be utilised in peaceful constructive activities instead of being dissipated in a futile armed encounter. One great harm done by violent activism is the breaking of social traditions in the launching of militant movements. Conversely, the great benefit that accrues from non-violent activism is that it can be initiated and prolonged with no damage to tradition.

Generally speaking, attempts to improve or replace the existing systems by violent activism are counter-productive. The truly desirable revolution is that which permits gradual and beneficial changes. And this can be achieved only on the basis of non-violence.

The Prophet of Islam fully adopted the way of pacifism or non-violence all his life. All his successes were achieved by non-violent methods. There were many such issues in Mecca at that time which could have been the subject of clash and confrontation. But the Prophet avoided all such issues, strictly limiting his sphere to peaceful propagation of his message.

In Mecca, when the *Qur'aysh* leaders were set to wage war against the Prophet, even then, instead of opting for the way of reaction and retaliation, the Prophet secretly migrated to Medina.

5. Fath al-Bari, 6/654.

Migration, by its very nature, was a clear example of non-violent activism. This peaceful strategy enabled the Prophet and his followers, about two hundred in number, to form a powerful center of Islam in Medina. Had they adopted the path of confrontation instead of peaceful migration, the history of Islam might have been buried right there in Mecca shortly after its inception.

A study of the *Qur'an* and *Seerah* (life of the Prophet) tells us that the actual goal of Islam has been, since beginning to end, to change people's hearts. But, in accordance with the creation plan, everyone has been given total freedom. It was as a result of this freedom that certain people turned against the Prophet of Islam; some even went to the extent of taking up arms in order to put an end to his mission by force. It was in situations such as these that the Prophet and his companions had to resort to arms, temporarily, in self-defense. In this context, it would be correct to say that peace in Islam is the rule rather than the exception.

The Prophet Muhammad (pbuh) lived on this earth for 23 years after receiving Prophethood. During these 23 years, the *Qur'an* was revealed at intervals and according to the circumstances. If this period is divided up under the headings of war and peace, we will find that one part of the *Qur'an*, which is almost covering a span of twenty years, relates to peaceful teachings on the subjects of faith, worship, ethics, justice, humanity, etc., whereas the verses relating to war were revealed during a period of only three years, and that too only when the believers were faced with armed aggression.

There are 114 chapters in the *Qur'an*, containing 6,666 verses in all. There are hardly 40 verses, which relate directly or indirectly to war. This means that the verses dealing with war represent barely 0.6 per cent of the entire text.

This kind of difference can be found in the constitutions of every country as well as in all religious books. For instance, while the *Bible* enshrines many teachings on the subject of peace, it also includes this saying of Jesus Christ:

"I did not come to bring peace but a sword."[6]

Similarly, while the *Bhagavad Gita* holds forth at length on wisdom and ethics. It also contains passages where Krishna insists

6. Matthew 10:34.

that Arjuna should go ahead and fight. Moreover, it is obvious that these injunctions in the *Bible* and the *Gita* are intended to cover only exceptional cases.

One important aspect of Islam as regards its peace-loving policy is that it differentiates between the enemy and the aggressor.

According to the teachings of Islam, if a group unilaterally attacks, thus opening hostilities, war can, as a matter of necessity, be waged in self-defense. The *Qur'an* states: "Permission to fight is given to those who are attacked." (*Qur'an* 22:39)

But so far as engaging in combat with the enemy is concerned, the *Qur'an* does not allow military action just on account of enmity. There is a verse in the *Qur'an* that gives clear guidance in this regard: "And good and evil are not alike. Requite evil with what is best. Then truly he, between whom and you there was enmity, will become your dearest friend." (*Qur'an* 41:34)

These verses teach us not to regard our enemies as objects of everlasting hostility, for a potential friend could be hiding in the guise of an enemy. Discover this friend and turn the potential into the actual. Then you will have no cause for complaint.

It is clear that there are two ways of settling an issue – one violent and one peaceful. When we compare the two, we find that, in any controversial matter, opting for violence is the harder course, while opting for non-violence is the easier course. The general rule in Islam is that whenever there is any controversy, we have to choose to tread the path of peace rather than that of violence. In present times, when freedom has been accepted as an irrevocable right of man, peaceful methods should invariably be adopted.

It would be appropriate to add here that, during the life of the Prophet, if certain wars of a limited duration took place, such engagement only reflected the conditions of those times. The wars that took place in the first half of the seventh century are explainable in terms of it being an age of religious coercion and religious persecution. The atmosphere of religious tolerance that prevails today was not to be found in those times, so that the opponents of monotheism, by initiating hostilities, forced the Prophet to fight. Today, religious tolerance has become an established right of every individual and every group. That is why, the question of going to war to secure religious rights should simply never arise.

Constructive Islamic activities are possible only in a peaceful and normal atmosphere. The importance of peace in Islam is, therefore, so great that we are commanded to ensure peace by bearing with all kinds of unpleasant situations. Even when countering persecution by opponents, the ways of peace and avoidance must be adopted, and peace must at all costs be unilaterally maintained — that is an important principle of Islam. There is only one exception to this rule, and that is in the case of physical aggression by opponents.

The Prophet of Islam began his Prophetic mission in ancient Mecca, where he lived for a period of thirteen years after receiving his Prophethood. During this period, his Meccan opponents repeatedly indulged in acts of persecution and violence. But the Prophet of Islam and his companions unilaterally tolerated all such acts of gross injustice. The emigration from Mecca to Medina was also a form of tolerance and avoidance, resorted to by the Prophet in order to avoid clashing with his opponents.

One example of this avoidance of armed confrontation is that of the signing of the *Hudaybiyah* peace treaty. When a pitched battle seemed imminent between the Prophet of Islam and his opponents, the Prophet successfully defused the situation by the initiation of peace negotiations which continued for two weeks. During these negotiations, which took place at *Hudaybiyah* near Mecca, the Prophet of Islam found the other party clinging obstinately to its demands. Therefore, the Prophet unilaterally accepted all the conditions of the enemy in order to arrive at a peaceful conclusion.

The purpose of this pact was to end tensions between the two parties and to maintain a normal atmosphere in order that the work of peaceful reconstruction might be performed – the actual goal of the mission of Islam. Immediately after the conclusion of the *Hudaybiyah* peace treaty, the atmosphere did return to normal and all the constructive activities of Islam were resumed in full force.

The present world is so structured that conflicts inevitably occur between individuals. On such occasions, Islam tells us not to allow the conflict to escalate to the point of a violent confrontation. The *Qur'an* calls this a policy of patience and avoidance. As a permanent principle, it says: "Reconciliation is best." (*Qur'an* 4:128) That is, at the time of mutual conflict, reconciliation should be resorted to in order to end the conflict. This is for the simple reason that, by adopting the path of conciliation, we can find opportunities to prevent our energy from being wasted in confrontational actions and to devote all this energy to constructive activities. It is this advantage of a conciliatory course that the Prophet of Islam recommended to his followers thus: "You should not desire confrontation with the enemy; you should ask God for peace."

There is a verse in the *Qur'an* that says:

"Whenever they kindle the fire of war, God puts it out." (*Qur'an* 5:64)

It was in this spirit of Islam that when the Prophet came into power in Medina, he did not start waging war in order to force people to surrender to him. Instead, he negotiated with tribes all over Arabia and ultimately brought about unity among them with a series of peace treaties.

If we make an in-depth study of the teachings of Islam, we will find that Islam wants to root out all those factors that lead to war. Why is a war waged? There are two main causes. First is to attempt to annihilate the enemy and second, to attempt to gain the political power. In the achievement of either of these goals, there is no justification in Islam.

With regard to the enemy, Islam teaches us to try to eliminate enmity – not the enemy.

According to the *Qur'an*, no enemy is everlastingly hostile. For in every enemy, there lies a potential friend. Therefore, what the believer ought to do is to reach out through unilateral good behavior to the man hidden within. By requiting good for evil, he should convert this enemy into a friend.

The Prophet of Islam was born in Mecca in 570 A.D. He received Prophethood in 610 and lived as a Prophet in this world for 23 years. During this 23-year period, he spent the first 13 years in Mecca and the last 10 years in Medina. Some verses of the *Qur'an* were revealed in *Mecca* and some verses were revealed in Medina. Now, what were his activities during this Prophetic period?

He taught people by reciting verses of the *Qur'an*, which said: 'Read in the name of your Lord...' and other such verses which were peaceful teachings, being non-militant in nature and ethical in value. He taught people how to pray, and to practice patience and tolerance even in the face of oppression, and, thus, avoid conflict.

He was a role model in that he showed that it was possible for a human being to work for the well-being of others without any ill-feeling, in spite of highly provocative circumstances.

All the tasks performed by the Prophet throughout his life were marked by the greatness, which comes from always choosing a non-violent course of action. Setting this kind of example formed the greater part for the Prophet's actual mission. And so far as war and violence are concerned, the jurists have characterised them as not being for the sake of Islam, but as being contingent upon exceptional circumstances.

❐

7

Peace and Mercy Gone for a Toss

On the publication of the *Satanic Verses* by Salman Rushdie, the Muslim reaction was to have him killed forthwith; he had committed an unpardonable offense against Islam and the Prophet. All over the world, Muslims demanded his head. They were not prepared to settle for anything less than that.

Even in this modern age, the campaign spread like wild fire. This gave the impression that Muslims were very vengeful and violent people. Consequently, in certain Western countries, notice boards were put saying, "Beware of Muslims." This showed the extreme fear engendered by the Muslim fundamentalist threat.

In all fairness, one can ask, "Is this Islam?" Never. God has been represented in Islam as an All Merciful, and the Prophet has been proclaimed as the Prophet of Mercy. It is ironical that in the name of such a magnanimous religion, a certain section of the fundamentalists could not appreciate such sentiments, far less promote them. Islam could never incite people to committing murder in the name of religion, simply because someone had written a book that ruffled their emotions. In fact, this is not the religion of Islam. It is the religion of certain bigoted Muslims.

In the days of the Prophet, a large number of Rushdies and Taslima Nasreens existed, but none of them were beheaded for the offence of insulting Islam and its Prophet. On the contrary, in the times of the Prophet, the principle of countering words with words was followed. That is why, those who spoke out against Islam, no matter to what lengths they went, were not penalised in any way. All that happened was that the Prophet appointed a poet called Hassan to give a befitting answer in verse to the offenders, poetry being the main mode of public expression and sentiments. This is the example we should follow for the resolution of all such problems in true Islamic spirit and earlier traditions.

In the present age, those who are overzealous in their approach to Islam are called fundamentalists, but a better name for them would be deviationists. For, the original meaning of fundamentalism was adherence to the principles of one's religion. But zealots have actually deviated from the fundamental principles of Islam. If they had been fundamentalists in the traditional sense of the word, they would have followed the example of the Holy Prophet. They would have fought ideas with ideas. But nowadays they are fighting words with bombs and bullets. Such people are not true fundamentalists; they are distorters of religion.

Religion is basically a matter of persuasion, but funda mentalists make it a matter of imposition. That is what begets violence. This is where fundamentalism assumes the form of extremism. But herein lies a fallacy. That is, if one takes fundamentalism in its literal sense, then it should be the same basic teachings and tenets of Islam as are emphasised in the Islamic scriptures themselves. There is a *Hadith,* which gives us clear guidance in this matter. The Prophet observed that Islam is founded on five pillars: bearing witness that there is no god, except the one indisputable God and that Muhammad is God's Messenger; the regular saying of prayers (*salah*), alms-giving (*zakat*); performing a pilgrimage to the *Kabah*, performing pilgrimage for the House of God in Mecca (*Hajj*) and fasting during the month of Ramadan (*sawm*).

The rest of the teachings of Islam fall into the category of detailed explanations of and elaborations upon five basic principles, which propagate a peaceful striving. Holding any other precept besides these to form part of the basic tenets of Islam is misguided and unacceptable.

Therefore, the objective set by the fundamentalists is that politics is only a relative part of Islam. That is why, we find no express injunction in the *Qur'an* pertaining to words such as these: "O, Muslims, establish the political system of Islam." But regarding the fundamental principles, the *Qur'an* gives specific Commands to establish them.

The absence of such directives clearly shows that politics in Islam is a relative concept, and not a real part of it. Since Islamic fundamentalists target the Islamisation of the state rather than reform of individuals, their only plan of action is to launch themselves on a collision course with the rulers, both Muslims and non-Muslims. And, thus, their movement takes the path of violence.

From the *Qur'an* and the *Hadith*, we learn that reform of the individuals through peaceful method is the goal of Islam. And once their targeted enemy is removed from the seat of power, fighting for the division of power goes on and on endlessly as we see in Afghanistan. Without doubt, idealism and perfection are highly desirable virtues in Islam, but the direct target of Islamic idealism is not society, nor the state but the making of an ideal individual. There is no express injunction in this regard in the *Qur'an* and the *Hadith*.

Furthermore, Islamic fundamentalism, launched in the name of Islam, has dealt a death blow to the image of Islam as a religion of peace and mercy. The basic weakness of the modern distorted version of fundamentalism lies in that it sees religion, or an ideology, as a matter of imposition rather than of persuasion. And in its practical shape, its inevitable logic of coercion turns it into barbarism.

January 24, 2001

❐

8

What the Prophet Means to the Muslim

Human destiny, by Islamic lights, is a matter of man having been placed on this earth by God that he may be put to the test – the test being of his capacity to make correct moral choices. It is for this purpose that man has been given complete freedom, for, without such freedom, the divine test would have no meaning, no validity.

It is required of man that he should lead his life on earth following a regimen of strict self-discipline. Wherein should he find the guiding principles for such a course? The answer, according to Islam, is in Prophethood. Throughout the history of mankind, God appointed certain human beings – Prophets – who would be the recipients and conveyors of His guidance as sent through his angels. The last in the series was Prophet Muhammad.

The concept of Prophethood is totally different from that of incarnation. According to the latter, God himself is re-born in human shape on earth in order to give succor to humanity. But a Prophet in the Islamic sense is a man just like any other; his uniqueness resides solely in him also being a messenger of God.

By Islamic tenets, Prophethood is dependent not on inspiration, but on divine revelation. Inspiration is a common psychological phenomenon, of the kind experienced by a poet, whereas revelation is a true and direct divine communication. The *Qur'an* is a collection of these divine revelations, which the Prophet received over a period of 23 years.

According to Islam, Prophethood is not acquired but God-given. That is, it is not possible to engage in spiritual exercises and then, as a result, be elevated to Prophethood. Not even the Prophet had any say in this matter of selection. The choice depends upon God alone.

The Prophet's responsibility was to communicate the divine message to humanity. In doing so, if he received a negative response from the people, or was even persecuted, he had nevertheless to follow a strict policy of non-confrontation, and had to unilaterally adopt the path of patience and forbearance. He was responsible only insofar as the conveying of the message was concerned. The response to, or acceptance of, the message, entirely depended on the addressees. But clearly, the greater the number who accepted the message, the greater the sphere in which a practical system of guidance sent by God became established.

The *Qur'an* testifies to the fact that God's messenger came in every age and in every region. According to a *Hadith*, more than one lakh messengers were sent to guide the people. However, the Prophets mentioned by name in the *Qur'an* are two dozens in number, Prophet Muhammad being the last. In the past, the need for new Prophets had always arisen because God's religion, suffering from the vagaries of time, had frequently been distorted from its original form. New Prophets had to come to the world time and time again in order to revivify the true spirit of religion, which had been lost when nations in ancient times, entrusted with the guardianship of the divine scriptures, repeatedly betrayed their trust, allowing the book of God to be laid waste. They had to right the wrongs done by human interpolations in the books they brought with them. But after the Prophet Muhammad, the world will see no further Prophets, for the Book which the Prophet gave to the world – the *Qur'an* – is still perfectly preserved in its original state. In the divine scheme of things, no further Prophets are then required.

It is not only the Prophet Muhammad's (pbuh) Scripture which is preserved in its pristine state but his very spirit, for his utterances, the events of his life, the struggle of his Prophetic mission, have all been fully recorded and have remained intact.

The *Qur'an* tells us that when the Prophet Muhammad proclaimed his Prophethood, people found it difficult to believe in him. They asked, "What kind of messenger is this? He eats and drinks and moves about in the markets. If God had to send a Prophet, why didn't He send an angel?"

In reply, the *Qur'an* has this to say: "If the earth had been inhabited by angels, We would have sent an angel as a Prophet, but since it is human beings who live on earth, a man has been selected as God's Messenger." (*Qur'an* 17:94,95)

The Prophet then, as the bearer of God's message, had to project himself as a model for other human beings. The *Qur'an*, indeed, describes the Prophet as a model character. He experienced all that was experienced by others: grief and solace, advantages and disadvantages, pain and pleasure, etc. Yet he never wavered from the truth, thus setting an example of how others must abide by the truth on all occasions. This deprived wrong-doers of the excuse that they had no role model to show them the path God desired them to follow.

The messenger of God was born just like any other human being. He led his life just as others did. In this way, he clearly demonstrated that the way of life, which he exhorted others to lead, was entirely practicable. His words and deeds, thus, became a realistic example of how God's servants should conduct themselves on earth and what path they must opt for to avert God's displeasure and earn His blessings.

Al-Risala, May 1997

❒

9

Secular Knowledge at Its Islamic Best

Revealed knowledge is the only source from which to learn how to make spiritual progress, while material progress is based on a knowledge of nature.

So far as success or failure in the hereafter is concerned, it rests entirely on the revealed knowledge passed on to mankind by the Prophet (2:120). The Prophet Muhammad is enjoined to proclaim to mankind that "God's guidance is the only guidance".

Nevertheless, Islam holds that while the principles for the attainment of salvation in the hereafter derive solely from divine revelation, the attainment of material progress is underlain by knowledge of the laws of nature as discovered and established by secular scientific research. Islamic schematism, therefore, by reason and by tradition, has always accorded to the secular sciences the status of an independent branch of learning. In fact, the *Qur'an* repeatedly urges us to give serious thought to the natural phenomena of the heavens and the earth, as being "signs for men of sense – those who remember God when standing, sitting and lying down, and reflect on the creation of the heavens and the earth, saying, "Lord, You have not created this in vain" (*Qur'an* 3:191). These verses clearly suggest that proceed to our own conclusions on the basis of human ratiocination in matters of the world.

The difference between the scientific and the religious approach to practical matters has been made clear in a *Hadith*. Fifty out of the 63 years of the Prophet's life were spent in Mecca, a desert city where there was no agriculture. Later, he migrated to Medina, where agriculture and horticulture were practiced – in particular, the growing of date palms. Naturally, the Prophet had no experience of either farming or fruit growing. One day, as the Prophet was passing through the outskirts of Medina, he noticed that some people, who had climbed up the date palms, were engaged in some activity. On inquiring what they were busy with, they explained that they were fertilizing the trees. Traditionally, they did this by the artificial pollination of the date flowers, and this ensured a good crop. But when the Prophet said, "What if you don't do it?" the people, in deference to his judgment climbed down the trees without completing their task. That year the yield was very low.

When the Prophet inquired why the yield was so low that particular year, the orchard keepers replied that the yield depended on the pollination, which they had been carrying out when he had stopped them. On hearing this, the Prophet replied: "Continue doing as you used to, since you know the matters of the world better than I do."[7]

This incident illustrates how the Prophet separated religious knowledge from a practical matter such as horticulture. In fact, the principle evidence in this was applicable not just to horticulture, but to all natural matters governed by the laws of nature. The clear inference is that what is demonstrable in nature, yielding itself to research and experiment, will be accepted by Islam as established, empirical knowledge.

The same principle may be applied – as well as in agriculture and horticulture – to all other scientific disciplines, for instance, to geology, astronomy, engineering, and so on. Islam is quite clear on this point that all of these are the subject matter not of religion but of scientific research.

For instance, if experiment shows that water boils at 100 degrees Celsius, it will be accepted as such without any dispute. Only that will be held valid which has been proved by scientific research experiment. All discoveries must be verifiable. Nothing will be accepted on the basis of mere speculation.

Historically, this Islamic policy of the division of religion and science is extremely important, as it opened the door to

7. Sahih Muslim, Sunan Ibn Maja.

scientific progress for the first time in human history. Prior to the advent of Islam, this policy of division had never been followed, so that science remained the mere handmaiden of religion. Any attempt at true scientific research was generally hampered or stopped altogether by the forces of dogmatism and superstition. Independent progress was impossibility. The division recognised by Islam was epoch-making precisely because it freed secular science from the grip of religion. This opened the way to the open conducting of research and experiment without any fear of interference. This process of liberation continued for a period of a thousand years, until that modern era came into existence, which is now known as the scientific age.

What is demonstrable in nature, yielding itself to research and experiment, will be accepted by Islam as an established, empirical knowledge.

Al-Risala, November 1998

❑

10

Cleanliness in Islam

Islam, as we learn from the *Qur'an* and *Hadith*, is a religion of nature. Islam and nature being indeed each other's counterparts. Nature loves cleanliness and abhors pollution: that is why, this highly desirable feature of human existence – cleanliness – is one of the basic tenets of the Islamic faith.

What is the nature of that faith? It is to lead a life in total consonance with the will of God. And such a life can have its beginnings only in a condition of exemplary personal hygiene.

According to a *Hadith*, the keeping of one-self clean is one-half of faith; this indicates the amount of emphasis laid upon hygiene in Islamic practice. The cleanliness factor is, thus, a major segment of the very essence of Islam.

This is clearly in evidence at the appointed times of worship – the most sublime form of worship being *salat* (*namaz*), which is engaged in five times a day. Each time the hour of prayer arrives, the first thing that a Muslim must do is perform his ablution. Ablution (*wudu*) entails the washing of all the exposed parts of the body. As a cleansing process, *wudu* is the equivalent of a half bath. In this way, the devout Muslim takes a half bath five times daily.

In the first phase of Islam, it was common practice amongst Muslims to take a bath daily before the *fajr* (dawn) prayers. Bathing, thus, became a regular daily feature of every Muslim's life.

The servant of *Uthman*, the third Caliph, tells of how the Caliph unfailingly used to take a bath once or twice daily. If Muslims have always attached great importance to cleanliness, it is because of the explicit commands on this subject in the *Qur'an*.

When the *Qur'an* began to be revealed, one of its signal injunctions was: "Cleanse your garments" (*Qur'an* 74:4) and thus keeping oneself away from all pollution.

The cleanliness of clothes is a necessary concomitant of the purity of the body. Without that, the body is not one hundred per cent clean. Indeed, as much stress is laid on cleanliness as on the avoidance of wearing showy apparel. In Islam, the devotee is required, ideally to worship in clothes, that are simple, and, above all, clean.

In the realm of spiritual development, one of the principal elements is purification through penitence. As the *Qur'an* says: "God loves those who turn to Him in penitence and He loves those who keep themselves clean. (*Qur'an* 2:222)"

Just as repentance frees body and soul of worldly moral dress, so does water remove impurities from body and clothing. Islam, accordingly, exhorts others to turn in remembrance to God, thus purifying his soul.

The mosque, the focal point of Islamic life, is called in a *Hadith* the 'home of the pious people'.

As the *Qur'an* puts it: "In it are men who love to be purified and God loves those who purify themselves." (*Qur'an* 9:108). We are asked, therefore, to clean the mosque, ridding it of noise and dust, just as Abraham and Ishmael have enjoined 'to Purify My House (the *Kabah*) for those who walk around it, those who stay there for devotion, and who bow down and prostrate themselves (*Qur'an* 2:125)'.

Following the examples of the sanitising of the mosque, Muslims are urged to keep their bodies pure by ablution and bathing, their clothes clean by regular washing and their houses and their surroundings spotless.

These practices are incumbent upon every Muslim.

According to a *Hadith*, the Prophet Muhammad said, "God is pure and loves purity,"[8] which means that cleanliness and purity are on the highest scale of cardinal virtues. What God loves is undoubtedly of supreme value.

Every Muslim must, in consequence, lead a life marked by its cleanliness and purity in order to earn the approval of his Creator.

---

8. Tirmidhi.

The cleanliness of clothes is a necessary concomitant of the purity of the body. Without that, the body is not one hundred per cent clean. Indeed, as much stress is laid on cleanliness as on the avoidance of wearing showy apparel. In Islam, the devotee is required, ideally to worship in clothes, that are simple, and above all, clean. If Muslims have always attached great importance to cleanliness, it is because of the explicit commands on this subject in the Qur'an.

Al-Risala, November 1998

❐

11

Islam on Fanaticism

What is fanaticism? It is defined by *Webster* as "excessive and unreasonable enthusiasm or zeal". Used in the religious context, it connotes "religious extremism". Zealots may act under the banner of religion, but it must be borne in mind that their actions are the very negation of the true religious spirit.

Whenever someone adopts a creed, he does so because he regards that as the truth. There is nothing wrong in this. Islam wants us to believe in the veracity of our creed and to practice it as far as possible in our daily living. But this should not be taken to extremes, for Islam does not approve of fanaticism, which it holds to be a kind of ideological madness, a form of *ghulu* (extremism), which, along with bigotry, has been expressly forbidden. (*Qur'an*, 4:171).

The Prophet of Islam once observed: "I have been sent with a religion which exhorts gentleness." That is, he had brought to mankind a religion, which makes concessions to others, and which was completely free of all rigidity. This is not to say that Islam has no distinct ideology: its moral principles are certainly very well defined. But, in practical matters, it advocates dealing gently with others, while adhering strictly to Islamic tenets, as being in the true spirit of religion.

The Prophet of Islam lived for the first thirteen years of his Prophethood in Mecca, during which period, there were no less than 360 idols within the precincts of the *Kabah*. By religous persuasion, the Prophet believed implicitly in One God. Even so, he went to the *Kabah* to say his prayers, He made no attempt to remove the idols, nor did he come into conflict with the idol-worshippers. If the Prophet had been an extremist, he would not have been able to exercise such restraint.

When the Prophet was in Mecca, he used to pray facing in the direction of the *Kabah*. On reaching Medina, he should have continued, to pray facing towards the *Kabah*. But, there being many Jews living in Medina at that time, the Prophet bowed to the established Jewish custom by praying in the direction of *Baital-Maqdis* (Jerusalem). Had the Prophet been a fanatic, he could never have acted in this way.

Once a Bedouin villager entered the Prophet's mosque in Medina and proceeded to defile the place by urinating. Now this particular mosque (Masjid-e-Nawabi) is held very sacred in Islam. And the Prophet's companions wanted to give the man a good beating. But the Prophet forbade this. Instead, he asked them to fetch a bucketful of water to wash the place clean. Had the Prophet been an extremist, he would have had the offender soundly thrashed.

During the early Meccan period, the city was under the domination of idolaters. Twenty years later, when Mecca was conquered, it came under the rule of the Prophet of Islam. Since ancient times, it has been the custom to place a cover (*ghilaf*) over the *Kabah*, and at the time of the conquest of Mecca, this holiest of shrines was shrouded in a cover prepared by the idolaters. In this new age of monotheism, such a symbol must have been anathema, and one of fanatic mentality would have immediately torn down the trappings of polytheism. Not so the Prophet. He left the cover where it was. But then, after some time, it caught fire and was destroyed. Only then did the Prophet have it replaced. Had he been a fanatic, he would have behaved very differently.

Religious fanaticism falls into two categories. One relates to the self and the other to one's conduct in society. On the individual plane, no one is supposed to exceed the bounds set by religion. If he does so, this amounts to fanaticism. For instance, fasting is a form of worship in Islam, to be performed for a certain period each year. However, if one started fasting the whole year round that would be transgressing the prescribed limits, which is anti-Islamic. In the second case, fanaticism in relation to others generally arises from being provoked by anything that runs counter to Islam, and then taking stern action. For instance, drinking is unlawful in Islam and is punishable by flogging. But if the would-be reformer started flogging just any drinker he came across, that would be sheer fanaticism and, as such, an un-Islamic act. It is only when all efforts to reform the alcoholic have proved unavailing that he should be punished. Even then, his punishment should not be by some irate individual, but by a properly constituted religious court. Islam's first imperative, in fact, is a proper religious education for all in order to ensure correct behavior at all times, in private and in public.

Islam wants us to believe in the veracity of our creed and to practice it as far as possible in our daily living.

Al-Risala, July 1998

❐

12
The Mosque in Islam

What is the role of the mosque in Islam? *Masjid*, or mosque, literally means 'a place for self-prostration', that is, a place formally designated for the saying of prayers. According to a *Hadith*, the Prophet of Islam observed: "The *masjid* is a house of God-fearing people." This means, in effect, that it is a center for the inculcation of reverence, where individuals learn what is meant by piety and are thus prepared for a life of devotion to the Almighty.

The *masjid* is built so that people may visit it to read the Book of God, to remember their Creator, silently and in prayer, and to hear His commandments on how they should lead their lives, that is, how to conduct themselves according to His will.

The most important of all these activities is the saying of prayers, a ritual to be carried out five times a day as prescribed by Islam. This act of worship, the greatest means of instilling a sense of awe in the devotee, may be carried out at any place, but ideally, is performed in an organised manner, in congregation, within the mosque. There the worshippers range themselves in orderly rows behind a single prayer leader, the *imam*. (The acceptance by the group of just one individual to lead to congregation avoids any dissension, which might arise from there being more than one.) The number of the worshippers may be ten or ten thousand; all have to stand in rows behind the *imam*. This teaches the lesson of unity. Nevertheless, *namaz* in essence, is an individual action. Everyone recites his own prayer and is rewarded an account of its innate rectitude and sincerity.

The prayer begins with ablution, that is, with the washing of the face, hands and feet. The bodily cleansing is a symbolic reminder that the Muslim should lead his life in this world in a state of purification of the feelings and the soul.

What is recited during prayer consists either of verses from the *Qur'an* or *dhikr*, remembrance, of God, and *dua*, invocations and supplications. All of this is aimed at bringing about a spiritual awakening such as will induce the worshipper to renounce his life of ignorance and heedlessness in favor of a life inspired by Islamic moral values.

Throughout the prayer (*namaz*), the phrase *God-is-Great*, God is great, is repeated several times. Implicit in these words is the idea that the person uttering them is not great. Their frequent repetition is a lesson in modesty, designed to rid the worshipper is conditioned by *namaz* to surrender himself to his Maker in all humility.

The various postures in the *namaz* climax in the act of self-prostration – the ultimate demonstration of submission. Real proof of this submission to God will only become manifest, however, in subsequent dealings with other human beings, in which it is clear that self-glorification has been replaced by glorification of the Almighty, and that feelings of superiority have given away to profound humility.

The *namaz* ends with each worshipper turning his face sideways and uttering these words: "May God's peace and blessings to upon you. Every day, all around the globe, Muslims perform these rites. It is as if they were saying to their fellow men all over the world: O people, we have no feelings for you but those of peace. Your lives, property and honour – all are safe. It is this spirit worshippers are enthused with before they return to society.

Besides the five daily obligatory prayers, there is a weekly Friday prayer, which is necessarily offered in the mosque. In practice and content, it is just like any other prayer which is but since a larger number of people gather on his occasion, a sermon (*khutba*), giving religious guidance, is also preached by the *imam* before the prayers begin.

In this, he reminds worshippers of their accountability to God, of the commandments, pertaining to Islamic character and of the proper way to deal with others in society. In this way, the Friday refreshes the memory on religious commitments.

The mosque, initially intended as a place to worship, has come to be built to serve other related purposes, such as housing the *madarsa*, library, lecture hall, guest house and dispensary. According to a *Hadith,* the Prophet advised the building of mosques in a simple style, so that there should be no dissipation or dilution of the true religious and spiritual atmosphere.

All mosques (with the execution of three) are of equal religious standing, whether large or small, plainly conceived or architecturally magnificent.

The three mosques, which have a greater degree of sanctity because of their historical and religious associations are the Grand mosques of Mecca, Prophet's mosque in Madina and the Dome of the Rock in Jerusalem.

Al-Risala, June 1998

❒

13

Dissent in Islam

The *Qur'an* has commanded us to settle all matters at issue through counseling (*Qur'an* 42:38). Unlike arbitration, counseling implies the freedom to dissent. If diversity of opinions were not allowed to emerge, no fruitful counseling could ever be done. That is why, Islam grants total freedom of expression. In the first phase of Islam, there is not a single instance of anyone being held blameworthy on account of a difference of opinion or the frank voicing of criticism.

There are many interesting instances of dissent in Islam. The first telling example to be set forth in the *Qur'an* is that of the angel's reaction to God's decision to create human beings and settle them on the earth as His creatures. When the Lord told the angles of this, they remonstrated: "Will you put there one that will do evil and shed blood...?" (*Qur'an* 2:30). This was an expression of dissent against God Himself. But God did not disapprove of this. Instead, he simply explained the matter to the angels, after which they were satisfied. This shows that putting a curb on dissent or criticism, or upbraiding dissenters, is not the Islamic way. The method of Islam is to listen to opposite viewpoints and then attempt, by well-reasoned argument, to remove the grounds for dissent.

In the *Qur'an*, the Prophet has been upheld as a model: "You have a good example in God's Apostle." (33:21). A study of the Prophet's life shows that he invariably adopted the same approach to dissent or criticism as the Almighty did on the very first day of creation.

This is illustrated by an incident in the life of the Prophet in Mecca. There one of his opponents denounced him, couching what he had to say in lines of verse. (In those ancient times, the recitation of poetry, a time-honored custom, was the best means of circulating an idea among the Arabs). The poetess from the opponents' side, who had composed the offending verses, approached, the Prophet and recited a couplet, one line of which is as follows: *Muzammaman asaina wa amrahu* (We have disobeyed the condemned – *muzammaman* meaning condemned – and rejected his teachings).

The Qur'aysh tribe of Mecca had called the Prophet Muzammam, and used to denounce him by this name. On hearing this line of verse, the Prophet remarked to his companions: "Are you not surprised that God has turned the abuses of the Qur'aysh away from me? They abuse one whom they call *Muzammam* and denigrate him. But I am Muhammad (meaning 'praiseworthy'), so their abuses are not going to apply to me."[9]

We learn from this example set by the Prophet that if anyone directs any unwanted criticism at one, the best response is to take it in good part, and to pass it off with a good-honored comment. We find an abundance of such examples in the Prophet's life. When he migrated to Medina, there, too, people used to abuse him. On such occasion, he would request one of his poet companions to arise and conduct his defense in verse.[10]

This shows that in Islam the best answer to invective is not in the meeting out of severe punishment to offenders, but in countering it with argument, the power of argument being a thousand times more effective than that of violence. This was the example set by God. Inspired by this precedent, His Prophet placed no curb on dissent in the society of the first phase of Islam. As we see from the above example, not even vituperation or calumny was suppressed. If healthy criticism can be responded in with an argument, then abuse and denigration can also be replied in the same manner.

Umar Ibn al-Khattab was a great and powerful Caliph of the first phase of Islamic history. He had granted such great freedom to the people that both men and women could freely criticize him

9. Seerat Ibn Hisham Vol. 1, p. 39.
10. Seerat Ibn Hisham.

in public. Umar then either coolly accepted their point of view, or gave reasons to them as to why his stand was right and proper.

Once as Caliph, Umar made a mistake in giving a judgment. When one of his companions pointed this out to him, he promptly admitted his fault, saying, "If this man had not been here, Umar would have been ruined." On another occasion, Umar once said prayers for someone who had sent him the 'gifts' of his own shortcomings.

Islam allows freedom of expression to the greatest possible extent: neither dissent nor criticism nor abuse is punishable crimes. Islam advocates finding solutions to all matters of contention by means of discussion rather than by violence.

Al-Risala, May 1998

❐

14

Islam and the Theory of Revolution

We learn from the *Qur'an* that the state of a community is changed by God only when its members have themselves moved on to a higher spiritual plane, whether by individual effort or under the benign influence of social reformers. Material social accomplishment means little without that inner core of virtue. The *Qur'an* expresses this with telling simplicity: "God does not change a people's lot unless they change what is in their hearts." (13:11)

The starting point of the Islamic revolution is, in fact, the individual. From the individual stems progress of the kind to give society a whole new ethical structure. Clearly, Islamic thinking on this subject is diametrically opposed to the communist ideology, which decrees that the individual be reformed by a change of system. The Islamic view is that when the individual voluntarily reforms, society will itself undergo a radical transformation. And that, from the Islamic standpoint is the ideal situation, obviating as it does the need for totalitarian 'incentives' to change, such as threats, coercion, intimidation and draconian punishments.

The theory of Islamic revolution recognises that the individual is the source of both corruption and reform. Therefore, if the rectification of any aspect of society is sought, the starting point must be the individual and his spiritual wholeness. There is a *Hadith,* which gives metaphorical expression to this. "Listen carefully. In the body there is a piece of flesh. If that is healthy, the whole body is healthy. But if that piece of flesh is not in proper shape, the whole body will become unfit. Listen, that piece of flesh is the heart."[11]

If a social revolution is to be brought about, emphasis must be laid primarily on producing good character. The importance of the good and the right – in though, word and deed – should, ideally, be inculcated from the very outset. A state of personal virtue must be arrived at, whether by early spiritual nurturing so that goodness becomes a matter of instinct, or by later initiatives in conditioning, so that reform takes place from within as a matter of mature and rational acceptance. Goodness then becomes the principle upon which all-healthy social interaction takes place. This generally has a pervasive effect on social institutions, which take their moral hue from the individuals responsible for their functioning at all levels in their hierarchies.

According to a *Hadith* recorded by *Mishkat*, the Prophet of Islam said that the rulers would be of the same level as that of the ruled. That is, whether a system is good or bad for a society will depend upon the individuals who manage it, and also who are managed by it, and whose lives as citizens of a country are quite inseparable from it. In a society formed of good citizens, the system, whatever it may be, will run on just and equitable lines. Conversely, in a society formed of miscreants and moral backsliders, no system per se can conceivably engender social progress, while the system itself, because of the corruption of individuals, will appear to be riddled with iniquities.

The strength of a society and its ability to endure are dependent on the personal worthiness of its members. Each member contributes his individual strength like a brick in a tall building. If the bricks are badly made, so that they erode and crumble, it will only be a matter of time before the entire building crumbles and falls. Can society survive if its constituents are of an inferior moral fiber? Society is also at risk from individuals who launch out on their own on perverse and ill-considered courses. When a single individual can wreak such havoc on society, should not change be in the direction of moderation?

Clearly, in a society that is entirely riven by corrupt and subversive forces, a revolution is called for. The most salient

---

11. Sahih Al Bukhari, Vol. 1 No. 49.

principle of Islamic revolution is that change must be brought about by peaceful efforts. There is a *Hadith,* which says: "God grants to non-violence what He does not grant to violence."[12] The Prophet Mohammed was eminently successful in bringing about major changes in both religious and secular beliefs and practices throughout seventh-century Arabia and the countries surrounding it. The fact, that this was done in the most gradual and pacific way with minimum of bloodshed, is a matter of historical record. It was only after a very long period of missionary work that the Prophet exhorted people, on the basis of divine revelations, for example, to give up drinking, gambling and adultery. Had he attempted to hasten matters by force or intimidation, people would have reacted negatively and might have decided never to comply with his requests. (*Sahih Al-Sahih Al Bukhari*).

It is a measure of the success of his persuasive methods that, despite the heavy addiction to liquor in Arab society, regular topers not only gave up the habit, but also destroyed all the liquor pots they had stored in their homes. Given the 15 years of his painstaking work just to condition individuals' minds to the sublimity of surrendering to their Creator, one might say that the Prophet's method was evolutionary rather than revolutionary.

Al-Risala, April 1998

❑

12. Sunan Abu Daud, 4/255.

15

Environmental Activism, Islam-Style

According to Islam, the virtuous are to be rewarded by God in the after-life by being admitted 'to gardens watered by running streams' and lodged in 'Pleasant mansions in the Gardens of Eternity'(*Qur'an* 61:12). The very fact that Paradise is represented in the *Qur'an* as a beautiful garden, shows the importance attached by Islam to vegetation: indeed, frequent mention is made in the Scriptures of green and growing things as being a blessing from God to mankind.

Referring to the initial stage of creation, the *Qur'an* states: "After that bringing forth from its water and its pasture land." (*Qur'an* 79:31) Nowhere in the vast expanses of universe is there any similar vegetation, which explains why it is that living things, including man, exist only on this earth and on no other celestial body.

In another verse, which is more admonitory in tone, man is enjoined to "reflect on the food he eats: how we pour down the rain in torrents and cleave the earth asunder; how we bring forth the gain and the grapes and the fresh vegetation, the olives and the palm, the thickets, the fruit trees and the green pasture for you and your cattle to delight in". (*Qur'an* 80:24-25).

This shows that God has made vegetation a special food for both men and animals, from which they receive all the nutrients essential to the sustenance of Life. The different fruits and vegetables have also been endowed with prophylactic and curative properties, and perhaps to show that life is more than mere biological existence, each food item has its own distinctive flavor to appeal to the human palate. Honey is specifically cited as a valued foodstuff produced from plants. Its therapeutic qualities are also emphasized in the verse, which says: "Herein lies healing for mankind."(*Qur'an* 16:69) Many effective medicines, from ancient times to the present day, have been produced from plants. The healing powers of plants are indeed so great that even that great carnivore, the tiger, will resort to eating grass when it falls ill.

People are urged in the Scriptures to engage in farming and gardening to provide both physical and spiritual sustenance for themselves, but, despite their Creator's largesse, are cautioned against waste. In verse 161 of the sixth *Surah* of the *Kur'an* after asserting that "it is He who brings forth all manner of plants and creepers and upright trees, the palm and the olive and the pomegranate" and exhorting mankind to "eat off their fruit in their season", goes on to admonish: But waste not by excess. For God loves not the wasters.

Perhaps the most telling references to plant life made in the *Qur'an* and *Hadith* fall within the realm of the metaphor. The Prophet has been recorded as saying: "The believer is like a gentle plant. When the winds blow, it does not show haughtiness: instead, it sways to and fro with the wind, and when the winds are not blowing, it reverts to its position once again." This simile is intended to show how the true believer, the worshipper of God, lives among others. He displays no arrogance, holding that adjustment is better than clashes and confrontation. He follows the principle of persuasion and avoids the path of violence.

In the *Qur'an*, the creature most favored in God's eyes, the believer has been likened to a tree. Just as the tree benefits mankind by its offerings of shade, fruit, flowers and a loveliness to gladden the eye, so should human beings live in society, giving comfort and bringing joy to their fellow men. Just as the tree affords the coolness of its shade to God's creatures, so should God's servants give respite and relief to all those around them.

Again, the tree is used in verse 14 of the 24th *Surah* of the *Qur'an* to symbolise the expression of good intentions towards others. "Do you not see how God compares a good word to a good tree? Its root is firm and its branches are in the sky; it yields its fruit in every season by God's leave. God speaks in parables to men so that they may take heed." Conversely, the verse explains: "But an evil word is like an evil tree torn out of the earth and shorn of all its roots."

Such traditions show what great importance, both physical and metaphysical, is attached to vegetation in Islam. To emphasise this point, the Prophet once observed: "If you have a plant in your hand, and you can see Doomsday approach, even then, without any further delay, you should embed it in the soil." It was ever the desire of Islam that man should make his surroundings verdant, even if in the next instant, his handiwork were to be destroyed by an earthquake. Perhaps the insight of the Prophet on this subject, which has as great a resonance in modern times as it had 14 centuries ago, is contained in his observation that he who plants a tree, whose fruits will eventually be eaten by birds and human beings, performs an act of charity.

Al-Risala, April 1998

❐

16

Hajj: A pilgrimage, Not a Tour

It is incumbent upon Muslims to perform *Hajj*, at least once in a lifetime, as long as they possess the means. As is clear from the following excerpts from the *Qur'an* and *Hadiths*, *Hajj* is one important pillar among the five foundation pillars of Islam.

"Pilgrimage to the House is a duty to God for all who can make the journey." (*Qur'an* 3:97).

"The first House ever to be built for men was the one at *Bakkah (*Mecca), it is a blessed place, a source of guidance for the whole world." (*Qur'an* 3:96)

"There are five basic pillars of Islam," said the Prophet Muhammad: "To bear testimony that there is no deity save God, and that Muhammad is His Prophet; to establish prayer and pay the poor-due; to make pilgrimage to the House and, fast during Ramadan."

The root meaning of the word '*Hajj*' is "to set out" or "to make pilgrimage." Canonically, it has come to refer to a Muslim act of worship, performed annually, in which the worshipper circumambulates the House of God in Mecca, stays awhile in the plain of Arafat and performs other rites, which together constitute *Hajj* – the act of pilgrimage.

Hajj is a comprehensive act of worship, involving both financial outlay and physical exertion. Both remembrance of God and sacrifice for His sake are part and parcel of *Hajj*. *Hajj* is an act of worship, in which the spirit of all acts of worship has, in some way or another, been brought into play.

The sacred duties of *Hajj* revolve around the House of God in Mecca. What does the House of God represent to a believer? It brings to life a whole Prophetic tradition, stretching from Abraham to Muhammad. The House of God stands as a model of true faith in God, and submission to the Master of the House. "The Prophets gave up everything and followed the Lord" is the message that rings out from the Lord's House; "leave all and follow Him. They were obedient to His will; be you so also. They served His cause on Earth; serve Him until you die, and you will prosper forever."

The journey to *Hajj* is a journey to God. It represents the ultimate closeness one can achieve to God while living in this world. Other acts of worship are ways of remembering God; *Hajj* is a way of reaching Him. Generally, we worship Him on an unseen level; in *Hajj* we worship Him as if we saw Him face-to-face, when a pilgrim stands before the House of God Himself. He is then moved to revolve around the Lord's House, like a butterfly encircling a flower, clinging to His doorstep as a slave begging for his master's mercy.

To make *Hajj* is to meet God. When the pilgrim reaches *Meeqat*, the border of the Sacred Territory, he is filled with awe of God; he feels that he is leaving his own world, and entering God's. Now he is touching the Lord, revolving around Him, running towards Him, journeying on His behalf, making sacrifice in His name, smiting His enemies, praying to the Lord and seeing his prayer answered.

Among all Muslim acts of worship, *Hajj* holds a prominent position. In one *Hadith*, the Prophet called it the supreme act of worship. But it is not just the rites of pilgrimage that constitute this importance, it is the spirit in which *Hajj* is performed. Let us put this other way and say that it is not merely a matter of going to *Mecca* and returning. There is much more to *Hajj* than that. *Hajj* has been prescribed so that it may inspire us with new religious fervor. To return from *Hajj* with one's faith in God strengthened and rekindled – that is the hallmark of a true pilgrim.

The House of God in Mecca is one of God's signs on earth. Their souls that have strayed from the Lord take comfort in Him once again; hearts which have become hard as stone are brought low before Almighty God; eyes which have lost their vision are filled with divine radiance. But these blessings of *Hajj* are only for those who come prepared for them. Otherwise, *Hajj* will be just a tour, a visit that leaves no lasting impression upon the tourist.

"*Hajj* is to stand in the plain of *Arafat*." These words of the Prophet Muhammad illustrate the importance of sojourning in the place. The plain of *Arafat*, in which pilgrims spend one day, presents a picture of the arena of Judgment Day. A huge number of God's servants flock in from all sides to witness the spectacle. And what a spectacle! All are dressed in similar, simple attire. There is nothing to single out any person. All are reciting the same words: "Here we are at Your service, Lord." How can one who witnesses this spectacle but call to mind the like of this verse of the *Qur'an*:

"When the trumpet is blown, and behold, from the graves they rush forth to their Lord." (36.51)

The pilgrims gather on the plain of *Arafat* in order to recall the time when they will gather on the plain of the last day. What they will experience in practice in the next world, they conjure up visions of in this world.

For all these reasons, Hajj reigns supreme among all acts of devotion. Like the Sacred Mosque in Mecca has a station above all other mosques, so the worship that is performed there – as part of the pilgrimage – stand head and shoulders above all other acts of devotion.

Al-Risala, March 1998

❐

17

Islam and Social Relations

What are the teachings of Islam on the subject of the multi-religious society? When Islam is studied with this question in mind, we find clear and consistent commandments for all social interaction. In chapter 109 of the *Qur'an*, the Prophet is enjoined to address non-Muslims thus: "I do not worship what you worship, nor do you worship what I worship. I shall never worship what you worship, nor will you ever worship what I worship. You have your own religion, and I have mine.

This verse of the *Qur'an*, coupled with others of its teachings, amounts to an unambiguous and easily applicable formula for mutual respect. It means simply that all believers, whatever their elected religion, must have due reverence for the religions adhered to by others.

What establishes the need for such a formula is the edifice of religion being founded on the total conviction that it is the whole truth. To have any followers at all, a religion must carry that conviction. It is in the nature of things. But religious conviction alone is not a broad enough base on which to form a just society, particularly if that conviction is publicly expressed by different groups through the widely differing practices of different faiths.

In the multi-religious context, it also takes broadmindedness, compassion and fellow feeling. Only when in possession of these virtues can members of society display that tolerance in their dealings with others, which will ensure a lasting peace.

The principle of mutual respect is a natural one and is to be found in all areas of civilized living. One of the major demands made by Islam is that this natural principle be upheld and acted upon by the adherents of different religions, so that societal structures may be strengthened by stable and enduring relationships.

For the greater part of his life, the Prophet of Islam lived in a society where adherents of other religions existed side-by-side with believers in Islam. The Prophet's behavior towards the former was invariably that of respect and tolerance. At a time when the majority of the denizens of Mecca were still idolaters, his conduct consistently conveyed his high moral character. On the one hand, he communicated to them the message of *tawheed* with love and kindness and, on the other, fulfilled all of their human rights. That is why the non-Muslims of Mecca had such great confidence in him – to the point of entrusting their belongings to his care. This they continued to do right up to the last days of his stay in Mecca.

After the attainment of his Prophethood, he lived in Mecca for a period of thirteen years, later migrating to Medina, where he lived for ten years until his death. For about half of this period in Medina, he was living among people belonging to three religions – Muslims, Jews and Pagans. The Prophet devised a constitution for these people, known in history as *Sahifa-tul-Medina* (Charter of Medina).

The charter expressly mentioned that issues concerning these three groups domiciled in Medina would be decided on the basis of their own religious traditions – those of Muslims according to their Islamic traditions, and those of pagans and Jews according to their respective traditions. This principle of Islam was intended to apply at all places where Muslims lived along with adherents of other religions. This *sunnah*, or practice of the Prophet, for a plural society carries the same moral authority as other of his practices.

Islam recognises no difference between Muslims and non-Muslims from the ethical standpoint. The rights granted to a Muslim are exactly the same as those granted to a non-Muslim.

A tradition in *Sahih Al Bukhari* gives us a telling example of how this principle should in practice be followed. When the Prophet was in Medina, he saw a funeral procession passing along a street. The Prophet was seated at that time. On seeing it, the Prophet stood up in deference to the deceased person. One of his companions said: "O God's messenger, it was the funeral of a Jew (not a Muslim)." The Prophet replied: "Was he not a human being?"

This tradition of the Prophet of Islam tells us that every human being is worthy of respect. There might be differences between people in religion, culture and traditions but it is incumbent upon everyone to accord equal respect to others, as all men and women are creatures of one and the same God. All are descendants of Adam and Eve.

Everyone has certainly the right to adopt one religion according to his beliefs. But with that choice comes the ineluctable responsibility of giving respect in full measure to adherents of other faiths and, in the light of those faiths, giving them what is ethically their due.

Al-Risala, February 1998

❐

18

Non-Violence and Islam

Islam is a religion that teaches non-violence. According to the *Qur'an*, God does not love *fasad* (violence). What is meant here by *fasad* clearly expressed in verse 205 of the second *Surah*: it is that action which results in disruption of the social system, causing huge losses in terms of lives and property.

Conversely, we can say with certainty that God loves non-violence. He abhors violent activity in human society, as a result of which people pay the price with their possessions and their lives. This is supported by other statements in the *Qur'an*. For instance, we are told in the *Qur'an* that peace is one of God's names (59:23). Those who seek to please God are assured by verse 5 of the sixteenth *Surah* that they will be guided by Him to "the paths of peace".

The entire spirit of the *Qur'an* is in consonance with this concept. For instance, the *Qur'an* attaches great importance to patience. In fact, patience is set above all other Islamic virtues with the exceptional promise of reward beyond measure. (39:10)

Patience implies a peaceful response or reaction, whereas impatience implies a violent response. The word *sabr* exactly expresses the notion of non-violence as it is understood in modern times. That patient action is non-violent action has been clearly expressed in the *Qur'an*. According to one tradition, the Prophet of Islam observed: God grants to *rifq* (gentleness) what he does not grant to *unf* (violence).[13]

The word *rifq* has been used in this *Hadith* as an antithesis to *unf*. These terms convey exactly what is meant by violence and

13. Sunan, Abu Daud, 4/255.

non-violence in present times. This *Hadith* clearly indicates the superiority of the non-violent method.

God grants to non-violence what He does not grant to violence is no simple matter. It has very wide and deep implications. It embodies an eternal law of nature. By the very law of nature all bad things are associated with violence, and all good things with non-violence.

Violent activities breed hatred in society, while non-violent activities elicit love. Violence is the way of destruction while non-violence is the way of construction. In an atmosphere of violence, it is enmity that flourishes, while in an atmosphere of non-violence, it is friendship, that flourishes. The method of violence gives way to negative values while the method of non-violence is marked by positive values. The method of violence embroils people in the problems, while the method of non-violence leads people to the exploiting of opportunities. In short, violence is death, non-violence is life.

Both the *Qur'an* and the *Hadith* have attached great importance to *jihad*. What is *jihad*? It mean struggle, to struggle one's utmost. It must be appreciated at the outset that this word is used for non-violent struggle as opposed to violent struggle. One clear proof of this is the verse of the *Qur'an* (25:52), which says: Perform *jihad* with this (i.e. the word of the *Qur'an*) most strenuously.

The *Qur'an* is not a sword or a gun. It is a book of ideology. In such a case performing *jihad* with the *Qur'an* would mean an ideological struggle to conquer peoples' hearts and minds through Islam's superior philosophy.

In the light of this verse of *Qur'an*, *jihad* in actual fact is another name for peaceful activism or non-violent activism. Where *qital* is violent activism, *jihad* is non-violent activism. No-violence, therefore, should never be confused with inaction or passivity. Non-violence is action in the full sense of the word. Rather, it is more forceful an action than that of violence.

Non-violent activism is not limited in its sphere. It is a course of action, which may be followed in all matters. Whenever individuals, groups or communities are faced with a problem, one way to solve it is by resorting to violence. The better way is to attempt to solve the problem by peaceful means, avoiding violence and confrontation.

When the *Qur'an* began to be revealed, the first verse of the revelation conveyed the injunction: 'Read!' (Iqra) (*Qur'an* 96:1). By persuing this verse, we learn about the initiation of Islamic action. It begins from the point where there is hope of continuing the movement along peaceful lines, and not from that point where there are chances of it being marred by violence.

Generally speaking, attempts to improve or replace existing systems by violent activism are counter-productive. One coup d'étatis often the signal for a series of coups and counter-coups, none of which benefit the common man. The truly desirable revolution is that which permits gradual and beneficial changes. And this can be achieved only on the basis of non-violence.

Al-Risala, January 1998

❐

19
How the Qur'an was Compiled

The *Qur'an*, according to Muslim belief, is a book of revelations from God. Today, it exists in the form of a book, but all the 114 chapters of the *Qur'an* were not revealed at one time. They were sent bit by bit, according to circumstances, over a period of 23 years.

The *Qur'an* is pivotal to all Muslim activities. Muslims recite the *Qur'an* daily, and read from it in their prayers five times a day. Over and above this, they also read it out to others. In this way, the *Qur'an* has remained at the center of Muslims' activities since the beginning.

In ancient times, information used to be preserved in human memory. The oral tradition in those days functioned as libraries do today. This system made it possible for the revelations of the *Qur'an* to be preserved in the memory of a large number of followers. And to this day, and despite printing presses, the institution of memorising the *Qur'an* is still alive all over the Muslim world.

But the message of the *Qur'an* was not transmitted purely by oral tradition even during the lifetime of the Prophet. Among his companions was a select group of about half a dozen *katib-e-wahy* – transcribers of the revelations. A few of these scribes were always present and whenever any part of the *Qur'an* was revealed, the Prophet would recite it to them. Thereupon, at the exact moment of revelation, they would not only commit it to memory, but would write it down on any available material, such as paper, bones, leather or skin. In former times, when the accepted way of disseminating the subject matter of a book was to memorise it and then recite it, it was quite exceptional that the *Qur'an* should have been both memorised and preserved in writing.

The second exceptional point concerns the arrangement of the verses and chapters of the *Qur'an*. When the *Qur'an* was revealed in parts, at different times according to the demand of circumstances, how did it come to be arranged in its present form? We find its answer in the books of *Hadith*. It has been proved from authentic traditions that the angel Gabriel, who conveyed the revelations of God to the Prophet had himself, arranged these verses. Each year during the month of Ramadan, the angel Gabriel would come to the Prophet and recited before him all the *Qur'anic* verses revealed up till that time. And after listening to the angel, the Prophet would repeat the verses in the order in which he had heard them. This dual process has been termed *al-Irza*, 'mutual presentation' in the books of *Hadith*.

In the last year of the Prophet's life, when the revelations were complete, Gabriel came to the Prophet and recited the entire *Qur'an* in the existing order twice, and the Prophet also recited to Gabriel the entire *Qur'an* twice. This final presentation is called *al-Arz al-Akhirah* in the *Hadith*.[14]

And, in this way, the *Qur'an* came to be in the form we are familiar with today, preserved in memories of tens of thousands of the Prophet's companions even during his lifetime.

When the Prophet died in 632 AD, at the age of 63, the *Qur'an* existed in two forms: in the memory of these companions, who had learned it by rote in what is now its present order; two, in writing – on pieces of paper and other materials, preserved by the companions. What must be noted here is that the order existed in memory, not in writing, though all the parts existed at that time in written form.

After the death of the Prophet, Abu Bakr Siddique was appointed the first Caliph, and it was during his caliphate that the compilation of *Qur'an* was carried out. Zaid ibn Thabit, the Prophet's foremost scribe and an authority on the *Qur'an*, was entrusted with this task. His work was more of collection than of compilation – the scattered bits and pieces of the *Qur'an* were put together, not that they could be bound in one volume, but that they could be used to crosscheck countless memories in oral tradition. Once this correspondence between the oral and written forms had

14. Fathul Bari, p. 659-663.

been established beyond any reasonable doubt, Zaid proceeded to put the verses of the *Qur'an* down on paper in their correct order. The volume he produced was then handed over to the Caliph, and this remained in the custody of the Prophet's wife, Hafsa.

The third Caliph, Osman, arranged for several copies of this text to be sent to all the states and placed in central mosques where the people could prepare further copies. In this way, the message of the *Qur'an* spread further and further, both through oral tradition and hand-written copies, until the age of the press dawned. Many printing presses were established in the Muslim world, where the beautiful calligraphy of the scriptures was reproduced after its content had been certified by memorizers of the *Qur'an*. Once again with the help of memorized versions and written texts, correct, authentic copies were prepared; and with the publication of these copies on a large scale, the *Qur'an* spread all over the world. Any copy of the *Qur'an* found in any part of the world at any time will be exactly the same as that handed down to the Muslims by the Prophet in his last days, arranged in the form still extant today.

Al-Risala, December 1997

❐

20
The Concept of Peace in Islam

If you read the *Qur'an* carefully, you will find that it is a book of peace. For example, the very first verse of the *Qur'an* reads: In the name of God, the Most Merciful, the Most Compassionate. This verse, which is repeated in the *Qur'an* 114 times, clearly shows that the God of Islam is the God of Mercy and Compassion, and the book of Islam too is the book of mercy. The people of Islam must also possess the quality of mercy and compassion otherwise they could not be true believers.

If you go through the *Qur'an* you will find that from most verses, either directly or indirectly there emanates the spirit of peace. There is a verse which says: "And God calls to the home of peace" (*Qur'an* 10:25). This means that the destination of Islam is peace. All the teachings of Islam are oriented towards the goal of peace.

Another example: 'Reconciliation is the best.' (*Qur'an* 4:128) When there is a conflict between two individuals or two groups, Muslims ought to follow the course of reconciliation. In controversial matters, the policy of Islam is one of adjustment and not of confrontation.

If you make a detailed study of the *Qur'an* you will discover many verses, which deal with the objects and events of the universe, as signs of nature. These verses project the universe as a model of peace and harmony. There are innumerable astronomical bodies in space. All are in motion, but all follow their own orbits without the slightest deviation. Holding up this phenomenon as an ideal, the *Qur'an* asks us to follow the same course of peace, that is, to move in one's own orbit and not trespass (3:83). Thus peaceful living is the religion for both: man and the universe.

Now I would like to present examples from the traditions of the Prophet. Once a man came to the Prophet and said to the Prophet: "Advise me!" "The Prophet said: "Do not become angry and furious." The man asked (the same) again and again, and the Prophet said in each case: "Do not become angry and furious."[15]

That is to say, stick to positive behavior in all situations. In fact, in normal conditions man is governed by his own nature. And nature always takes the course of peace. When people are provoked their nature is upset, and they are derailed into negativity. So, the Prophet advised people never to take a negative course of action, and to keep to peaceful and positive behavior in all situations, even in the face of provocation.

According to another tradition, the Prophet of Islam once observed: Don't wish for confrontation with your enemy, instead always ask for peace from God.

This means that even when they have enemies. Muslims are not allowed to take the course of confrontation. They must rather seek the way of avoidance. The *Qur'an* further states in chapter 41, verse 34, that if you deal with your enemy positively and return good for evil, he will become your closest friend. These references from the *Qur'an* and *Sunnah* make it clear that peace is the greatest concern of Islam. The Islamic method is a peaceful method. Islamic activism is a peaceful activism.

Why Islam lays down such a great emphasis on peace? Because all the good things that Islam wants to see in human life can be brought about only in peaceful environment. For instance, such constructive activities like spiritual uplift, character-building, educational activity, social welfare, worship and prayer can be performed only in peaceful conditions. No peace, no progress; no peace, no development.

Peace in Islam is not required for the sake of peace. It is required for the sake of God that is for the sake of a greater purpose. It is because no Islamic activity can be carried out except in peaceful conditions. Due to this great importance, the Prophet of Islam always wanted to maintain peace even at the price of unilateral adjustment.

---

15. Sahih Al Bukhari, Vol. 8, Book 73.

Some people portray the picture of Islam as a religion of violence by using the word *jihad*. They say that *jihad* in Islam is a holy war. But it is totally untrue there is no concept of holy war in Islam. *Jihad* has nothing to do with war or violence, it actually means a struggle, a peaceful struggle. "And make *jihad* on them, with the help of the *Qur'an*" (25:52), says the *Qur'an*. Nowhere does it say: "with the help of a sword".

Clearly, *Jihad* is an act to be performed by the power of ideology rather than the power of the sword; it is only another name for peaceful activism along Islamic lines.

The *Qur'an* says that on the day of Judgment, God will say: 'O peaceful soul, come and enter my paradise' (*Qur'an* 89:28). And only those who have followed the path of peace in this world will be allowed an entrance into God's Paradise.

Peace in Islam is not required for the sake of peace. It is required for the sake of God, because no Islamic activity can be carried out except in peace.

Al-Risala, November 1997

❐

21

In the Service of God and Man

All the teachings of Islam are based on two basic principles – worship of God and service of men. Without putting both of these principles into practice, there can be no true fulfillment of one's religious duties.

Islam inculcates in its followers the spirit of love and respect for all human beings. By serving human beings, on one hand they please their God, and on the other, they achieve spiritual progress for themselves.

According to one *Hadith* (tradition), should you be merciful to people on earth, God will be merciful to you. In this manner Islam link personal salvation to the service of people. One can receive God's reward in the Hereafter only if one has done something to alleviate the sufferings of mankind in this world.

On Doomsday, it is said, God will say to a person: "I was ill, but you did not come to nurse Me." The man will reply: "God, You being the Lord of the Universe, how can You be ill?" God will answer: "Such and such servant of Mine was ill. Had you gone there, you would have found Me there with him." Then God will say to another person: "I was hungry, but you did not feed me." The person will reply: "God, You are the Lord of the worlds, how could You go hungry?" God will say: "Such and such of my servants came to you, but you did not feed him. Had you done so, you would have found Me with him."

The Islamic principle is that if someone wants to find God, he shall first have to make himself deserving of this by helping the poor and the needy. This act becomes a means of spiritual progress for him, and there is no doubt that it is only those people who have elevated themselves spiritually, who find God.

This culture of mercy and compassion approved by God is not limited towards human beings, but extends also to the animal world. We must be equally sympathetic to animals. *Hadith* gives us many guidelines on how to look after animals and treat them with fairness. There are duties laid down by God. One who is cruel to animal's risks depriving himself of God's mercy.

Two significant examples have been mentioned in a *Hadith*. One devoutly religious woman, who spent most of her time in worship, one day became enraged with a cat and trussed it up with a rope, depriving it of food and water, in which state it remained until it died of thirst and hunger. God so strongly disapproved of this that, despite the woman's great devotion, He decreed that she be cast into Hell.[16]

Another woman, a prostitute by profession, was generally despised by people. One day she found a dog lying on the ground dying of thirst. This woman felt sympathy for it. She searched high and low, till she found a well – but there was nothing with which to draw water from it. She tied her shoe to her shawl, and by lowering this into the well, she was able to draw water, which she gave to the dog. She did this several times until the dog's thirst was quenched. Then it revived and walked happily away. According to the *Hadith*, God was so pleased with this gesture that He decreed that she should enter Paradise.[17]

Islamic belief softens the hearts of its believers. That is why, when people imbibe Islamic belief their will of necessity become kind and compassionate towards others. But if even after adopting the beliefs of Islam, feelings of love and compassion do not well up in the heart of its believer, he should rethink on whether or not Islamic beliefs have truly found a place in his heart and mind, whether or not he is able to fully practice what he believes and whether or not he has succeeded in moulding himself entirely into the path of Islam.

When Umar ibn Khattab, the second Caliph of Islam, travelled from Medina to Palestine, he had taken only one camel along with him. He felt that if he rode the camel for the entire journey, it would be cruelty to the animal, so it must be given rest. Therefore,

16. Sahih Al Bukhari Book 3, p. 553.
17. Sahih Al Bukhari Book 54, p. 538.

he rode and walked by turn, so that the camel should have periods of rest, until he reached his destination.

If the true spirit of Islam is inculcated in a person, he becomes so compassionate to all living beings that even at the cost of his own comforts, he extends a helping hand to others.

As it is put in a *Hadith*: "He is not a Muslim whose stomach is filled while the neighbor to his side goes hungry."[18] This shows that a Muslim is one who is as concerned with others' hunger and thirst as he is with his own; who is concerned not only with his own person but with the whole of humanity.

According to another *Hadith*, you should "extend greetings to people, feed them and earn your place in heaven". This shows that according to Islam, that person is worthy of Heaven whose heart is impatient for others' peace and goodwill, who is eager to share with everyone, whether it be food, clothes or medical help, etc. In short, one should share in people's pain and suffering.

Islam is a religion of humanity. Islam considers serving others a great act of worship. According to the teachings of Islam, it is only in serving people that we shall have a share in God's mercy.

Al-Risala, October 1997

❐

18. Sahih Al Bukhari Book. 4, p. 112.

22

The Sacred Book of Islam

The *Qur'an*, according to Muslim belief, is a revealed book; it is not authored by a human being, but is the true word of God in human language. A medium-sized book so far as its length is concerned, it comprises 114 chapters or *Surahs* (77, 439 words). Its revelation to the Prophet Muhammad, upon whom be peace, through the Angel Gabriel, began in AD 610, while the Prophet was sitting in (*Jabal-an-Noor*) seclusion in the cave of Hira at the top of the Mountain of Light, two miles from Mecca. The scriptures were not revealed at one point of time. Their various parts were revealed as and when the occasion demanded. The entire process was completed over a period of 23 years, the last passage being revealed to the Prophet while he was addressing a gathering at Mount Arafat on the occasion of his last and only *Hajj* in A.D. 622. The entire volume was later compiled in Medina during the last days of the Prophet.

Since the *Qur'an* came into existence long before the days of the printing press, there were only two ways of preserving it: either by committing the entire text to memory, or writing it down. That is why, there have always been a great number of *hafiz* (those who committed the entire *Qur'an* to memory) in every age, right from the moment of the *Qur'an's* first revelation. The earliest written copies are still available in different museums, one of these being in Tashkent.

The *Qur'an,* addressed directly to mankind, tells us of God's scheme for human existence: that man is placed on this earth for the purpose of being tested. The freedom he has here has not been given him as a matter of right, but as a means to allow him to prove his moral fiber. It is the outcome of this test that will ultimately decide man's eternal fate. It is asserted in the holy book that human beings are eternal creatures, yet only an infinitesimal part of their lifespan has been assigned to the present world, while the remainder has been ordained for the Hereafter.

As we learn from the scriptures, all the previously revealed books had been sent by God so that man might be informed of the nature of his life. The *Qur'an*, the last of the revealed books, endorses all the revealed books, which preceded it. But this endorsement applies to them only in their original, pristine versions. The religious scriptures preceding the *Qur'an* were – as is claimed by their followers – divine in origin. But from the point of view of academic authenticity they have lost their original credibility. This is due to alteration, deletion and interpolation. According to the *Qur'an,* the only authentic version of God's message to mankind is that revealed by Him to His final Prophet.

The study of the *Qur'an* tells us that it is individual-based rather than system-oriented. That is, the actual target of the holy book is to change the thinking of the individual. Changing the system is not the *Qur'an's* objective. For the system is subservient to the individual and not the individual to the system. That is why, the utmost emphasis is placed on inculcating right thinking in man. Yet, it is not the method of the *Qur'an* to set out everything in advance, in detail. It rather encourages individuals to think for themselves along the proper lines, so that they may discover for themselves the great truths of life. In educational terminology, this is called the discovery method.

Islamic teachings can be summed up under two basic headings: believing in One God and worshipping Him alone; regarding all human beings as equal and according equal rights to all.

In brief, it says monotheism and justice for all. The *Qur'an* enshrines these basic teachings, dealing with them in their abstract and practical forms, but for a detailed application of their wisdom, one must go to the *Hadith* (the sayings and deeds of Prophet Muhammad).

As far as social life is concerned, the essence of Islamic teaching is that God has granted freedom to everyone. This freedom in itself demands that people should lead their lives with proper restraint.

For if freedom is exercised without restraint it will inevitably result in friction, outright clashes and the descent of society into chaos. Social equilibrium can be maintained only if conscience (*nafs lawwama*) prevails over ego (*ammara*). In social life, our actions elicit good or evil depending upon whether we have activated the ego or the conscience of the person or persons concerned.

Whenever one initiates any undertaking, the *Qur'an* states expressly that one should begin by uttering the name of God. One thus always reminds oneself, at the outset, of God's attributes of benevolence and compassion. It is also a way of determining that all projects will be launched not with personal but with divine intentions, and that all actions stemming therefrom will be merciful rather than exploitative in nature. The most frequently repeated invocation in the *Qur'an* is: "In the name of God, the most Beneficent, the most Merciful." The recurrence of this phrase no less than 114 times is in itself a clear indication of how important it is.

Al-Risala, September 1997

❐

23

The Concept of Jihad

Jihad is regularly misconstrued as war, with all its connotations of violence and bloodshed. However, in the Islamic context, and in the literal sense, the word '*jihad*' simply means a struggle – doing one's utmost to further a worthy cause. This is an entirely peaceful struggle, with no overtones even of aggression. The actual Arabic equivalent of war is *qital*, and even this is meant in a defensive sense.

According to Islamic teachings, *jihad* is of two kinds. One is with the self (*jihad bin nafs*), that is making the maximum effort to keep control over negative feelings in one's self, for instance, arrogance, jealousy, greed, revenge anger, etc. The psychological efforts to lead such a life of restraint, is what *jihad bin nafs* is about. In social life, it happens time and again that all sorts of base, negative feelings well up within a man, causing him to lead his life succumbing to desires and temptations. The internal effort made in such a situation to overcome the temptations of the self and to continue to lead a life guided by principles is the truly Islamic *jihad bin nafs*.

According to one *Hadith*, a believer is one who wages *jihad* with himself in the path of obedience to God. That is, at moments when the self (*nafs*), lured by some temptation, desires to deviate from the path of God, he keeps control over it and remains unswervingly on the divine path. This is his *jihad* – a permanent nature of life of a believer, continuing day and night, and ending only with death.

The other form of *jihad* is to propagate the constructive message of Islam. All those who embark upon which a course must first of all study the *Qur'an* and *sunnah* in a dispassionate and objective manner. No kind of conditioning should be allowed to come in the way of such study. Only after passing through this intellectual *jihad* will they would be proponent of Islam be in a position to make a true representation of his religion to the world.

Two conditions have been laid down in the *Qur'an* for the communication of the teachings of Islam to other – *naasih*, well-wishing and *amin*, trustworthiness. The former appertains to God and the latter to man.

What is meant by *naasih* is an earnest desire on the part of the preacher of truth for the well-being not just of his immediate interlocutors, but of the whole of humanity. This well-wishing should be so steadfast that it remains undiluted even in the face of injustice and oppression. Overlooking people's negative behavior towards him, the preacher should continue to remain their well-wisher. The element of trustworthiness (*amin*) is important in that it ensures that the religion which God has sent to the world will be presented to the people without deletion, addition or distortion. For instance, if the Islam sent by God is *akhirah* (Hereafter) oriented, it should not become world-oriented; if it is spirituality based, it should not become politics-based; if it confines *jihad* to peaceful struggle, it should not become violence-based. Islam asks us to perform *jihad* by means of the *Qur'an*, calling this 'greater' *jihad* (25:52). But it never asks its believers to do the 'greater' *jihad* by means of the gun.

This is a clear proof that *jihad* is, in actual fact, a wholly peaceful activity, carried out through peaceful methods. It has nothing to do with violent activities or violent threats.

Jihad through the *Qur'an* means striving to the utmost to present the teachings of the *Qur'an* before the people. That is, presenting the concept of One God as opposed to the concept of many Gods; presenting *akhirah*-oriented life as superior to world-oriented life; principle-oriented life as against interest-oriented life; a humanitarian-oriented life as more elevated than a self-oriented life and a duty-oriented life as a categorical imperative, taking moral precedence over a rights-oriented life.

Jihad, according to Islam, is not something about which there is any mystery. It is simply a natural requirement of daily living. It is vital both as a concept and as a practice because, while leading his life in this world, man is repeatedly confronted by such circumstances as are likely to derail him from the humanitarian path of the highest order.

These factors sometimes appear within man in the form of negative feelings. This is something everyone must remain intellectually alert, to, so that if for any reason there is some danger of a negative mindset gaining the upper hand, he may consciously and deliberately turn himself to positive thinking. Even if circumstances repeatedly place him in situations, which are depressing and demoralizing, he must never on such occasions lose course or lose sight of noble goals. The reassertion of his ethical sense is the real *jihad,* which he has to wage.

From the Islamic standpoint, intention is all-important. Any undertaking carried out with good intentions will win God's approval, while anything done with bad intention is bound to be disapproved of and rejected by God. In actual fact, intentions are the sole criteria of good or bad actions, in the divine scheme of thing, and it is one's intense inner struggle to make all activities God-oriented, which is truly Islamic *jihad*.

Al-Risala, August 1997

❐

24

Islam and the Concept of a Single God

Fundamental to the religious structure of Islam is the concept of *tawheed*, or monotheism. As the seed is to tree, so is *tawheed* to Islam. Just as the tree is a wonderfully developed extension of the seed, so is the religious system of Islam a multi-faceted expression of a single basic concept. For, monotheism in Islam does not mean simply belief in one God, but in God's oneness in all respects. No one shares in this oneness of God.

Anthropologists would have us believe that the concept of God in religion began with polytheism, that polytheism gradually developed into monotheism. That is, the concept of *tawheed* was an evolutionary feature of religion which emerged at a later stage. But according to Islamic belief, *tawheed* has existed since the beginning of human life. The first man was also the first messenger who taught human beings the religion of *tawheed*.

It was in later generations that this system began to change. This happened principally because people began to make the assumption that divinity was inherent in natural phenomena. They wondered at the loftiness of the mountains, the unceasing flow of the rivers and the extraordinary brilliance of the sun and moon, and took it to mean that things possessed of such awesome attributes must necessarily share in God's divinity. Men gifted with special talents, likewise, came to be included in the category of the divine; they were supposed to be incarnations of God Himself. It was in this manner that polytheism crept into the religion.

In consonance with the view that human religions began with *tawheed*, and polytheism developed later, the basic mission of all the Prophets who appeared at intervals in this world was to lead people away from the worship of many gods and back to the worship of the One God. In other words we can say that they wanted to turn people away from the adulation of creatures and towards reverence for the Creator.

As proof of the Creator's existence, the *Qur'an* advances the fact of the very existence of the universe. All studies of the universe show it cannot be *Sui Generis*: some other agent is essential for the universe to have come into existence. This means the choice is not between a universe with God or one without God, rather it is between a universe with God, or no universe at all. And so we are left with only the option of a universe with God – a condition also necessary for the existence of human beings.

God created man and settled him on the earth. After settling him here, he has kept an unceasing watch over him. Life and death are equally in His hands. Whatever man gains or lose, it is all a matter of the will of God. As expressed in the *Qur'an*: "God; there is no God but He the Living, the Eternal One. Neither slumber nor sleep overtakes Him. His is what the heavens and the earth contain. Who can intercede with Him, unless by His leave? He knows all that is before them and all that is behind them. They can grasp only that part of His knowledge, which He wills. His throne is as vast as the heavens and the earth, and the preservation of both does not weary Him. He is the Exalted, the Immense One." (2:255).

While *tawheed* means the oneness of God, it must be stressed that this concept differs radically from pantheistic or animist notions that all the forms of existence are diverse manifestations of one and the same reality. On the contrary, the oneness of God as defined in Islam means there is only one Being of the nature of God. All other things of the universe, physical or non-physical, are the creations of this One God: they are in no respect constituents of, or partners in, the divine godhead.

However, in Islamic theology, *tawheed* does have two aspects to it: *tawheed fi az-Zat* and *tawheed fi as-Sifat*, that is, oneness of being and oneness of attributes. This means that in addition to the fact of there being only one Being who enjoys that status of divinity and possesses divine powers, there is also the fact that no one else can have a share in, or lay claim to God's attributes. These include the power of creating and sustaining the universe with all its countless bodies in motion, of sustaining and nourishing our world; in short, of governing all the happenings in the heavens and on earth; all of these are directly managed by God. No representative or deputy of God has any power – either independent or delegated – over the events of the universe: "He throws the veil of night over the day. Swiftly they follow one another. It was He who created the sun, the moon and the stars and made them subservient to His will. His is the creation, His is the command. Blessed be God, the Lord of all creatures." (*Qur'an* 7:54)

The divisibility of the divine attributes is totally alien to Islam. Just as God is alone in His being, so is He alone in His attributes. In recognition of His uniqueness, the *Qur'an* opens with the following invocation: "Praise be to God, Lord of the universe, the Compassionate, the Merciful, Sovereign of the Day of Judgment. You alone we worship, and to You alone we turn for help. Guide us to the straight path, the path of those whom You have favored, not of those who have incurred Your wrath, nor of those who have gone astray." (1:1-7)

Al-Risala, June 1997

❒

25

Monism and Monotheism

The major religions of the world can be divided into two broad categories – the Aryan and the Semitic, with Hinduism, Buddhism and Jainism in the first and Judaism, Christianity and Islam in the second. So far as their theological aspects are concerned, there is a marked difference between these two kinds of religions. While the Aryan religions are basically philosophy-based, the Semitic religions are revelation-based. The former represent the culmination of the philosophical pursuit of truth by the great minds of the world. In the quest for reality, meditation and contemplation brought these saintly souls to the conclusions, which gave rise to the principal, organized religions of the eastern hemisphere.

The creeds of the Semitic religions, on the other hand, are based on divine revelation. That is, God chose a series of Semites to be His apostles and then imparted to them His commandments. These messengers became not only the bearers of divine scriptures but also their divinely inspired interpretations, which provided the fundamentals of the Semitic religions as they exist today.

The basic difference in respect to beliefs of the Aryan and Semitic religions can be briefly described in terms of monism and monotheism respectively.

Although both traditions – monism and monotheism – have the idea of God in common, there are fundamental differences in their conceptualisation of God. In the Aryan tradition, God is an all-pervasive force rather than an independent reality. Monism posits the totality of a single reality, with all the diverse phenomena of the natural world seen as different manifestations of the same reality. According to this concept, therefore, there is no real difference between the creator and the creation. Thus, in monistic theorising, the concept of an individual, personalised God does not exist.

In Semitic religions, particularly in Islam, the concept of God is entirely based on monotheism. This concept can also be termed dualism – that the Creator and the creation are completely different from one another. God has a real and eternal existence. As the Creator of all things, he is distinct from all He has created. His creatures in their seemingly independent existence totally depend upon the will of God. The sole possessor of all power, God has created man to live for a specific period of time, during which he is sent into the world to be tested. It is this concept of the Creator as totally distinct from the creation that sets the Semitic religions apart from the Aryan.

The philosophy of Islam is explicitly that of monotheism. It is true that the Sufi system has incorporated monistic concepts. This is in actual fact a deviation from the original Islam, and is held by the majority of Islamic scholars to be an incorrect interpretation, not truly representative of Islam.

Other presentations of Islam also figure in the books which were produced in the later period of Islam. But all of these, based as they are on personal interpretations, do not have the status of sacred books. In Islam, only the *Qur'an* and *Sunnah* (the Prophet's words and deeds) enjoy the status of the only authentic sources, and it is to them that we must turn if we are to have a true appreciation of the essence of the religion.

The mainstay of Islam is its monotheism – *tawheed* – belief in the oneness of God in the complete sense of the word. God is One. He has no partner. He created all things and has complete control over the universe. We should serve Him and submit to Him alone. Though He cannot be seen, He is so close to us that He hears and answers us when we call upon Him.

The distinctive aspect of this monotheism is that no intermediary link exists between the Creator and the creation. By remembering Him, any individual at any point in time may, quite independently, establish contact with God. There is no need for any go-between. Indeed belief in an intermediary link with God is alien to the Islamic religious system. Called *shirk* (associating others with God) it is deemed to be an unpardonable offence.

According to the *Qur'an,* God in Islam is not a symbol, but a reality. God is not a kind of working hypothesis on which to found a religious system. On the contrary, God in Islam is a Personality. He has a real and independent existence. He is alive and self-sustaining, self-perpetuating. He has knowledge. He takes decisions, rewards and punishes. He is the Controller and Sustainer of human history.

The chapter of the *Qur'an, Al-Ikhlas* (Purity) sums up in a few terse words the unity of the Godhead. Say:

God is One, the Eternal God. He begot none nor was He begotten. None is equal to Him.

Al-Risala, April 1997

❐

26

Innumerable Bounties of Fasting

Fasting (*sawm*) is the third pillar of Islam. Right from dawn till dusk, a man who is strictly on a fast will neither eat as much as one morsel of food nor drink a single drop of water. By submitting to this discipline, that is, by depriving himself of the prime necessities of life, man learns the valuable lesson of fortitude. With no food and drink, he naturally feels hungry and thirsty, and his strength begins to ebb.

The entire routine of his life is severely disturbed and his whole system is upset. But, out of a high sense of discipline, he braves all the difficulties and discomfort, and remaining alert and never losing heart, he steadfastly discharges his duties. Food and drink may be temptingly placed before him, but, despite an overwhelming urge to have both, he will not even touch them. In this way, he prepares himself for a well-regulated and responsible life, doing only what is his duty and refraining from pernicious acts and habits. He is strengthened to continue with his mission in life, no matter how much he may be beset by adversity.

God has endowed man with innumerable gifts, but, all too often, he takes them for granted without any feelings of gratitude. Countless benefits like the air, the sun, the water have been showered upon man, the absence of any one of which would cast his delicately balanced system into a living hell. But because he has received these things without any effort on his part, he sets no great value upon them, and hardly ever stops to ponder upon how they came to be his.

It is only when fasting temporarily curbs the satisfying of his desires that his consciousness of the value of these divine gifts is awakened. When, at sunset, after a whole day's hunger, thirst and the accompanying discomfort and fatigue, a man begins to eat and drink, he becomes fully aware of his utter dependence on God's bounty. He is then filled with gratitude towards God and the realisation comes to him that, even were he to lay down his life for this Bountiful Creator, the price he should have to pay would not be too high.

The life of a believer in this world is one of fortitude and forbearance, limited as it is to the enjoyment of whatever is allowed by God and avoidance of whatever is forbidden by Him. It will naturally be beset by all the difficulties encountered in the path of righteousness and truth, and the believer must staunchly face up to them.

Much of his time must be given to such activity, and no precious moment can be wasted in stooping to revenge himself upon adversaries who have made him the object of their spite and malice. On the contrary, the slights and injuries of this world should leave him undaunted; he should be able simply to take such untoward incidents in his stride so that he may continue unflinchingly to discharge his duties. Whenever his pride has been hurt, or whenever some unpleasantness has left him in a state of agitation, he must guard against adopting a negative attitude – for this is sheer weakness – and must continue to devote his energies in a positive manner to worthy objectives. Nothing, in fact, should stop him, or even slow him down in his progress towards the Hereafter.

All of this demands enormous fortitude, and, without it, no one can travel along the path of Islam. The annual month-long period of fasting builds up the strength of character which is essential, if devout Muslims are to tread the path of righteousness for the rest of the year, avoiding impatience, cruelty and all such evil acts, and making no attempt to meddle with divine commandments. While in its outward form, fasting means abstinence from food and drink for a given period in essence, it is training for a whole life of self-denial, inculcating patience, fortitude and forbearance.

It is only when fasting temporarily curbs the satisfying of man's desires that his consciousness of the value of these divine gifts is awakened. When, at sunset, after a whole day's hunger and thirst, a man begins to eat and drink, he becomes aware of his utter dependence on God's bounty. He is filled with gratitude towards God and the realisation comes to him that, even if he were to lay down his life for this Bountiful Creator, the price he should have to pay would not be too high.

Al-Risala, January 1999

❒

27

A Muslim's Behaviour – Part-I

The behaviour of a Muslim in his environment is one of love, mercy and compassion. Here are some relevant references from the sayings of the Prophet of Islam in this regard:

1. "You are helped and are provided for only because of the weak and poor ones among you." *(Sahih Al Bukhari)*
2. "I and the guardian of orphans (whether the orphan be of one's near or distant relation or of strangers) will be in one place in paradise like my two fingers," said the Prophet and his fingers were nearly touching each other at the time (*Sahih Muslim*).
3. On one occasion, a man complained to the Prophet of having a hard heart. The Prophet prescribed the following remedy – "Touch an orphan's head and feed the poor." (*Musnad Ahmad*).
4. Someone said: "O Prophet of God, teach me something." "Abuse no one," replied the Prophet, "and despise not anything good and speak to your fellow-men with open countenance." (*Tirmidhi*).
5. "God has no mercy for him who has no mercy for his fellows." (*Sahih Al Bukhari& Muslim*).
6. "A man came to the Prophet and said, "How many times should I forgive a servant?" The Prophet kept silent. The man repeated the question thrice. "Forgive your servant seventy times everyday," said the Prophet (*Abu Dawud*).
7. "He who does not behave kindly towards younger people and does not show due respect to older ones is not of us." (*Tirmidhi*)

8. Someone asked: "What is Islam?" The Prophet said: "Purity of speech and hospitality." (*Musnad Ahmad*)
9. The Prophet said: "On the Day of Judgement God will question: 'O Man, I was sick and you did not visit Me.' My Lord, the man will wonder, "How could I visit you when You are the Lord of the universe?" God will remind: "My so and so servant was sick and you did not visit him. Had you visited him, you would have found Me there, with him?" (*Sahih Muslim*)
10. "Visit the sick, feed the hungry, and help to relieve people's misery." (*Sahih Al Bukhari*).
11. "Muslims who live in the midst of society and bear with patience the afflictions that come to them are better than those who shun society and cannot bear any wrong done to them." (*Abu Dawud*).
12. "Every good deed is a charity, and it is a good deed that you meet your fellowmen with a cheerful countenance and you pour water from your bucket into the vessel of your fellow. Answering a questioneer with mildness is charity. Removing that which is inconvenience to wayfarers, such as thorns and stones is charity." (*Tirmidhi*).
13. "The leader of a people is truly their servant." (*As-Suyuti*)
14. "Faith (iman) is to restrain oneself against all violence, let no believer commit any violence." (*Abu Dawud*).
15. "Good has forbidden you disobedience of parents, miserliness, false claims, and the burying alive of female infants." (*Sahih Al Bukhari & Muslim*)
16. "Give the worker his wages before his sweat dries." (*Ibn Majah*).
17. "The seller is under obligation to disclose any defect in the article offered for sale." (*Sahih Al Bukhari*)
18. "No one should be subjected to chastisement by fire." (*Sahih Al Bukhari*)
19. "Honest difference of opinion among my people should be accounted a blessing." (*As-Suyuti*)
20. Someone asked the Prophet, "What fanaticism was?" And he replied: "That you help your people in wrongdoing." (*Abu Dawud*)

21. "That one will not enter Paradise whose neighbour is not secure against his mischief." (*Sahih Muslim*)
22. "He who believes in God and the Last Day must not put his neighbour to inconvenience." (*Sahih Al Bukhari& Muslim*)
23. "He is not a believer who eats to his fill while his neighbour goes without food." (*Ibn Abbas, Al-Baihiqi*)
24. The Prophet said: "A person passing through a street carrying anything pointed or with a sharp edge should cover it up, so that nobody is exposed to the risk of injury due to his carelessness." (*Sahih Muslim*)
25. "To remove anything from the street that causes inconvenience is charity." (*Sahih Al Bukhari*)

"Muslims who live in the midst of society and bear with patience the afflictions that come to them are better than those who shun society and cannot bear any wrong done to them." (*Abu Dawud*).

Al-Risala, March 1999

❐

28

A Muslim's Behaviour – Part-II

This is second in the series of sayings of Prophet Muhammed regarding the merciful and compassionate behavior of a Muslim.

26. God is Gentle and loves gentleness in all things. (*Sahih Al Bukhari & Muslim*)
27. Gentleness adorns everything and its absence leaves everything defective. (*Sahih Muslim*)
28. Honour your children (especially daughters) and make provisions for their proper upbringing. (*Ibn Majah*)
29. One who brings up three daughters, teaches them good manners and morals, arranges their marriages and treats them with fairness, deserves to be ushered into Paradise. (*Abu Dawud*)
30. Paradise lies at the feet of the mothers. (*As-Suyuti*)
31. On one occasion the Prophet observed: "Most unfortunate is the person whose parents are aged and who fails to win Paradise through taking good care of them." (*Sahih Al Bukhari*)
32. A man came seeking permission to participate in *jihad* (holy war). The Prophet asked him: "Are your parents alive?" The man said: "Yes." He sent him away saying: "Then go back and find your *jihad* in serving them." (*Sahih Muslim*)
33. He who wishes to enter Paradise through the best door must please his father and mother.
34. The most perfect of believers in the matter of faith is he whose behaviour is best; and the best of you are those who behave best towards their wives. (*Tirmidhi*)

35. You will not enter Paradise until you have faith, and you will not complete your faith until you love one another. (*Sahih Al Bukhari & Muslim*)
36. He who eases the hardship of another, will have ease bestowed upon him by God in this world and the next... God goes on helping a servant so long as he goes on helping his fellow-man. (*Sahih Muslim*)
37. In his farewell address, the Prophet said: "You are all brothers and are all equals. None of you can claim any privilege or any superiority over any other. An Arab is not to be preferred to a non-Arab, nor is a non-Arab to be preferred to an Arab; nor is a white man to be preferred to a coloured one, or a coloured one to a white, except on the basis of righteousness." (*Musnad Ahmad*)
38. The Prophet, during his night prayer, used to say: "O God! I hear witness that all human beings are brothers. (*An-Nasai*)
39. Even with regard to servants, the Prophet said: "They are your brothers, and you must treat them as such. Provide them with the kind of clothes that you wear, and if you set them a hard task, join them in it to help them complete it" (*Abu Dawud*)
40. The Prophet observed: "None of you can be a believer unless you desire for your fellow-man what you desire for yourself." (*Sahih Al Bukhari*)
41. He who defends the honour of his fellow-man, God will shield his face against the fire on the Day of Judgement. (*Tirmidhi*)
42. God is not merciful to him who is not merciful to mankind. (*Sahih Al Bukhari*)
43. He who keeps away from his brother and fellowman for a year is as if he had slain him. (*Abu Dawud*)
44. The Prophet was very insistent upon kindness towards animals. On one occasion, he noticed a dove flying around agitatedly, and discovered that somebody had caught its young. He was very annoyed and asked the person to restore the young to the mother immediately. (*Abu Dawud*)

45. A woman was tormented on account of a cat which she had shut up till it died. On that account, she entered the Fire. (*Sahih Muslim*)
46. Forgiveness was granted to an unchaste woman who, coming up on a dog panting and almost dead with thirst at the mouth of a well, took off her shoe, tied it with her head covering, and drew some water for it. On that account, she was forgiven. (*Sahih Al Bukhari*)
47. The Prophet forbade beating or branding an animal on its face. (*Sahih Muslim*)
49. There is no man who kills a sparrow, or any other living creature (even it may be more despicable than a little sparrow) without its deserving it, but God will ask him about it. (*An-Nasai*)
50. For a Muslim, it is an act of charity to plant a tree or till a land where birds or people or animal come and eat its fruits. (*al-Bazzar*)

He who eases the hardship of another will have ease bestowed upon him by God in this world and the next... God goes on helping a servant so long as he goes on helping his fellow-man (*Sahih Muslim*).

Al-Risala, April 1999

❐

29

Islam on Conversion

Conversion in Islamic thinking is not synonymous with proselytisation in the formal sense. It is an event that takes place in a person's life as a result of intellectual revolution or spiritual transformation. It is not simply leaving one religious tradition for another. What is meant by conversion is that the individual has discovered the truth after an exhaustive search for it and then by his own choice, he chooses one religion over another.

During his final phase in 6 AH, the Prophet of Islam sent invitation letters to the neighboring rulers of his time, by which they were directly invited to accept the message of Islam. For instance, in his letter to the Byzantine emperor Heraclius I, the Prophet wrote these words: "Accept Islam and you will be blessed with peace."

Similarly, at any gathering in Mecca, the Prophet would make a point of going to that place and address the gathering thus: "O people, say there is no God but God and you will attain God's grace."

At first glance, this was an invitation to people to change their religion. But the study of the *Qur'an* tells us that it was in actual fact an invitation to a transformation in thinking, instead of a change of religion in the simple sense.

In the first phase of Islam, some Arab Bedouins had accepted Islam just by reciting the *Kalima*, the creed of Islam, while they had not undergone any change in character at a deeper level. The *Qur'an* admonished them in strong terms:

The Arabs of the desert say, 'We believe', Say, "You have not believed yet; but rather say, 'We have accepted Islam, for the true faith has not yet entered into your hearts." (49:14)

From this we learn that conversion according to Islam means a thorough transformation of the person and not just a change of religion in the everyday sense. Similarly, criticising the ways of Jews and Christians, the *Qur'an* says: "Say: 'We take on God's own dye – and who has a better than God's? And we are His worshippers."' (2:138)

A formal method of religious conversion was prevalent among the Jews and Christians known as baptism. In this ritual ceremony, the convert is dipped in water. The hue of water was considered to symbolise purity, and their priests believed that dipping someone in pure clean water purified him, and he was thus converted to a new religion.

According to the verse quoted above, pouring water outwardly does not purify a person, for the attainment of purity necessitates a transformation of the total human personality. The convert is suffused with the hue of God and he adopts God's ways in thought, word and deed.

The *Qur'an* refuses to give its seal of approval to conversions which are mere formalities. In ancient Medina, about 300 people had become Muslims by reciting the Islamic creed. Apparently they even said their prayers, and fasted, but they did all this in a hypocritical manner, paying only lip service: their inner state did not correspond to their outward pronouncements.

They claimed allegiance to Islam by word of mouth but, with regards to the state of their hearts the Islamic spirit was lacking. The *Qur'an* brands the 'Islam' of such people as a falsity: "When the hypocrites come to you, they say: 'We bear witness that you are God's apostle.' God knows that you are indeed His Messenger, and God bears witness that the hypocrites are lying." (63:1)

What is meant by true religious conversion is illustrated by an incident in which some verses from the *Qur'an* were read to a gathering of Christians, about 70 of them were so deeply moved that they abandoned their ancestral religion and converted to Islam.

As the *Qur'an* puts it: "When they listen to that which was revealed to the Messenger, you will see their eyes filled with tears as they recognize its truth. They say: 'Lord, we believe. Count us among Your witnesses. Why should we not believe in God and in the truth that has come down to us ? Why should we not hope for admission among the righteous?" (5:83-84)

Religious conversion in actual fact is the result of a realisation. When the individual's search for truth finds a convincing answer, his heart is intensely moved. His eyes are filled with tears. His whole existence is moulded in the hue of truth. It is then that he emerges a new and altogether different person, having undergone a transformation.

Religious conversion in actual fact is the result of a realisation. When the individual's search for truth finds a convincing answer, his heart is intensely moved. His eyes are filled with tears. His whole existence is moulded in the hue of truth.

Al-Risala, May 1999

❐

30

Islamic Interpretation of Life

Man is a pleasure-seeking animal. He has an abundance of desires and thus seeks to create a world where he may fulfill all of them. Yet there is no one who can achieve that goal; everyone is destined to die with desires unfulfilled.

This destiny, however, is special to man – no other creature shares this fate. As is known, the physical world, the mountains, the rivers, the stars, etc. have no desires at all, saving them from the problem of unfulfilled wants.

Animals as well are not much different from the physical world in this regard. Their desires are very limited. For example, their desire for food is limited in scope to the immediate present. Animals have no concern for tomorrow and do not desire to store food for tomorrow. They require food for the moment and that is achievable to them. So, when they die, there is not a single regret in their existence – they have no cause for lamenting: I have failed to achieve what I wanted to achieve.

Then why is it exceptionally the case for man that even so-called super achievers feel at their moment of death, that their life was a case of missed opportunities; they wanted so much yet achieved so little? What is worse, they are compelled to leave even those little achievements in this world and proceed to an unknown destination, completely alone.

Why this tragic state of affairs? The reason according to Islam is that man is born with a dual personality. Intellectually, he is unlimited in capability but physically he is a limited being. This disparity in his inner nature causes the problem.

After great labour, man acquires much wealth but he dies without completely enjoying it. He builds his dream house. Yet sadly, upon entering it, he feels unable to fully enjoy it due to his limitations and disadvantages. Any conceivable thing that he obtains is inherently imperfect, whereas man is intellectually a perfectionist. After experiencing each new goal that he has so long sought to achieve, he desires it no more because after achieving it he realises that this latest goal too, is less than perfect.

If man were to live according to his physical being, then there would be no problem with this world. Man would live like an animal with some limited kind of immediate desires and would die without any feeling of failure for not achieving his desires.

Herein Islam provides the silver lining for man. If nature was capable of creating a world that satisfies man's physical needs, then logically it must be capable of creating a world that suits his intellectual needs.

This world for the intellect exists but with only one difference – the world according to his physical nature was given to him for his pre-death period of life and the world according to his intellectual needs will be given to him for his post-death period of life. So, according to Islam, man's life is like an iceberg. This worldly life is only the tip of the iceberg and the other-worldly life will be like the hidden majority of the iceberg.

Thus, there is no need for man to fall prey to frustration. Adopt a two-fold plan for your life. One based on your needs of the present world and the other according to your needs of the future world. So, a successful life in this world is one based on the following concept: that the present life is where we can only sow and we shall harvest in the next world.

If we were to plant a seed in the morning with the hope of enjoying the fruit by dinner time, we are sure to be frustrated. Had we planned to reap the fruit a hundred years from now, however, then we would not meet any frustration for frustration is but the name of misplaced hope. The problem for man thus lies not in the nature of life but in his concept of life.

Is there any proof of the existence of a world, as envisaged by Islam, other than this world? Yes, there is a clear proof. The *Qur'an* says that the present world itself is sufficient proof of the future world. If God was capable of creating the present world in all its complexity, then there is no room left to doubt his capability of creating the next world.

The *Qur'anic* call in brief is that man should take the present world as an opportunity to develop in himself such a divine personality that is deserving of permanent residency in the eternal world of paradise. A world that the *Qur'an* praises as a house that lies neighbor to none other than God Alimighty Himself!

If man were to live according to his physical being, then there would be no problem with this world. Man would live like an animal with some limited kind of immediate desires and would die without any feeling of failure for not achieving his desires.

Al-Risala, June 1999

❐

31

Common Sense in Islam

There is a very significant verse in the *Qur'an* that states: *"Therefore set your face in devotion to the true faith, the up-right nature with which God has endowed man. God's creation cannot be changed. This is surely the true religion, although most men do not know it." (30:30)*

According to this verse, Islam is based on nature. Islam and nature, both are counterparts to each other. What is in nature in an unwritten form is in Islamic scriptures in written form.

It is because of this that common sense is also a source of Islam. When a right point comes to your mind, provided that you are not preoccupied with some artificial ideas, this point is as valid an Islamic teaching as those found in scriptures in a written form. There is no difference between the two except that those written points are certainly true, whereas what is derived from your inner nature is probably true.

Once, a man came to the Prophet of Islam seeking some advice for his daily life. The Prophet said: "Consult your heart..." There is also another saying of the Prophet: "Take that which is clear and leave that which seems to you not clear." These kinds of sayings of the Prophet tell us that what comes from a non-corrupt mind is true, at least in nature. What a man's inner voice speaks is a kind of revelation from God.

The Prophet of Islam appointed Mu'adh bin Jabal the governor of Yemen. When he was leaving to take charge of his post, the Prophet asked: "How will you decide matters as a governor?" He replied: "I will decide according to the Book of God – the *Qur'an*." The Prophet then asked: "If you fail to find it in the *Qur'an* what will you do?" He replied: "I will decide on it according to the teachings of the Prophet of God (*Sunnah*)." Then the Prophet again asked: "What if you fail to find it even in my *Sunnah*, what will you do then?" He replied: "Then I will try to form my own opinion." This means that a man has a good knowledge of *Qur'an* and *Sunnah* and has also successfully preserved his God given nature in its original form, is in a position to make the right judgment even if it is not directly stated in the *Qur'an* or *Sunnah*.

There is a very meaningful and relevant incident in the early period of Islam. The Prophet of Islam sent a troop from Medina to Banu Quraidhah, a Jewish settlement at that time. Bidding them farewell, the Prophet said: "None of you should pray *Asr* until we reach *Banu Quraidhah*."

These troops of Sahaba were on the way when they noticed that the sun was about to set and then a difference arisen between the members of the troop. Some of them said: "We should pray *Asr* before reaching the destination, otherwise we won't be able to pray' *Asr* on time." Obviously, this was against the injunction of the Prophet, but they justified it by saying: "What the Prophet meant was only rapidity. So, some of them prayed *Asr* during the journey while the others adhered to the literal meaning of the injunction and after arriving prayed *Asr* albeit late.

On their return to Medina, the story was narrated to the Prophet, who endorsed both practices. From this Prophetic precedent, we learn a principle of great significance – that common sense is applicable also to those matters which are clearly described in *Shar'iah*, with the only condition that the concerned man is truly sincere.

From these references, it becomes clear that Islam is religion of common sense. Anyone, literate or illiterate, can follow Islam with the condition that he is sincere, his concern should be only to follow the divine path and not his own whims and desires in the name of Islam.

But it does mean that Man himself is the master of his own destiny. He himself has the right to judge what is or is not good for him. The human nature provided by God is only to facilitate his task and not to make him his own judge.

Even after both these equipments, Man is not free from God's control. In the last resort, it is for God to judge whether he was right or wrong.

Man has to be extremely cautious to read his nature, to save himself from all types of false conviction and self-deception and to consult divine scriptures with all seriousness and sincerity.

Otherwise, he will be doomed to failure even if he claims that he always obeys his nature or claims to follow the word of God. Being the victim of one's own falsehood is not an excuse under any circumstances.

Anyone, literate or illiterate, can follow Islam, provided he is sincere and his concern should be only to follow the divine path and not his own whims and desires in the name of Islam.

Al-Risala, July 1999

❒

32

The Political Philosophy of Islam

The political philosophy of Islam is flexible. It is not based on any rigid principles. Basically, it is the real circumstances of any given situation that determine the Islamic political system. In spirit, the Islamic political philosophy is eternal but in form, it is flexible.

A study of the *Qur'an* shows that there is no such thing as a detailed political philosophy or a complete political system revealed. For example, the appointment of a *khalifah* or head of state is the most important part of any political system, but in this respect, no clear cut directions are given in the *Qur'an*. It was because of this that after the Prophet of Islam, there were four subsequence heads of the Islamic State but all four were appointed in four different ways.

The fact that the *Qur'an* or Islam does not explicitly outline a detailed political system is not due to any shortcoming or incompleteness of the religion.

To be sure, there is no doubt that Islam is a complete ideology. The fact that Islam does not clearly outline a political system is exactly what is wanted because politics by its very nature should be flexible and malleable. Otherwise, it would go against nature and would not be sustainable.

Thus, what would be the point of detailing something that is not sustainable? Hence, it is just according to nature that the *Qur'an* sets forth only the basic ideological principles and does not ordain a detailed political system in a practical form.

This nature of the Islamic political system can clearly be seen in the Prophet's life. The life of the Prophet of Islam as a Prophet was twenty-three years long but during this period, he did not opt for any single political system.

Instead, his political behavior would depend upon the circumstances that prevailed at the time. The entire life of the Prophet, as regards to politics, may broadly be divided into three parts. During the early period of his Prophethood, the Prophet of Islam lived in Mecca for thirteen years. During this period, the political system of Mecca was based around the *Dar-al-Nadwa*, which was a sort of tribal parliament. But the Prophet did not ever attempt to enter or seize control of this *Dar-al-Nadwa*. He completely ignored the *Dar-al-Nadwa* and immersed himself in peaceful work.

From this behavior of the Prophet, we learn that the first principle of Islamic political philosophy is to accept the existing political status quo as it is and to avail the constructive opportunities in non-political fields in a peaceful manner. This principle is not simply status quoism but it is a positive status quoism because it provides room to continue peaceful activity in fields other than politics.

The second principle of Islamic political philosophy can be gleaned from the period in the Prophet's life after migration to Medina. The life of the Prophet in Medina was for ten years. This period can be further divided into two broad parts. During the first half of the Medina period, three communities were present in the city – the Muslims, the idolators and the Jews. In other words, at that time, Medina was a multi-cultural society.

Due to this circumstance, the Prophet opted for a kind of common politics. He issued a charter, which is known in Islamic history as *Sahija-tul-Madinah*. In this charter, he declared that all three communities were to enjoy cultural and religious freedom.

Even the Jewish judicial system which had been running for a long time now was allowed to continue as it was under Kaab ibn Ashraf, a Jew. So, the first half of the Medina period was, in present terms, much akin to a democratic system.

Modern democracy is a system of power-sharing. The Medina period was quite similar to this.

So, according to the Prophetic precedent above, a power-sharing system under a democratic setup is also permissible under Islam, if circumstances so require.

The third principle of Islamic political philosophy is a system governed completely by Islam. The Prophet adopted this third method only after Medina had become virtually a homogeneously religious society.

The wisdom behind the above three principles of Islamic political philosophy is given in this *Hadith*: "How you are, that is how your rulers will be (*Mishkat-al-Masabih*)."

In short, the well-known saying that politics is the art of the possible is very near to the spirit of Islam.

Islam does not clearly outline a political system because politics by its very nature should be flexible and malleable. Otherwise, it would go against nature and would not be sustainable.

Al-Risala, August 1999

□

33

The Essential Guide to Society

The *Qur'an* leads us to true guidance. It says: "God is He besides Whom there is no god, the Ever-living, the Self-subsisting by Whom all subsist; slumber does not overtake Him nor sleep; whatever is in the heavens and whatever is in the earth is His; who is he that can intercede with Him but by His permission? He knows what is before them and what is behind them, and they cannot comprehend anything out of His knowledge except what He wills. His knowledge encompasses the heavens and the earth, and the preservation of them both tires Him not, and He is the Most High, the Great." (*Qur'an* 2:255)

"There is no compulsion in religion; truly the right way has become clearly distinct from error; therefore, whoever disbelieves in the Satan and believes in God, he indeed has laid hold on the firmest handle, which shall not break off, and God is Hearing, Knowing." (*Qur'an* 2:256)

"God is the guardian of those who believe. He brings them out of the darkness into the light; and (as to) those who disbelieve, their guardians are satan who take them out of the light into the darkness; they are the inmates of the fire, in it they shall abide." (*Qur'an* 2:257)

Now, let us try to visualise the passage in its applied form so that we may have an idea of the kind of individual, society and the type of state that would emerge when Islam is consciously accepted and practised in letter and spirit.

A. **Individual :**The *Qur'an* says: "Do they seek for other than the Religion of God? While all creatures in the heaven and on earth have, willingly or unwillingly bowed to His will." (3:83)

It means that submission to God is the only true religion for both man and the universe. All other things on earth and space – water, trees and stars are following the divine command.

The *Qur'an* says: "Neither is it allowable for the sun to catch up with the moon, nor can the night outstrip the day. Each swims along in (its own) orbit." (36:40)

The same is required by all human beings. "A believer with his faith is like a horse with its tether."[19] A true believer has a highly disciplined life. He adheres to the set of do's and don'ts ordained by the Almighty. He exercises full control over his speech and always subordinates his intention and thinking to God's will. He is always God's servant.

B. **Society:** The foundation of a society is based on mutual well-wishing. In Chapter *Al-Asr* (Time) the *Qur'an* says: Man is in loss, except those who believe and do good works and exhort one another to truth and patience. (103:1-3)

How must a believer live in society? The Hadith says: "If anyone sees evil, he must rectify it on his own. If he has no capacity to do so, he should do it with his tongue. If he is unable to discourage, then let him condemn the same in his own heart." (*Sahih Al Sahih Al Bukhari*)

Good will naturally flourish in a society based on these principles. The roots of evil, even if not totally eradicated, will dry up because of public discouragement. As the truth is openly propagated and the virtue of patience highly recommended, peace will prevail in society as a whole. This is conducive to healthy growth and development. The rights of individuals will be secured, communal harmony ensured, higher values of brotherhood, cooperation and altruism sincerely observed, and finally, the projects of common welfare, progress and prosperity will be achieved.

C. **State:** A state is an organised political community under one government. Islam does not prescribe any particular form or structure of the state. Nevertheless, Islamic teachings are so comprehensive that they embrace all

---

19. Mishal Al Masabih, Vol. 2/1226.

essential issues including state and its related national or international problems.

What is an Islamic state? Any state governed by Muslims is not an Islamic state. Apart from its monotheistic doctrinal basis, an Islamic state would practically be identified with the "no-compulsion" principle. For the power gained through compulsion or the power used for compulsion in any manner, particularly in religious matters, is strictly prohibited and condemned in Islam. That is why, states governed by Muslim dictators have never been considered ideal by Islamic scholars themselves. However, Islam does not allow its followers to rebel against any established state even though it may not seem to be in accordance with the Islamic ideal. That state should never be resisted by means of a counter-compulsion, say revolt, but by means of conviction and negotiation. This ensures stability in law and order, which subsequently promotes Islamic values and prepares a foundation for a true Islamic state. To establish an ideal state is not Islam's main target as wrongly projected by some groups of Muslims. It is something that may ultimately emerge from a society of sincere practicing Muslims. It is not predictable. Such a state, according to the *Qur'an* (24:55), "is a worldly reward God grants to His righteous servants when He wills". It is not a goal the community may struggle for.

To establish an ideal state is not Islam's main target as wrongly projected by some Muslim groups. It ultimately emerges from a society of sincere practicing Muslims. It is not predictable.

Al-Risala, September 1999

❐

34

What is Man's Purpose in Life?

Man attains distinction only when he leads a purposeful life. A purposeful life is one in which a man discovers his supreme status.

An animal strives to obtain food; a bird flies in search of a better country when the seasons change; a wasp busies itself building up its own home from tiny dust particles; a herd of deer protects itself from wild beasts of prey. All these appear to be purposeful actions. But when the phrase "a purposeful life" is applied to man, it does not refer to efforts of this nature. Without doubt man, too, has to arrange for food, clothes and habitation for bare survival.

Man's life becomes purposeful only when it goes beyond common animalism and takes the form of superior humanism.

God's creations fall into two categories: animate and inanimate. Obviously, animate objects enjoy a certain superiority over inanimate objects. The former can be divided into three classes: the vegetable, the animal and the human. Modern scientific research has shown that plants also possess life, nourish themselves, grow and have feelings.

But animals and men represent a higher form of life. In what way does man excel animals? Many theories have been advanced over the ages and great minds are still studying it. But modern biologists have come to the conclusion that it is man's capacity for conceptual thought which distinguishes him from other life forms. Animals lack this quality, whereas man is conscious of the fact that he is thinking. He consciously forms a plan of action in his mind; he determines actions everyday. Though many animals act like men, they are not the result of thought; they all stem from pure instinct. Animal actions are governed by environmental stresses from without and physical pressures from within.

Man can use his conceptual quality to search for his purpose. It does not result from the pressures of desire or of immediate exigencies. It must emanate from his own urge to worship God. It has been explained in the *Qur'an*: "I created mankind ...... that they might worship Me. I demand no livelihood of them nor do I ask that they should feed Me. God alone is the Munificent Giver, the Mighty One, the Invincible." (51:56-58)

These verses specify man's purpose in life as worship. This is a purpose that elicits from man his uniqueness in its ultimate form. God does not demand of you a livelihood, the verse says. Rather He himself is responsible for your livelihood. This means that worship of God is a purpose, which is motivated neither by inward desires nor outward influences. Rather it comes into being through thought alone.

When a person works, makes money, builds a house, makes an effort to improve his standard of living, he appears to be engaged in efforts towards some worthy end. But this cannot be called purposeful life, for these activities do not demonstrate man's unique status. These functions might seem to be the result of deliberation, but are actually born out of the struggle for survival.

When man grows, he realises that there are certain material necessities without which he cannot live. He requires food, clothes, a place to live; he requires a reliable source of income to sustain him throughout his life. Then he sees that those who have material abundance enjoy respect and apparently possess every form of happiness and luxury in this world. Thus, he is driven on to do more than just seek a livelihood; he wishes to earn a degree greatly in excess of his actual requirements.

In the bustling market, grandiose offices, and opulent buildings, he is not really being guided by deliberate thought. Rather, he is guided by inflated ideas of his own needs, desires, longing and ambition to achieve fame and status. These activities, therefore, cannot be considered as being directed towards the purpose which sets man apart from the animal and lends him a higher distinction.

Man's true purpose can only be to seek the pleasure of God. It is only then that his human qualities find full manifestation. This is loftier than the efforts towards which an animal directs its energies. It is the ultimate station of human dignity.

To determine the purpose of life is, in short, the effort to make it meaningful. It must surely, therefore, be one that is in accordance with a man's unique status; it must be one which leads man on the path to success and progress in terms of his true nature.

Man's true purpose can only be to seek the pleasure of God. It is then that his human qualities find full manifestation. This is loftier than the efforts towards which an animal directs its energies. It is the ultimate station of human dignity.

Al-Risala, October 1999

❐

35

Towards the Right Thought

What is spirituality or *rabbaniyat*, to use the *Qur'anic* term? It is the elevation of man to a plane where the mind is focused on the higher, non-material realities of a godly existence. Its opposite is materialism, a course followed all too often in this world.

To put it another way, he who focuses on mere appearances is material-minded. And the one who rises above it is spiritual. He obeys the injunction of the *Qur'an*: "Be devoted servants of God" (3:79) or alternatively, "O people be godly servants of God."

To understand what constitutes materialism, imagine yourself looking at a palatial house or an attractive car and being overcome by the desire to possess it. A person who is unmoved by these objects and the notions of luxury, they convey lives in a more rarefied sphere. For him, there is little attraction in the world of superficiality, being engrossed as he is in the higher realities of a supremely spiritual life. A truly non-material person's soul exists at a profound level of spirituality. This is the unadulterated truth.

Those who live for worldly pleasures believe that gratification cannot be had except through the enjoyment of material goods. But this kind of thinking is the result of sheer ignorance. Having only experienced worldly pleasures, these people come to believe that every kind of enjoyment depends on it alone. If they were to experience spiritual pleasure, they would quickly forget about material pleasures, which are transient, whereas the spiritual kind may be savored eternally.

The taste of good food is enjoyable, but it is only when the experience of eating results in an outpouring of thanks-giving to God that we attain complete pleasure. A car ride can be exhilarating, but the pleasure that comes from a deep perception of reality – or sensing the indescribably unique power of God as manifested in cars, airplanes and all the other modern amenities created for man's comfort – is far superior to that which one experiences while travelling in a luxurious automobile.

A materially minded person finds pleasure only in something which he or she actually experiences. The spiritual person will thank God even at the sight of another person's object. Rather, he transforms his friend's material pleasure into spiritual pleasure for himself. A materially minded person only sees the creation while a spiritually inclined person sees the splendor of the Creator through the creation. It is obvious that the spiritual riches accruing from the discovery of the Creator cannot be gained through objects he created.

Furthermore, in the spiritual world, there is no great difference between comfort and deprivation. What one gains from material experiences is of lesser value than what one learns from deprivation. Tears of pain give greater satisfaction than laughter.

The greatest source of pleasure is in the remembrance of God. It is this reality that finds expression in the following verse of the *Qur'an*: "Only in the remembrance of God are hearts comforted." (13:28) Comfort here implies peace of mind that stems only from God, and not merely temporary solace. Man is an idealist by nature. Anything short of ideals only attracts fitful attention.

Existing only at the materialistic level is like descending into animalistic level. Materialism is, in other words, a form of shallowness. The real man is one who discovers the secret of spirituality.

If in materialism, there is pleasure of laughter, in spirituality, there is the pleasure of pain. If materialism is to live a life of limitations, spirituality is to be free.

Al-Risala, January 2000

❒

36

The Concept of Fatwa

The Shahi Imam of the Tipu Sultan mosque at Kolkata had issued a *fatwa* against Taslima Nasrin, the controversial Bangladeshi writer and announced an award of ` 20,000 to anyone who "tarred her face or is able to make her wear a garland of footwear" according to *The Hindu* of January 20, 2004. This was deservedly condemned by the All-India Democratic Women's Association as 'highly provocative and objectionable statements by SOQ1e fundamentalist forces'. However, surprisingly no other organisation protested against the statement. The Muslim community as usual remained mute not mustering enough courage to speak out against the Imam. For a long time, the *imams* and some *maulvis* with their half-baked knowledge of Islam have got away with such objectionable statements without being challenged. The best persons to object would have been the well-known Islamic institutions or the *ulema*. But once in a while, a Fatwa issued by these institutions and *ulema* leave you wondering whether the issue has been examined in depth with proper insight.

The recent *fatwa* against cow slaughter by Darul Uloom Deoband is one such example. As rightly pointed out in the editorial of the *Pioneer* of 3rd February, 2004, this *fatwa* is lacking in sensitivity. It should have told the Muslims to sacrifice animals other than the cow in all the states and not just where it is already banned. This instruction would have been in keeping with the teaching of the Prophet who had said: 'He is not a believer who hurts his neighbor.' The neighborhood in the age of information technology extends as far as the TV is viewed. By sacrificing other animals on Eid, the Muslims are fulfilling the same obligation and in no way become entitled to lesser reward from their Creator.

When it comes to obligatory (*fard*) prayer, the Muslims have to perform but there again is it proper to block the road or use the loud-speaker at wee hours? Which causes inconvenience to others? An ordinary Muslim easily believes the Maulvis, whom he accepts to be an authority on the matter related to faith thus it is their responsibility to mend the ways and teach Muslims how to respect their neighbors.

Every now and then, one hears of a *fatwa* being issued by someone or the other. In Gujarat, an Imam issued a *fatwa* on the eve of the last assembly election to vote against a particular political party. Some years ago, two contradictory *fatwas* were issued on whether it was correct for the Muslims to march to Ayodhya to protest. There appears to be no clear concept of *fatwa* even among the educated Muslims, leave alone the press or other communities. So, what exactly is a *fatwa*?

The Sharia or Islamic law is based on *Qur'an* and *Hadith*, or the tradition of the Prophet. During the lifetime of the Prophet, his companions often consulted him on important matters to ascertain the correctness of the course available to them. The *Meccan* revelations declared God unique entity, the only entity with power and authority. Also the *Meccan* verses give examples of earlier civilizations that were destroyed when they denied their obligation to God. It is also noteworthy that of the five pillars of Islam, only Faith and Five times a day Salah were ordained at Mecca, the other three; *Zakat*, Fasting and *Hajj* were ordained at Medina.

After the migration, the situation changed for the Muslims. The Prophet was appointed as the head and the Muslim community became a fledging state. Therefore, the revelation was concerned primarily with the organization of Muslim state and economic law. A number of Medina verses answered the question raised by the Jews in order to befuddle the Prophet and discredit Islam. The decree enjoined by the *Qur'an* can be broadly placed in two categories÷ One pertains to dealings between God and man and the other between man and man. In the first case, it deals with religious rites whose validity depends on the correct intention. A great deal of emphasis has been placed on the intention in Islam. The dealing among men comprises family law that protects family structure and they include marriage, divorce and inheritance, trade laws that govern business transaction, rental contracts, etc. Criminal laws specify punishment and compensation for various crimes.

The *Qur'an* itself announces that it was revealed to reform human condition. Islam did not erase all pre-Islamic customs and practices. Instead, it removed the very facet of corruption and eradicated customs harmful to the society. If Islam forbade interest, it was because it takes unfair advantage of less fortunate member of the society; fornication was forbidden due to its exploitation of women and destruction of family bonds. Psychological and spiritual damages that it inflicts on individuals and the society, making the trade basis of mutual consent reformed trade practices. Islam looked at everything from the perspective of human welfare. What was harmful was removed and what was beneficial was confirmed. Islam is fundamentally a system of building and one of destruction and its goal is reformation and not merely control and government. It is important to understand that Islam's confirmation of some custom does not mean that it has taken its laws and principles from other sources. Also it does not mean that those practices confirmed by Islam are not divine. Some of the practices were inherited from the earlier generation to which the Prophets had been sent. For example, *Hajj* is the tradition of Prophet Abraham.

The system of Islam has been revealed for man's benefit. It provides him with guidance in all walks of life in order to ensure for him a righteous lifestyle within a just society. Islamic laws are not meant to be burden. Because of this, God has enacted along with divine laws variety of concessions like permission to break the fast and shorten and join the prayers during travel. Even consumption of prohibited substance (pork and alcohol) to be allowed in case of dire necessities was adopted during the time of the four Caliphs. However, with the expansion of Islamic territory during the Abbasid dynasty, the companions and the sub-companions had dispersed widely and consultations were not possible. And often situations arose with changing time, which did not have direct references either in the *Qur'an* or the *Hadith*.

The *fatwa* is meant to serve exactly that purpose. The system of *fatwa* is undoubtedly peculiar to Islam. Its importance lies in its ability to keep Islam abreast with the fast-changing world and accompanied aspirations of its followers. Such a provision also answers the question: Whether this religion was suited only for a particular time or a community living in a desert, or whether it is for all times to come.

Imagine if the *Qur'an* were to cover every situation arising in future, and certainly with human life constantly evolving the situations too would get numerous and more complex, it would have been an unwieldy and voluminous book, difficult to handle and refer. Since Islam is a religion for all times to come, it must also be able to deal with changing time, new challenges and new problems that will confront its followers. A provision, therefore, had to be made to find a right way out of the ordinary as well as complex matters that may not have been addressed in the two books that are available to the Muslims.

"As stated earlier, the *fatwa* has its base in *Fi'qh* and *Shar'iah*. While *Fiqh,* means understanding of the religion, the *Shar'iah,* refers to the sum" total of Islamic laws, which were revealed to the Prophet Muhammad, and which were rerecorded in the *Qur'an* as well as deducible from the Prophet life (called *Sunnah*). *Shar'iah* is fixed and unchangeable welfare as *Fiqh* changes according to circumstances under which it is applied. (Give examples to illustrate). The development of *Fiqh* started during the life of the Prophet, roughly in the 609 CE and went through different stages. The stagnation and decline set in 1258 CE with the sacking of Baghdad by the Mongols. Evolution of schools of Islamic thought has generously contributed to the development of *Fiqh*. However, no single school of thought can be claimed to solely represent Islam in its totality. This honor is reserved for the interpretations of *Shar'iah* by the Prophet himself, who was divinely guided, *Imam Shaf'ii*, the founder of the *Shaf'ii* school of thought, has said.

Initially, the only source of Islamic law was divine revelation in the form of either the *Qur'an* or the *Sunnah* (the sayings and actions of the Prophet): 'The *Qur'an* represented the blueprint for the Islamic way of life on which the Prophet attuned his actions, which served as practical demonstration in ordinary day-to-day life. The revelation of *Qur'an* began with the beginning of the Prophethood in 609 CE till close to the death of the Prophet in 632 CE. The *Qur'an* was revealed over a period of 23 years. The last ten years were in Medina where the Prophet had migrated. The Meccan period was particularly difficult for the Muslims. At Medina, they enjoyed more freedom. Also it was here that they came in contact with Jews and Christians in large numbers. The verses revealed at Mecca and Medina were quite distinct from each other. The earlier revelations at Mecca were basically designed to build faith in God. Most of the Meccans believed in a Supreme Being and called him God long before they were exposed to Islam. However, they had other Gods.

❐

37

The Concept of the State in Islam

In order to explain the concept of the state in Islam, I would like to quote some of the relevant verses from the *Qur'an*.

Say: "O God! Lord of Power, You give power to whom You please, and You take away power from whom You please." (3:26).

Some points are made here very clearly: one being that the actual possessor of power is God and that it is He who grants power on earth to whom He wants and who takes away power from whoever He wants. So, the whole matter in this regard rests with God. If someone receives power, it is not due to his own effort: it is given to him by God alone. Similarly, when power is taken away from him, it is done by God alone.

Thus, the dominance or subjugation of any group is ultimately for God to decide. According to this verse, no human being has any power whatsoever. The theory that comes to light is that political power is totally governed by God, just as the entire universe is running in accordance with the divine plan. It is like saying that God alone is the controller of the universe and that He alone has the final word as to who is going to be given political power. Just as God exercises full power over the setting and rising of the sun, so also He has full power over the granting of political ascendancy.

This is an incontrovertible fact. There is another verse in this connection that throws further light on the issue:

"And He will bestow upon you other blessings that you desire; help from God and a speedy victory." (*Qur'an* 61:14).

In this verse, "other blessings" means political power. This has been characterized as something secondary. When we take this verse in its literal sense, it transpires that the status of political power has a secondary rather than a primary position in Islam. Primary position is given to the purification of the self through intellectual and spiritual development.

Another point made clear in this verse is that the receiving of political power depends solely upon divine succor. Victory and defeat apparently belong to the human world, but both are totally governed by God.

As we learn from the *Qur'an*:

Whomsoever may God grant victory and whomsoever may God grant defeat.

The above another verse from the *Qur'an* that explains this matter further. If we take this verse literally, it emerges that political power is a promise from God, and not a target. That is, it is not something that Muslims should aim at for they can receive it only by divine edict.

Another point that we learn from this verse is that power is not granted to any group simply because of its struggle to that end, but rather on the fulfillment of two specific conditions. The *Qur'an* makes it clear that true faith and virtuous character alone are the deciding factors in receiving political power.

What is meant by faith is that the group who is to be the recipient of political power should have undergone the intellectual and spiritual revolution called *Iman* (Faith) in the *Qur'an*, that is, they should have absolute trust in God, total submission to the Prophet, full conviction on the existence of the angels, of the hereafter, of hell and heaven; in short, they should display a keen desire to mould their lives in accordance with the spirit of the *Qur'an*. When such qualities of faith are produced within a group, the time will come for it to be considered by God for the grant of political power. Good deeds necessarily entail full conformance to the divine commands regarding worship, moral character and the upholding of justice. In the words of the *Qur'an*, our lives should be wholly dyed in God's hue. When this quality of good character has been developed in the majority of the people, only then is political power given to that group by God's command.

Then there is another verse in this connection which throws further light on the subject.

This is in the context of the granting of political power to the Prophet David. The words uttered by the Prophet David after receiving power was 'Leabluani' (This is meant as a test). These words tell us that political power is given in order to try us. The test contrives to separate the grateful from the insolent servants of God.

Thus, according to the *Qur'an*, the nature of political power in this world is exactly the same as that of other things. That is, when an individual is given wealth, children or anything of a material, worldly nature like success, all that is designed to test him. All these blessings serve as test papers. Thus, political power is also a test paper.

Therefore, according to the *Qur'an*, whoever receives power should realize that power is given to him in order to test him. It is not something to take pride in, nor is it nearly a matter of being a gift from God.

The concept of the State that emerges from these verses of the *Qur'an* makes it clear that political power is not the target or goal of our activities or actions. Rather it is the result of some other set of actions. That is to say, according to the *Qur'an*, the objectives of our struggle should be faith and good character. These conditions have to be fulfilled and only then can a group be blessed with political power by God, if He so desires. We might say, by way of analogy, that the position of faith is that of the seed and the position of power is that of the fruit.

According the *Qur'an*, the whole matter can be likened to a tree. The position of the seed in this example is that of action and the position of the fruit is that of receiving the reward of that action. In this way, those who sow the seed of *Faith* and good deeds may receive political power, the gift from God.

We must then consult the *Qur'an* and *Sunnah* as to what is the structure of political power in Islam. In the *Qur'an*, the first principle that comes before us is in the form of approbation of: "Those who conduct their affairs by mutual consultation." (42:38).

This verse alludes to a basic principle of conduct so far as the political structure of Islam is concerned. This shows that the political system of Islam is based on mutual adjustment this being one of the most important social principles of Islam, which is equally desirable, both prior to and after receiving political power.

It is noteworthy that this verse enjoining Muslims to settle their affairs by consultation was revealed in Mecca, whereas Muslims received political power only in Medina after their migration. The revelation of this verse in Mecca shows that this principle of consultation is an all-time social principle. The practical proof of this principle at all times is made clear by the fact that whenever any social problems arose, the Prophet would always call his companions for consultation.

Therefore, we find in the books of *Seerah* (Prophet's biography) a number of examples which begin with these words, "O people, give me advice."

After the death of the Prophet in Medina in 632, Abu Bakr Siddique was appointed a leader of the Believers, and first successor of the Prophet. Events tell us that the Prophet was of the opinion that this task of leadership should go to Abu Bakr, but he never nominated the latter, nor did he prepare a will.

There were, however, certain indications doing the lifetime of his wishes. For instance, the task of congregational prayer is such as performed only by the head of the State. That is why, the Prophet of Islam used to lead the prayer himself. For, according to Islam, the Imam of the mosque should be one who is the leader of the political institution, or he could be one appointed by the head of the State his deputy. It is significant that the Prophet of Islam made *Abu Bakr* lead the prayer several times. This stand of the Prophet was to make it clear to the people that the appointment of the leader of the believers should be in accordance with the opinion of the people and not by appointment. That is why, after his death, when the companions gathered together at *Saqifa Bani Saeda*, an assembly hall in Medina, Abu Bakr was appointed the successor of the Prophet, after a long consultation. Although the Islamic system is democratic in its nature, it would be, however, more appropriate to say that democracy in Islam is indirect democracy rather than direct. That is to say, the entire public is not consulted in the Islamic democratic system. Instead, we find different methods in that golden period of Islam known as the pious caliphate.

None of the caliphs of this period were appointed after consulting the public. Only the senior people available in Medina were consulted.

This pattern was adopted concerning the appointment of all the four caliphs. With these standard examples during the pious caliphate before us, we should not be wrong in saying that the democratic system of Islam is almost the same as that is called indirect democracy in the jargon of today.

This system entailed selecting a central body after seeking the opinion of the public. This body then selected the caliph. That is why, certain scholars have called this method '*Arbab hallo Aqd*', that is, the intellectuals, the leaders, those who have a say in society are responsible for selecting the caliph or their leader. That is to say that this decision-making body will be formed by public opinion and this body, in turn, will be entrusted with the task of selecting the leader.

We gather from our study that the political structure of Islam is not an unchangeable, rigid structure but has sufficient flexibility to suit the circumstances. For instance, the selection of Abu Bakr at Saqifa Banu Saida took place after a discussion among the companions, while Umar ibn Khattab was appointed by Abu Bakr Siddique, the leader of the believers himself, during his last days. Then the third caliph was selected by a six-member board nominated by caliph Umar. So far as the selection of the fourth caliph is concerned, it took place in an emergency situation, due to the murder of the third caliph Usman; the circumstances did not allow holding normal discussions. Therefore, a group of Muslims declared Ali ibn Abi Talib to be the fourth caliph and the Muslim community accepted his caliphate. Then during the Umayyad period, Umar ibn Abdul Aziz (8th Umayyad caliph) as caliph, who is known as the fifth pious caliph was selected. His election took place in the following manner. The preceding caliph Sulaiman ibn Abdul Malik, had left his will in a sealed envelope with instructions that it should be opened only after his death. So, this letter was opened in the mosque of Damascus after his demise.

This announcement was made by Reja ibn Haywa, who was appointed by Sulaiman to read out this will to the large number of people gathered in the mosque. It was an official announcement of the nomination of Umar ibn Abdul Aziz as caliph. But Umar ibn Abdul Aziz declared it publicly that he was returning this nomination to the people and it was up to them to choose whoever they wanted. At this turn of events, all the people gathered in the mosque chorused: "We accept you as our caliph." Only after this general consent did Umar ibn Abdul Aziz accept the caliphate.

The first phase of Islamic history is known as the golden phase. There is no doubt about it that consultation is an established practice in Islam and we see this from the precedent set in this golden period. Yet there is a high degree of flexibility in the principle of consultation in Islam. It is not a hard and fast rule. That is why, we find that all the five caliphs were appointed by different methods. Then another fact is that the area of this principle of flexibility in Islamic democracy is very vast. As we see during the Umayyad period, Muawiya ibn Abi Sufyan, the founder of the Umayyad Caliphate, nominated his son to succeed him. This was clearly the way of kingship or dynastic rule, going patently against the precedents set in the golden period. But this method introduced by Muawiya became so common that it was adopted by almost all the succeeding Muslim rulers right from Muawiya to Aurangzeb. Yet the Islamic scholars in general accepted their rule giving them their silent approval. This shows that there is great flexibility in the Islamic concept of democracy based on consultation.

This flexibility goes to the extent of even accepting dynastic kingship, if circumstances demand it. As for the governments established on the principle of dynastic rule, the scholars held the view that a government's fulfilling its social, economic and religious responsibilities was more important than this or that political structure.

That is why, in later history, we find that although the Muslim scholars did not react to this dynastic rule, they did speak out openly about their responsibilities towards social justice.

The religious (*ulema*) scholars never shirked their role of reminding the kings of their social duty. Most of the scholars refrained from accepting any government post so that they might not have to yield to any undue pressure. They thought that by remaining independent, they would be able to play their role of censuring the policies of the government and of reminding the rulers of their duties. Shaykh Ahmad Sirhindi, known as Mujaddid Alafsani, provides an excellent example of what role the religious scholars had to play to keep the kings in check.

That is why, in later periods of Islamic history, when dynastic rule had become the order of the day among the Muslims, the rulers, more or less, could not deviate far from the Islamic principles of justice. For instance, the ruler had to come to the mosque to pray with the public, he had to spend the money of the Treasury to fulfill the requirements of the public, he had to discharge his religious responsibilities and see to it that the public had no difficulty in discharging its religious rites.

Anyone could approach the kings to register his or her complaint. And there was a proper arrangement by the government for the free religious education of the people, etc.

From our study of the *Qur'an*, *Hadith* and Islamic history, we come to this conclusion:

1. The position of political rule in Islam is not that of the target of action, but is rather the result of action. That is to say, fulfilling the criteria of faith and good deeds alone makes one deserving of political power.
2. There is no hard and fast rule for the political structure in Islam. Rather, we find great flexibility.
3. Although there may be adjustment so far as the political structure is concerned, there can be no adjustment or concession so far as the Islamic spirit is concerned.
4. According to the study of the hadith, our actions towards political reform will be limited to the giving of advice, i.e., by peaceful means. This will never go to the extent of launching violent movements aimed at ousting the rulers. As the traditions have it: "When you find corruption among the rulers, you still must pay your due to the ruler and seek your due from God. It is as if the principle of Jesus Christ is also accepted in Islam: "Render, therefore, to Caesar the things that are Caesar's, and to God the things that are God's."[20]

20. Luke: 20:26.

The *Qur'an* tells us: "God enjoins you to do justice. This justice in its basic sense pertains to individual character. It demands that everyone in his personal life should develop a character based on justice. When the number of these just people grows into a large group, they desire to lead their lives based on justice at the congregational or social level. Thus, when this social life manifests itself in the form of an organised social institution, it is called the state in Islamic terminology. This action (the desire to lead a just life) will be called just character from the individual point of view and this same action at the social level will be the mainspring of the just state."

❐

38

Missionary Maulana

August 5, 1990, Organiser (Men And Matters – V.P. Bhatia)

A most welcome visitor to our office last week was Maulana Wahiduddin Khan, Chairman of the local Islamic Centre. He was invited by the editorial staff of our sister publication '*Panchjanya*' for a get-together over a cup of tea. Also present on the occasion were Prof. Rajendra Singhji (Rajju Bhaiya), *Sah-Sarkaryavah* of the *RSS*, Shri Murli Manohar Joshi, General Secretary, *BJP*, and Shri Kaushal Kishore, *Sah-Boudhik Pramukh* of the *RSS*.

Incidentally, Maulana Saheb belongs to Azamgarh, a place in UP near Godabad. And Rajju Bhaiya has taught in the Physics Department of the Godabad University for 24 years, including four-five years as its Head of Department before seeking voluntary retirement for the whole-time Sangh work in 1966. And Shri Murli Manohar Joshi is still a serving Professor in the same department of the same university. The present Prime Minister, Shri V.P. Singh is among those who came into contact with Rajju Bhaiya as students.

Coming back to Maulana Saheb, his is, in fact, a one-man or one-institution crusade for cooling down the crusading ardour of Muslims. He has been threatened often without being cowed down. And he repeated his ideas with undiminished conviction to bring the community to the constructive path.

Regular readers of '*Organiser*' would at once recall the startling interview of the Maulana, which this paper had published (in summary) in the Dewali 1987 issue and which introduced him to the non-Muslim world. That way he may be described as the discovery of '*Organiser*'. The article was spotted by us in a local Urdu daily '*Mashriqi Awaz*'. It made a very sensational copy, as it dittoed or rather improved upon what many enquiry commissions had been saying about the genesis of communal riots. For, he blamed the Muslims of the subcontinent for every riot whether in India or Pakistan because of their easily excitable, inflammable nature and called upon them to declare a 'unilateral ceasefire' for the sake of social and political peace as well as good image of Islam. Since then, the interview has been making the rounds in a number of publications and I found the Maulana's ideas reproduced in a recent publication '*The Role of Islam in South India*' by G.D. Gadre. Shri Gadre has tried to be as sympathetic to Islam as possible and painted it even as the religion of the future but not without much success, because of the unforgettable record of the vandalism of Muslim kings who are still considered as heroes by the mass of Muslims.

Before coming to how the Maulana repeated his earlier ideas about the roots of communal mischief, I may summarize what he had said in 1987 as follows: "The present-day Muslim is the most quarrelsome community in the world. This is not so only with the nature of Muslims in India but of those all over the world. Their (aggressive) behavior is worse in Pakistan where hardly a day passes without a riot. They get flared up over minor matters, which get transformed into riots. Since Hindus are now in a strong position, their (Hindus) reaction turns out to be quite terrible against Muslims who may have to suffer a loss of one to one hundred. In the light of their statistics (community-wise casualties) of riots, Hindus would appear to be aggressors, but I do not accept the analysis as correct, because according to the *Qur'an*, the real culprit is one who starts (the riot). The basic problem with Muslims is that they treated God's creation in a manner which is wholly against what has been ordained by God. During their rule, they regarded Hindus as their inferiors. But now when they have lost political power, they regard Hindus as their enemies. Both these actions fall in the realm of crime."

How to mend the situation? As a real well-wisher of the community as well as of the country, Maulana Saheb calls upon Muslims to give up their belligerence. They should declare peace even unilaterally, because end of communal riots through mutually agreed action would never come about. The Prophet did so to end the feud between Mecca and Medina. Japan accepted all US terms to end Second World War. Muslims too should do so as they are the biggest losers in the ongoing strife. They are projecting a wrong image of Islam and hindering its spread by peaceful means. They have been living with Hindus for centuries but not a single significant movement or personality has come up to tell them about (the ideal way of) extending the invitation of Islam to others. Instead, they have been cursing their countrymen for the last 50 years. It will never help them; it is against the wishes of God.

That the Maulana's views remain unchanged was clear from the fact that at the last week's function, he paid a handsome tribute to '*Organiser*' for publishing the only correct report of Bhagalpur riots, which, he said, were precipitated because the Muslims went back on their undertaking to allow the Ram Navami procession pass through their strongholds. He had pointed out to Muslims about this lapse of theirs, resulting in huge loss of life and property. Incidentally, M.J. Akbar too says the same thing in his report on the Meerut riots of 1987, collection of his articles '*Riots after Riots*', a book of very mixed motives.

Thus, it would appear that Maulana Saheb represents the true spirit and message of his religion and, in fact, of all religions. For, what he says about avoiding conflict is bound to have a favorable response. One may differ or vehemently disagree about the necessity of proselytisation or conversion, which Islam considers God-ordained for, extending true blessings of God to all-mankind, but one cannot quarrel with the means preached by him – that it is only through good conduct and one's own ideal life that one can attract others to one's fold. This is, in fact, what we used to be taught as a first lesson to increase the *sankhya* (numbers) in the *Shakha* in our childhood days.

Though religious conversion is an altogether different and highly controversial thing, it is astonishing. Many people still believe in it even in 20th century. Every man should have a cause to strive for in life, otherwise life becomes a spiritless, pointless affair. But some strive peacefully for what they consider promotes spiritual salvation of others, while others do it violently. Most of conversions in India have been through terror or political and economic pressure while the entire Islamic world is in the grip of restlessness and violence it is trying to export to other countries.

Coming to what the Maulana Saheb said at the get-together last week, it may be summed up as follows: True Islam came to India peacefully through the Arab sailors in Kerala first of all. There was exchange of Indo-Arab books and knowledge also. I preach only that type of peaceful Islam. I do not make the poisonous and explosive speeches like Imam Sahih Al Bukhari. Imam is not a very educated being. He can only shout. The progress of the country lies in Hindu-Muslim amity, spread of nationalistic ideas and end to all bickering and misunderstandings. Muslims should not distrust Hindus who can be very good to Muslims. (He gave a couple of examples.) People all over the world are human beings first and Hindu, Muslim, Christian, etc. afterwards. We should rouse their conscience by appealing to their humanity rather than challenging their ego or self-pride. If you stop any religious procession, it hurts the ego of others and rouses the worst passion reaction. We should follow the rule of the road in real life: avoid confrontation, give way to the one coming from the opposite side. Even if the other party shouts provocative slogans, forbearance will save many an ugly situation, and even change the heart of others. This Maulana Saheb is a missionary with a difference – one who believes in winning over others through pristine sincerity alone.

Another part of the discussion about how the Muslim kings hijacked Islam will be discussed next time.

Al-Risala, August 5, 1990

❐

39

'Hinduism is the only Tolerant Faith'

says Maulana Wahiduddin Khan, who blames "incompetent Muslim leadership" for Hindu militancy.

Maulana Wahiduddin Khan, the eminent Islamic Scholar and President of the Islamic Centre, New Delhi, is noted for his independent views on subjects concerning Muslim Society. He does not confine himself solely to religious matters but is also a sort of social activist. He has authored over 100 books on various subjects. Said Michael L. Fitzgerald Secretary Pontifical Council for Inter-Religious dialogue, Vatican City on 21-9-1993: Maulana Wahiduddin Khan, though a Muslim, as appears from his name, spoke to us in such a positive and gentle way that we might have thought he was a Hindu. What I mean is that he is a great spirit of tolerance. *Organiser* specially interviewed him to find out his views on the Ayodhya incident. Excerpts:

Q. What is your viewpoint on December 6?

Ans. My views on this subject have been absolutely clear – right from the beginning. It is best to forget an unpleasant incident, whether in personal life or in society. I had said on a fateful day that both Hindus and Muslims would have to take a positive position and stick to it. I had suggested that Muslims should forget about the Babri monument and Hindus should also tear up the long list of mosques intended to be taken over.

Muslims should forget about this one and Hindus the others that they want to follow. This is how the country will progress. And my proposal is within the confines of the law. The places of worship bill passed in 1991 had the same proposal that status quo will be maintained in respect of all other mosques as they stood on 15 August, 1947.

Q. What signal does the 6th of December send out to Hindus? To Muslims?

A. Signal... (silent). Not an easy question answer (again goes silent). I am not sure you would agree with my view but when at several places I talked of the message of December 6 or what it points to, well, all that was based on experience.

I have since my childhood observed that the Hindus respect a mosque, whether in the countryside or in the urban towns. It is, therefore, a moot question why Hindus suddenly pulled down what we regarded as a mosque, why did the Hindu who normally respected mosques suddenly turn aggressive, he turned an egoist. And I have been saying the same thing to the Muslims. Now how could the Hindu's ego come to the fore? The reason is the Babri movement was taken over by an "incompetent Muslim leadership". What fed the Hindu's ego was the plethora of rallies, marches, boycotts and bands indulged in by the Muslims. Had the Muslims not adopted agitational approach and left the Babri structure to Hindus' mercy, I am hundred percent confident that the structure would never have been pulled down.

As for the lesson of December 6, I will say that if any time in future a controversy surfaces involving Hindus and Muslims, we should see to it that no one's ego is hurt. Both should coolly thrash out the matter to find a solution to the problem.

Q. Has there been a rise in Muslim militancy after December 6?

A. No, Muslims have not grown more militant. I can cite two instances. After December 6, the Muslims have not reacted in any conspicuous manner, although before December 6 they used to express their strong reaction to even minor pin-pricks by issuing statements or through other agitational means. Had the Muslim militancy grown, their reaction would have been much wider. Actually, their capacity to appreciate ground reality has grown, which has restrained their tendency to react. Secondly, the Muslim Personal Law Board has called upon them to observe December 3 as *'Yaumudduwa'*, a day of community prayer. Now the question is what is the relevance of holding the collective prayer on December 3 when the Babri monument was felled on

December 6? The fact is not many Muslims would come out for the collective prayers on December 6 and these leaders would be exposed. They, therefore, selected December 3 which is a Friday when Muslims customarily congregate in mosques for the *Jumma namaz* (Friday Congregational Prayer). The Board's appeal also proves that the Muslims no more wish to get involved in pointless controversies. Besides, it was impossible that Muslims would throng the country's three lakh mosques on December 6 for the '*Yaumudduwa*'. All this shows that Muslims have not grown more militant.

Q. Has the incident awakened the Muslims to concern themselves more with education and other developmental activities rather than concentrating on matters pertaining to their father?

A. Yes it has. Let me quote from a survey in India Today in support of it, which says that there has been a change in the Muslim thinking. They have realized that besides going in for science, technology, industry, they will have to think about social reform as well. The common Muslim has had a surfeit of dharnas, demonstrations, demands and the like, the staple of the so-called Muslim leadership. During my tours, I came across a number of Muslims who have begun to think positively over all this. A Muslim industrialist of Mumbai has opened a number of schools.

Q. You are sure schools, not *madarsas*?

A. No. Not *madarsas*, schools, where all subjects will be taught, including Urdu.

Q. Do you think the present Muslim leadership is in danger of losing its hold over the community?

A. Yes. The position of the so-called Muslim leadership is jeopardised because the Muslim masses have begun to challenge the so-called leaders of the Qaum. Their opposition to the established leaders is reflected in the readers' columns of the Urdu press. These leaders have a vested interest in the Muslim masses remaining illiterate and backward. They could then exploit the Muslim sentiments.

Q. Then can it be said that there has been an awakening following the 6th of December last year?

A. It is a confirmed fact. No doubt about that.

Q. Would you then consider the event in a way beneficial to the Muslims?

A. Look. Anything that happens benefits everyone one way or another. It is not applicable exclusively to Muslims. When Mahatma Gandhi was thrown out of a railway compartment by the British police, did it not prove for him a boon in disguise? What I mean to say is it made a hero of Gandhiji. It is quite right that circumstances make a man.

Q. And how about the Hindus? Has there been a rise in their militancy?

A. Hindus.... Well, I don't think that is so. Of course that the Hindus grown somewhat militant. Else they would not have gone in for the demolition. Hinduism by its very nature opposed militancy. It believes that if we are true to ourselves, others will also be true to themselves. If the *mandir* is a genuine expression of truth, so is a mosque. Hinduism is the only faith in the world which believes in the genuineness of all places of worship.

All I have come to believe is that there was some provocation for the Hindus, which, of course, could be only temporary as it is against the nature for a flare up to sustain for any length of time. That is why, the vehemence before and after December 6 has over the year gradually cooled down, although it has not totally subsided.

Q. In that case, would the Hindu vehemence disappear once the Shri Ram temple is reconstructed?

A. Yes. I am of the opinion that it will put an end to the Hindu vehemence.

Q. As a solution to the problem, the government recently announced the formation of two trusts for building a temple and a mosque. Do you think an official decision to build a temple and a mosque could truly bring about the rapprochement?

A. I support the Shankarcharyas' view that the Ayodhya issue should be taken out of the politicians' hands and entrusted to the *dharmacharyas*. A solution is possible if the matter is transferred to the Hindu and Muslim religious leaders.

Q. The government talks of building both a temple and a mosque. Will that solve the problem?

A. ....(long silence) I would not like to take names but in principle, I am of the opinion that if the politicians quit, the issue can be solved. Politicians are the cause of the dispute; religious leaders can bring about an amicable settlement. After meeting the Shankarcharyas, it was clear from our discussion that everyone wanted to have a peaceful solution.

Q. I would again ask you if a temple and mosque come up, will that be the end of the dispute?

A. You see. I cannot independently say anything in the matter. Nothing is going to happen simply at my instance. All I wish is that somehow the matter should be taken out of the politicians' hands. The religious leaders can also deliberate on what would bring about Hindu-Muslim unity. A mere lime and stone structure by itself is not going to be of any consequence. What is needed is that such an edifice results in Hindu-Muslim unity. The matter also needs to be taken out of government's jurisdiction.

Q. The Supreme Court is seized of the case under Section 143. If the Supreme Court decides that a temple did exist, will the Muslims accept the verdict?

A. I think the Muslims should abide by the Supreme Court's verdict. In fact, I am quite hopeful that they would accept the verdict. I would like to emphasize that the Muslims' prime 'concern' is not the *Babri* monument. They want to put a full stop at Ayodhya not a semi-colon. No controversy should be raised regarding any other mosque. If the Muslims are thoroughly convinced that with Ayodhya it would be thus far and no further and that Hindus and Muslims will hereafter live in amity, they will let the Hindus do what they like.

Q. The average Muslim wants that after Ayodhya, no other mosque should be the subject of a controversy and they would let there be a temple in Ayodhya. But the Muslim leaders want a mosque to be built at the very site where the Babri structure was. Do you think it will lead to a settlement?

A. I am confident that those who are now masquerading as so-called Muslim leaders, on the sole basis of having issued some statements regarding the *Babri* issue, do not represent the Muslim masses. The fact that they did not call upon the Muslims to participate in the *'Yaumudduwa'* on December 6 confirms my statement. Had they been truly representating the Muslims, they would have called upon the fraternity to assemble on December 6. Obviously, getting Muslims gathered in a mosque for offering namaz to say amen to any issue is no indication of Muslim leader's popularity. It is nothing more than a sham.

Q. Has December 6 led to polarisation among Hindus and Muslims?

A. There was some polarisation following the incident. But the process has now stopped. Polarisation and forming of blocs do not go forever. We can live in a society only with mutual understanding. Our cultures are intricately interwoven. We are partners in trades and professions. I believe all this is contrary to nature. And anything that goes against nature cannot endure.

Organiser, 5 December, 1993

❐

40

Selfish Muslim Leaders Pushing Babri Masjid Issue to Boiling Point

says Maulanas and Muftis (By Organiser Correspondent)

July 10, 1988, Organiser

The Babri Masjid Action Committee's proposed march to Ayodhya on October 14 and the decision to force entry and hold prayers in the Babri Mosque will lead to a more disastrous situation than what happened in Meerut last year, warns Maulana Wahiduddin Khan, Muslim Scholar and President of Islamic Centre, New Delhi.

In the latest issue (July) of Islamic Centre's Urdu monthly 'Al-Risala', the Maulana briefly recounts the events connected with the Babri Mosque-Ram Janmabhoomi dispute, which in his view is more than a century old, though, in its present phase, it began on February 1, 1986, when the Faizabad Court ordered the unlocking of the Ramjanmabhoomi closed since 1949.

He considers the court action as wrong but adds that even more wrong was what the Muslims did after that as they transformed the dispute into a national question by resorting to agitation, which is for the benefit of the leaders and not in the service of Islam. Their action has only pushed the problem to point of no return. The Muslims, he says, should have taken the help of either court or negotiations. But the Muslim leadership instead brought the Muslim feelings on the issue to a high pitch by making highly sentimental appeals and, thus, pushed the dispute to the street level leading to tension-ridden confrontation between Hindus and Muslims.

Without naming him, Maulana refers to Syed Shahabuddin's assertions that constant efforts were made at all levels for a negotiated settlement but no solution could be found. He, however, points out that his personal experience is that his (Shahabuddin's) statement is against facts. Here the Maulana recounts what happened at the March 27 meeting between Babri Committee leaders and Hindu leaders including Mahant Adityanath at Vithal Bhai Patel House in New Delhi.

At the meeting while Hindu leaders, according to him, adopted a cooperative attitude, Muslim representatives in their speeches displayed a stiff attitude. When Hindu leaders like Mahant Avaidyanath were ready to hand over matter to a mutually agreed board of historians, whose decision would be binding on both sides, the Chairman of the Babri Masjid Coordination Committee (Syed Shahabuddin) who is an MP also, flared up and started shouting. He was speaking so loudly that it was difficult to follow him except that 'This proposal is not acceptable to us'.

The Maulana is of the view that Ayodhya and Ramjanmabhoomi are holy places according to Hindu belief and are a highly sensitive issue for them. To transform such a delicate affair from the local to a national affair is a criminal act besides being an impediment in the solution of the dispute as it amounts to inviting the opposition of all Hindus of the country.

In his view, it is no way of solving this problem. He recalls many disputes about mosques having been solved amicably by resorting to negotiations rather than agitation. The Ramjanmabhoomi-Babri mosque dispute can also be solved in that manner. But, he surmises, it does not suit the Muslim leaders' interest.

Meanwhile, some Muslim theologians called Muftis who alone are authorised to pronounce *fatwa* (declaration) on contentious religious issues have declared the proposed march as 'Against Islamic tenets'.

The question was referred to the groups of Muftis belonging to Darul-Uloom Deoband, by M. Afzal, editor of Urdu weekly '*Akhbare-Nau*' and a staunch supporter of the Babri movement. According to a report in *Jansatta* (July 2), Mufti Jaferuddin, in his personal opinion, has opposed the march; the death of any Muslim during the course of which would amount to suicide, forbidden in Islam. But he along with two other Muftis, Nizamuddin and Habiburrahmn Khairbadi have suggested following the advice of a board of Muslim scholars (*ulemas*) who understand politics, the mind of the government and the laws of the land.

Mufti Sayeed Ahmed Ali of Wakf Darul Uloom has said that India being a *Darul Aman* (Zone of Peace) as against either *Darul Islam* or *Darul Harab*, the Muslims are enjoined upon by Islam to obey its laws and maintain peace.

If any law of decision of a court of law is against Muslim personal law or interferes with it, Muslims have the right to adopt any course of agitation by which peace is not disturbed and no harm is done to Muslim lives and property.

The Mufti declared the move to push the Muslims against the government and non-Muslim citizens as a proof positive of lack of understanding of both the religious strategy and country's politics. He further declared the march as 'not justified' under Islamic *Shar'iah*. Instead he has recommended to Muslims to demand to setting-up of a joint bench of Muslim-non-Muslims which can decide the issue overriding communal considerations.

❐

41

The Elusive Dialogue

Sub Heading: *Before December 6, the problem was how to save the 'Mosque'. After December 6, the question is how to save the Muslims, says Maulana Wahiduddin Khan.*

Our problem before December 6 was how to save the Babri Masjid, but the problem after December 6 is how to save the Muslims and how to prevent the Ayodhya type of event repeating itself at any other place.

"Muslims built up very big agitations on the Babri Masjid question, especially in the last six years even at the cost of huge sacrifices of life and property. But it could not be possible to save the mosque. In such a situation, it would be height of foolishness to continue the old type of protest movement. Such an agitation would have no sanction in Islam, as Islam ordains result-ordained action. An action that can yield no result is not in consonance with Islamic teachings.

"After December 6, the situation has changed completely. The mosque has been razed to the ground. The whole site has been cleared and a make-shift temple put up on it where worship and darshan are going on daily. As the situation has completely changed after December 6, we have to chalk out a new strategy in keeping with the new situation. Such a change in our course of action will be perfectly in keeping with the Islamic *Shar'iah*, as it is the permanent principle of the *Shar'iah* that injections change with the change of circumstances.

"Hence, in the light of the new situation, I suggested a three-point formula as follows:

1) That the Muslims should end their agitation about recovery of the Babri site.

2) That Hindus should stop their movement at Ayodhya itself forever. That is, they should not extend it to other places like Mathura and Kashi.

3) The government should make the Protection of Places of Warship Act (1992) a part of the Indian Constitution (to give permanent constitutional protection to the alleged converted places)."

That is what Maulana Wahiduddin Khan, the crusader for a Hindu-Muslim dialogue for permanent reconciliation, has said in a recent article in a local urdu daily *Qaumi Awaz* (April 3) in reply to a spate of articles and letters of criticism appearing in various Urdu and non-Urdu papers advising him not to mislead and confuse the Muslims by 'misinterpretation' of the *Shar'iah* and have mercy on them in their present depressed state of mind when they are in search of a messiah who can steer them to self-confidence to pursue their Islamic goal of "enforcing the Islamic *Shar'iah* in India" as another Maulana has said in the same paper.

This is, however, not to say that Maulana has no supporter in his community. A number of Muslims including Muslim intellectuals have been fretting and fuming against the "Babri Masjid" leaders for complete defeat of Muslims but it is doubtful whether this 'rational' or chastened section can hold out for long because of the near-total stranglehold of sabre-rattling *maulanas* over a medieval-minded crusading society, which even according to poet Mohd. Iqbal was the most backward of Muslim communities in the world.

Moreover, it is to be noted that with honourable exceptions, the rethinking among a section of Muslim has been triggered by pressure of circumstances and not by any change of heart or conviction. There can, in fact, be relapse even in this small group when the Hindutva pressure is lifted. For, even in case of Maulana Wahiduddin Khan, the plea for truce is based on the need for a change of strategy in an impossible situation where continuation of the mosque agitation would amount to courting "mass suicide" and even "loss of fundamental rights" if the Hindu majority is provoked any further.

Thus, he says, his is an interpretation of the *Shar'iah* in an extreme situation analogous to one in which it is ordained that "even eating of pork is permissible to save oneself from starvation death when nothing else is available". *Shar'iah*, he says, has always advised safer course of action, when the worst comes to the worst. Moreover, Muslims have done the maximum for the protection of the so-called mosque. Now they should "leave it to God and the conscience of the (Indian) nation". They should try to secure the best possible terms in arriving at an agreement with the Hindus and the government, by securing permanent protection of other (converted) mosques in exchange for abdication of their claim on Ayodhya.

Thus, appearing to commit the mistake of viewing Ayodhya movement simply as a drive for recovery of temples lost to imperialist vandals for political gains, and not for one of reassertion of Hindu pride in a Hindu country and cultural and spiritual rejuvenation for a total national renewal, he sticks to the Islamic hegemonistic stand by refusing to concede the genuineness of the Hindu urge for emancipation of their cultural and national symbols. In a typical Islamic style, he talks only in terms of two warring parties – one of which has emerged victorious for the time being. It is interesting to note that while he advocates surrender of the Muslim claim on Ramjanmabhoomi under compulsion after the Hindus have emancipated the site themselves by mass power in the teeth of Islamic-secular offensive, he refuses to see justification of Hindu claim on Krishanajanmabhoomi and Kashi Vishwanath.

In fact, he makes fun of Hindus for claiming these sites, even though they are more glaring examples of Islamic usurpation. As even a leftist writer Kamleshwar put it in the local Hindi daily Jagaran, you may dispute endlessly on Ramjanmabhoomi on the pretext of lack of clear historical evidence, but how will you dodge Krishnajanmabhoomi and Kashi Vishwanath issues about the demolition and conversion of which there is a clear *shahi farman* of Aurangzeb still preserved in the Kashi museum. However, the Maulana seems to depend on the Hindus' fear of riots, especially those of Hindu traders for loss of business, for preservation of status quo in Mathura and Kashi.

But one would not like to rub this point too hard if the aim is genuine reconciliation and peace by giving Muslims a sense of achievement at least over two places in exchange for one. But, as said earlier, the formula envisages no change of heart. It is only a forced concession for coexistence. For, the real hub of the matter is the warring Islamic mentality permanently at odds with the mother society for supremacy.

From Kashmir to communal riots to infiltration of millions both from Pakistan and Bangladesh, and now hi-tech holocaust in Bombay, certain dominant sections of the Muslims have, in fact, never allowed Hindus to forget that they and their country are under attack both from within and without, even after vivisection of the Motherland.

Not all the secular whitewashing can erase this adverse Islamic image, especially after large-scale attacks on peaceful citizens and police forces on the pretext of anti-Ayodhya protests as well as destruction of temples in areas like Mewat. Not all the deceptive reports like that of B.G. Verghese, condoning the desecration or destruction of some 40 temples or Shivalayas in Kashmir even in February 1986, long before the pretext of the December 6 demolition at Ayodhya, can help in confidence-building exercises. One can, in fact, be sure that someone like Verghese would undertake the job of condoning the destruction of hundreds of temples not only in India but even in Pakistan and Bangladesh a few years later on the plea that they have been rebuilt or repaired and are, hence, a "closed chapter". But that would only be adding insult to injury to put it mildly.

But then, as it is said, politics is art of the possible. It would, therefore, be fruitful to watch how Maulana Wahiduddin succeeds in his mission of the evergreen problem of Hindu-Muslim reconciliation. One may even pray for the success of his limited mission to usher in a piping period of peace and plenty in this country. But the intrepid Maulana himself seems to be chafing with impotent rage at the latest resolve of the pampered fat cats of the Muslim Personal Law Board to go ahead with another countrywide agitation to build the mosque "at the same place".

In a long letter to *Qaumi Awaz* (April 12), the Maulana rails at this perverse stand as an anachronistic (out of time) and regressive decision reminiscent of "the old imperialist mentality". He criticises the new Babri high command for ignoring the wishes of the majority of the people of India and looking to the government for striking a bargain, thinking that it could help them like the erstwhile British rulers. This attitude of confrontation with the Hindu masses, he says, will prove disastrous and like the fruitless Babri movement of the past, is worst example of bankruptcy, the incompetence of Muslim leadership.

As he points out, the Prime Minister's 15th August, 1992 promise from Red Fort could not save the mosque. Ten companies of security force could not protect it. What the people wanted has happened. The *kar sevaks* wiped out every trace of the mosque and removed every particle of its debris. Then the High Court too legitimised the new make-shift temple and allowed *darshan* of the idol. No man in his senses can believe that the Government which could not save the structure can now forcibly pull down the new temple, remove the idols and build mosque at the same place. It could not go against the wishes of the majority in a democracy, he says.

However, in total disregard of these realities and will of the people, "1500 leaders" of the Muslim Personal Law Board gathered in Delhi on April 5, 1992, to frame an unanimous memorandum demanding rebuilding of the mosque "at the same place" and met the Prime Minister to present it to him.

How strange it is, says the Maulana, that instead of going to the Hindu masses for better social relations and starting a dialogue to remove misunderstandings and achieve reconciliation, Muslim leaders are still looking to the corridors of power in Delhi as they used to do 50 years ago. "But the solution of our problem does not lie in deals with the government but in people-to-people contact and a heart-to-heart all-India dialogue with influential persons to end present conflict and to discover common ground for good neighbourly existence."

Such a dialogue, he says, would be in keeping with the spirit of *Shar'iah*. Here he refers to Prophet Muhammad's talks and agreement with non-Muslim chiefs at a place called Hudaibiyah near Mecca in 628 Hijri year (Islamic Calender). The agreement is famous in history as Hudaibiyah agreement. A similar agreement in India can start a new chapter in history of India to normalize

Hindu-Muslim relations and remove the only roadblock to the progress of the country, says the Maulana.

Thus, a Muslim leader, however well-meaning and well-intentioned in quest of peace, must search for a precedent in *Hadith* for talks with non-Muslims. But then everybody knows the fate of Hudaibiyah agreement which proved only a convenient truce to bail them out of a difficult situation, for a total conquest of Mecca ultimately.

Organiser weekly, 25 April, 1993

❑

42

Muslims Start the Riots

Sub Heading: Muslims are neither repressed nor discriminated against in free India; in fact, the level of affluence achieved by them since 1947 is unbelievable, says Maulana Wahiduddin Khan

Today the press and the leadership of Muslims are in the hands of those persons who unfortunately are a superficial type of people and for whom the easy formula of making themselves successful is to exploit Muslims by rousing a fear psychosis in them by focusing on some particular events and exaggerating them by focusing on some particular events and exaggerating them out of all proportions to give the Muslims a wrong impression that they are victims of tyranny and excesses in this country.

"After careful study and investigation of the conditions of Muslims in this country, I have come across a new revelation that their lot has improved a great deal since 1947 and whichever individual Muslim or whichever Muslim colony I have studied, I have found them, without exception, in a much better condition than before.

"My research about the plight of Muslim has led to quite the opposite results rather than what is usually published in Muslim papers and magazines and is falsely repeated as a settled fact that Muslims are the victims of discrimination in this country. The reality is different. You undertake a survey of any Muslim family and compare its social and economic condition with the pre-1947 one and you will find that every Muslim is in a far better material condition than before. Anyone can find this for himself from a survey of the Muslims close to him. And if you study the personal condition of those leaders who are going about championing the Muslim cause by alleging that Muslims have been reduced to misery and rain as a community, you will find their material condition a hundred times better than before. In any case, the Muslim site has more than its share of general affluence. They roll in riches no less than other sections of society. The affluence that they have achieved since 1947 is, in fact, unbelievable."

These are not the observations of a so-called 'Fascist-communalist" BJP-RSS-VHP leader or a much maligned Hindutva stalwart, but those of Maulana Wahiduddin Khan, President of the local Islamic Centre, expressed in his magazine *Al-Risala*. The Maulana, it may be pointed out, has recently shot into media limelight by his pragmatic and practical advice to the Muslims of India to forget about retaking the Babri site of construction of a new mosque on it completely. If they want to live and prosper in peace in this country. What they should actually sue for from the Hindu in exchange for this belated concession to Hindu as moments is he says, processes abdication of their claim on all slurped temples and temple sites desecrated and converted into mosques, especially the *idgah* on Krishnajanmabhoomi at Mathura and Gyanyapi mosque topping Kashi Vishwanath at Varanasi, which incidentally are models of 'composite culture' for the Islamic zealots and their secular patrons.

The Maulana's 'sage' advice to Muslims comes, of course, in a particular context of the need for model behaviour for the achievement of a long-term Islamic mission as set by the Prophet himself, to strive for the spread of Islam – the truest and final religion of God – all over the world. Being a true-blue Tablighi Maulana, he thinks this cannot be done in India in the present tarnished state of Muslim image and that if they want Islam to make any further headway in India, it will have to be the fine conduct of the Muslims themselves and not by other means as in the past. The volatile, over-emotional, easily excitable nature of the Muslims and the low state of their education is a great hurdle in the way of the progress of Muslim society as well as Islam. They take to violence too quickly and thoughtlessly and the Muslim leaders, instead of setting right these inbuilt aberrations are only adding fuel to the fire by blind and selfish behavior.

These are in brief the parameters of the distressed Maulana's loud thinking who was dubbed "RSS Maulana" not long ago by the likes of Shahabuddin for bluntly telling Muslims that almost every riot in free India was started by them and that they should undertake serious self-introspection and self-correction measures for winning the goodwill of the Hindus to reassure them about bonafides of Islam as a religion of peace and hope. It is another matter that very few Maulanas, the established religious leaders or Babri committee leaders are heeding to his advice.

While some like Maulana Qasmi are expressing their resolve to take back the Babri site peacefully and constitutionally even if it takes 300 years to do so, others are raising the war cry of "*masjid wahin banaenge*" and are pushing the Rao government to fulfill its disastrous promise made in a buff.

In any case, the top Islamic body of India, the Muslim Personal Law Board, headed by the most venerable Maulana Abul Hasan Ali Nadvi (alias Ali Mian), Rector of Nadwatul Ulema, the Islamic University of Lucknow, has pledged to get the mosque reconstructed at "the same place". The MPLB, it may be pointed out, has assumed the leadership of Babri movement after the collapse of the Babri Action Committee's leadership in the wake of the structure's demolition on December 6.

Anyway, while some may consider Maulana Wahiduddin's long-term motives not quite reassuring, it is interesting to watch him throwing a spanner in the fashionable propaganda line of the so-called secular press that the Indian Muslims are a poor miserable lot forcibly led to ghettoisation by the uncaring, communal Hindu majority and that special efforts and concessions are needed to lift them out of their morass. Flying in the face of such propaganda, which has been lapped up by anti-Indian and anti-Hindu elements all over the world, the Maulana says that the stories of "the persecution and repression" of Muslims of India are a handiwork of "yellow journalism" and that they are far removed from reality. He raps Syed Shahabuddin for putting out motivated stories of denial of Muslim backwardness and lack of talent or interest in government service as they are doing much better in other fields.

So well might the secular press cry, "Et tu Brute", for rendering some of the usual sob stories and highly selective reporting of the state and plight of Muslims of India totally unrealistic, irrelevant and mischievous. He debunks the secular stories about one sided riots as well.

Thus, the studied secular silence and almost total suppression of the genesis of the post-demolition riots in India, sparked off by violent Muslim protests, becomes highly suspect. While for weeks and months together, there have been stories about Muslims suffering after the inevitable backlash, there is total back-out of the plight of Hindu victims of Babri zealots all over India, especially in Mewat and Assam. Similarly, while highly motivated media mullahs and popes go on blaming the Shiv Sena for the second phase of rioting in Bombay from January 6 onwards no mention is made of the dire provocation provided by the burning of a Hindu family in Jogeshwari or the stabbing spree that led to a backlash in Bombay or Ahmedabad. No attempt is made to analyze why the proverbially mild and timid Hindu is compelled to come to streets and how the Shiv Sena's popularity touched dizzy heights in Bombay obviously because it is seen as the only force capable of setting scores with the Babri crusaders and even beating back their offensive.

It would be instructive to note what Mahatma Gandhi said about the Hindus' proverbial defensive nature in the wake of post-Khilafat riots in 1922-23 when they were mercilessly butchered or thrown out from places such as Malabar, Multan and Kohat. There is his famous anguished judgment: "There is no doubt in my mind that in majority of quarrels, the Hindus come out second best. But my own experience confirms the opinion that the Mussalman (Muslim) as a rule is a bully and the Hindu as a rule is a coward. I have noticed this in railway trains, on public roads, and in quarrels which I had the privilege of settling... Those Hindus who ran away to save their lives would have been truly non-violent and would have covered themselves with glory and added luster to their faith and won the friendship of their Mussalman (Muslim) assailants, if they had stood bare breast with smiles on their lips, and died at their post. They would have done less well, though still well, if they had stood at their post, and returned the blow. If the Hindus wish to convert the Mussalman (Muslim) bully into a respecting friend, they have to learn to die in the face of the heaviest odds." (Vide "*Hindu-Muslim Tension. Its Causes and Cure*", pp. 110-111. Young India, 5-6 1924)

Again, Gandhi said in the same context: "Hindus must cease to fear the Mussalman bully, and the Mussalmans should consider it beneath their dignity to bully their Hindu brothers." (p. 127, *Young India*)

In this context, there is another telltale quotation from Gandhiji about why the Muslim society as a whole is aggressive:

"The Mussalman being generally in a minority has as a class, developed into a bully... the thirteen hundred years of imperialist expansion has made the Mussalmans fighters as a body. They are, therefore, aggressive. Bullying is the natural excrescence of an aggressive spirit.

"The Hindu has an age-old civilization. He is essentially non-violent... Predominance of non-violent... non-violent spirit has restricted the use of arms to a small minority. The Hindus, as a body, are, therefore, not equipped for fighting... not knowing their (arms') use nor having an aptitude for them, they have become docile to the point of timidity or cowardice. This voice is, therefore, a natural excrescence of gentleness." (*Young India*, 30-12-1926; p. 226)

It should be obvious what the Hindus would do, if Gandhiji's advice falls flat on Muslims even so long after Partition or the Hindus refuse to be the guinea pigs. For sheer survival, when even the security forces are under secular attack for confronting the aggressor.

Excess of anything never goes unpunished, say the Greek tragedians. Secular sins are a legion and they are singing the psyche of both Hindus and Muslims. But the secular fundamentalists, particularly those in the media, even though discredited, go on peddling old myths, especially that the Muslims are grossly discriminated in free India and that they are a persecuted minority, whereas the reality is quite the reverse. For, they are in face the super-citizens, whom even the Pakistanis envy.

So, we come back to the Tablighi Maulana Wahiduddin Khan, to confront the lying philosophers of the incorrigible secular media. In a telling example about the reality of riots, the Maulana says that every Muslim is "a crusader by nature". But, unfortunately, this crusading zeal is being used for political hue and cry and mutual confrontations, rather than for spreading the deen (religion of Islam). The *qaum* is being drunk on "the liquor of emotionalism" by its writers and speakers for "cheap popularity". As a result, today's Muslim becomes "either escapist or confrontationist". He becomes frustrated or hypersensitive. Constructive attitude includes his thinking. The Muslim runs towards destructive paths as a result. He needs to be gainfully employed. Problem of Muslims is not riots or enemy's conspiracies, but how to defuse their own mischief, he says. It is not time for *jihad*, but for patience.

The Muslim, he says, is given the wrong impression that he is victim of discrimination and persecution, as a result of which he acts recklessly. One such example is the riot of February 1989 in Bombay when the Muslims' feelings were inflamed over British citizen, Rushdie's book (*Satanic Verses*). "They brought out a big procession against it, vitiating the atmosphere, leading to police firing. Some Muslims were killed for nothing as a result. They suffered economic loss also. Muslim papers kept printing stories of police excesses for weeks. It was all because of the emotional exploitation of Muslims by their press and leadership although India was the first country which had banned the book."

Similarly, he gives the examples of Aligarh riots of October 1978 and Moradabad riots of August 1980. The first started because a Muslim wrestler Ansar Ahmed and his men killed a Hindu wrestler Suresh Bhure who had defeated him in a *dangal*. The second started because of the Muslims' attack on a marriage party of Balmikis when they refused to stop the playing of band, etc. near a mosque. Later, the straying of pigs in an *idgah* pitted Muslims against the police in a big way.

The Muslim society, he says, does not stop its own over-emotional individual miscreants from triggering a riot but participate in it collectively. No attempt is made to nip the evil in the bud. Muslims are particularly aggressive at places where they are economically strong.

Interestingly, this is an outright contradiction and severe castigation of the secularists' theory that riots are staged by Hindu-vested interests in Muslim strongholds to cripple the latter economically. He pleads that instead of raising a hue and cry after the riots, Muslims would do better to restrain their own over-emotional co-religionists from taking offence over minor provocations, because it harms Muslims much more ultimately. In any case, he concedes that hot-headed nature and actions of Muslims are the first cause of riots.

Organiser weekly, 7 March, 1993

❐

43

Vande Mataram and Sare Jahan se Achchha are not different

Maulana Wahiduddin Khan at Sarv Panth Samadara Manch meet in Nagpur.

Sub-Heading:Long-term, positive and intensive efforts needed to usher in communal harmony—D.B. Thengadi

Nagpur instituting a sense of belonging towards the country and the society and creating capacity to look beyond one's religion was necessary for ensuring communal harmony and peace in India, observed Maulana Wahiduddin Khan, noted Islamic scholar, here on April 16.

He was delivering the inaugural address at the meeting of Serv Panth Samadara Manch of Bharatiya Mazdoor Sangh at Dr. Hedgewar Smriti Bhavan, Reshmbag. Former Vice-Chancellor of Nagpur University and President of the Manch, Shri Jal P. Gimi was in the chair. Renowned thinker and founder of the BMS, Shri Dattopant Thengadi was also present on the dais.

Describing this first meet of the Manch as the meet of the pioneers, Shri Dattopant Thengadi said that the idea of Sarva Panth Samadara Manch was conceived some couple of years ago on the auspicious day coinciding with the birthdays of Dr. Babasaheb Ambedkar and Dr. Hedgewar, founder of RSS.

The March was floated with a view to containing communal tensions and it has done a "silent but solid" work during the last couple of years since its inception, he added.

The idea of Sarva Panth Samadara Manch came to his mind through the teachings of late M.S. Golwalkar alias "Guruji" who was the second Sarsanghchalak of the RSS, and his association with people belonging to various religions in the BMS, Shri Thengadi said.

He said the organisation like BMS was the right place to implement the philosophy of *Sarva Panth Samadara* as the field of labour movement was above religious considerations.

He said while economics united some sections of the people, culture united the entire nation. But politics divided the whole country. We have to work rising above political and religious limitations, Shri Thengadi said adding that spreading communal harmony was welcomed by all.

BMS workers belonging to various religions here participated in the two-day meeting. Nearly 100-odd workers of Bharatiya Mazdoor Sangh belonging to various religious sects such as Islam, Christianity, Sikh, Hindu and others hailing from Kerala to Kashmir and Gujarat to Bengal also participated in the meet. All the participants sang *Vande Mataram*, paid respects to the *Bhagwa* flag of the BMS without any reservations or prejudices, a gesture which impressed the Maulana Wahiduddin Khan.

The Maulana said that misunderstanding amongst different religious sects was the root cause of communal disharmony and tensions and underscored the need to remove misgivings from the minds of the people.

He said we have always pampered the ego of different communities, which has led us to tensions and riots and added that the need of the hour was to arouse humanity if we want to make progress.

Stating that before 1947 there was no such tension between the Hindus and Muslims and even great Islamic poets like Iqbal used to sing the glory of Lord Rama in his couplet "*Hai Ram ke wajud par Hindustan ko naz ahale watan samajhate hain usko Imam-e-Hind*", but they were not confronted with criticism in those days, he said. Today, however, we have become more sensitive and this unnecessary sensitivity should be removed forthwith to bring back the era of peace and tranquity, the Maulana said.

Launching a scathing attack on the "self-styled" leaders of the Muslim community, who were opposed to singing *Vande Mataram* the Maulana said he did not see any difference in Iqbal's Sare Jahan se Achha and Vande Mataram and, therefore, could not justify the opposition to *Vande Mataram*. Such steps of these self-styled Muslim leaders widen the rift and encourage misgivings among Hindus and Muslims, he said.

The Maulana said that no Muslim leader today declared openly that he was proud to be an Indian Muslim. If they do so, the communal tension would vanish in just one single day, he said with confidence. If we want peace, we must be ready to pay the price for it and to take pride in being an Indian Muslim was precisely that price he said.

He said that the Muslims should feel that India was their country also. They belong to India as much as Hindus belong to this country. Once this feeling was developed, there could be no communal tensions, he said.

He said: "I have devoted myself for propagating communal harmony and this has become my mission for the life." He congratulated the Muslims for initiating efforts in this direction through the formation of this Manch. This was a right step at a very appropriate time, he said.

Shri Jai P. Gami in his presidential address said that Maulana Wahiduddin's speech had removed many misunderstandings from our minds. He said that religion had never deceived humanity. On the other hand, it was the rituality that had divided the people, he added.

He said we Parsis came to India. We were welcomed by the people here and, in due course of time, we merged with the people of this country "This country belongs to me and I respect it as I respect my parents," Shri Gimi said.

If we confined religious rituals to our own houses, then there would be no cause for communal tension, the former VC said.

Long-term positive and intensive efforts were needed to usher in an era of communal harmony in India, observed Shri Dattopant Thengadi, noted thinker and founder of the Bharatiya Mazdoor Sangh here today.

He was delivering the concluding address at the two-day session of Sarva Panth Samadara Manch floated by the BMS to create communal harmony amongst different religious communities in India held at Dr. Hedgewar Smriti Bhavan in Reshmbag.

Elaborating, Shri Thengadi said that the disease of communal hatred was very old and has become chronic. To remove such a chronic disease, long-term intensive treatment was required.

Although every political and social leader was stressing the need for social and communal harmony, the conflicts between various communities were on the rise. This was mainly because of the gap between what these leaders said and what they practiced, he said. He added that we had to set an example before the people to make them believe in what we preach.

Quoting noted social personality, Dr. Albert Shwaltzer, Shri Thengadi said that example was not the main thing in moulding the men's minds, it was the only thing. Therefore, it was imperative on our part to follow the ideals we preach, he added.

To remove misgivings, we have to work at the grass root level and build up contacts with individual's families and communities, he said. We must go step by step Shri. Thengadi advised, saying that nature of our work was slow but the results were solid. Since haste causes delay, we start our work slowly and achieve desired results in due course of time, Shri Thengadi said.

Organiser Correspondent, 25 April, 1994

❐

44

Maulana Wahiduddin Khan at RSS Karyalaya in Bangalore

The talk of separate Muslim identity is another way of harping on the two-nation theory

Maulana Wahiduddin Khan, renowned Muslim theologist and President, Islamic Studies centre, Delhi, visited Keshava at his RSS office in Bangalore, on 31/1/1994. He was accompanied by Shri Vinaya Chandra, State Secretary and Abbas Ali Bohra, Secretary, BJP Minorities Cell.

The Maulana had his meal with the inmates and interacted finely with them for a couple of hours. He recited with interest the Sanskrit prayer before the meals and very much appreciated its significance. Shri B.S.N. Mallya, Editor, *Vikrama*, K.S. Nagaraja Editor, *Pungava* and Chandrasekhara Bhandari, Prakashan Vibhag Pramukh, RSS, participated in the discussion.

In his opening remarks, the Maulana observed that his organisation – both an institution and an intellectual social movement – intends to extricate the existing separatism and help create a fair and free atmosphere of complete peace in the country. He said that the Muslim intelligentsia is fast taking interest in his movement.

It is no secret that the Muslim masses have come to the conclusion that a *masjid* cannot come up at the site, from where one was demolished on December 6, 1992. He strongly felt that, while on one hand, the Muslim community should defer its claim to the particular site and, on the other, the Hindus should not buttress any further claims on other religious places. Muslim fundamentalists should clearly understand that Muslims in general have discarded their association with the old structure and it was for this stipulated reason that they called a meeting to offer protest on a Friday – December 3, 1993 – when Muslims would customarily congregate and not on December 6, 1993, which happened to be a Sunday.

Organiser weekly, 13 February, 1994

❐

45

The Greatness of Simplicity

"Where are the people who used to come here? They were thin, as if from hunger. They had black marks on their foreheads, and their footwear was made from palm leaves."

In the time of Caliph Muawiyah, Afghanistan (known at that time as Sijistan) became a part of his kingdom. At first Sijistan's ruler, a Turkish Raja by the name of Rutbail, who was Buddhist by faith, put up stiff resistance, but after agreeing to pay an annual tax of 100,000 dirhams, he was granted immunity. For several years in succession he paid this tax regularly, but then one year, he refused to do so. Forces were repeatedly sent to his country but he was obdurate. When during the reign of Yazidibn Abdul Malik, the Caliph's envoys went to Rutbail to demand payment of the tax, the latter asked: "where are the people who used to come here? They were thin, as if from hunger. They had black marks on their foreheads, and their footwear was made from palm leaves." He then refused to pay the tax and, for the next quarter of a century, he lived independently of the Islamic empire.

It was clear that the simplicity of the companions of the Prophet had impressed Rutbail much more than the grandeur of the Umayyads. Formerly, the Islamic envoys had been unprepossessing in appearance, but had been possessed of great inner strength.

Anyone with real strength of character has very few material needs. Such an individual places a limit on his desires, shunning the world of fame and luxury. He actually takes pleasure in being humble, unlike those with pretensions to greatness. Free of any such complexes, his decision-making is never distorted by self-interest. The goals he sets before himself are worthy and wholesome, and he is ready to make any sacrifice to achieve them.

By contrast, those who seek artificial pleasures find themselves ensnared by them and, as a result, can never achieve religious fulfillment. They can never appreciate God's truth, because their lives are so cluttered with material encumbrances. They cannot see things as they are, and, this being so, are unable to associate themselves with any proper scale of human values. Living only for themselves, they lose sight of the divine goal of existence.

Al-Risala, January 1989

❒

46

On Silence

According to Abdullah ibn Umar, the Prophet once said: "The man who remained silent earned his salvation."[21]According to another tradition the Prophet once said: "Silence is wisdom. However there are few who practice it."[22]

A human being's greatest possession is his brain, and one of the first indications that he does possess a brain is his ability to remain silent. Maintaining silence then is not inaction. It is on the contrary a superior form of activity, indicative of the highest intelligence.

Keeping quiet and thinking are almost synonymous. In a silent state one is actually engaged in deep thought – undoubtedly one of the greatest of human actions. Where speech requires the activity of certain organs, silence requires the full activity of the brain. Silence, as an activity, has double the value of speech.

Silence is an indication of seriousness, denoting a man's efforts to have an in-depth appreciation of the matter in hand. Before venturing to speak, he realises the necessity to reflect. Before addressing his audience, he first addresses himself. He never rushes into anything; it is his silence that tells us that he is planning well-considered moves.

Speaking is the mark of impatience. Silence is the mark of patience. Where speaking can be indiscreet, silence is invariably discreet. Where speaking can be irresponsible, silence is a sure sign of responsibility.

Speaking demonstrates a man's limitations. Once he has spoken, his hearers may take his measure. Silence, on the other

21. Mishkat Al Masabih, 3/1360.
22. Al-Mafredat fi Gharib al Qur'an. p. 127.

hand, sets no such limits. One who remains silent is boundless, unfathomable. He is a man whose limits have yet to be revealed, and he speaks only when others have exhausted their funds of words.

Talkers are legion in this world, but those who love silence more than speech are as rare as the rarest of gems.

Al-Risala, August-September 1992

❐

47

Islam in the Present Age

In its issue of June 15, 1992, *Time* Magazine has made Islam its cover story with this title on the front page: 'Islam: Should the World be Afraid?' Another title inside the magazine on page 22 reads: 'The Sword of Islam.'

The aggressive picture of Islam as presented in the articles is no exception. Such references to Islam are common occurrences in modern times. Once during a journey to a European country, I met a Muslim youth who told me of an experience he had during an interview, which started as follows:

'Are you a Muslim?'

'Yes.'

'Then you are a terrorist.'

This is a clear indication of what the image of Islam has become in modern times – that of a terrorist religion. For this reason, people have come to regard Islam as a constant threat to universal peace, co-existence and solidarity. This, however, is a complete misunderstanding and is totally unrelated to the actual state of affairs.

The only acceptable way to determine the real position of Islam is to find out first of all what Islam sets out to achieve. Its God is very clearly expressed in this verse of the *Qur'an*: "O, Believers, be worshippers of the Lord." (3:79)The word used in this text is *rabbani*, i.e. devoting oneself to god and to no other. That is to say that, your love and your fear should all be for God and to God alone. The True Goal of Islam is thus to form such devout individuals. Obviously, a human being of this kind cannot be formed through violence and war. This is entirely a matter of intellectual revolution and of a change of heart. And such a change of heart and mind can be brought about only by advice, counseling, and not by recourse to violence.

If one were to speak of a 'militant businessman' or a 'violent merchant', this would be a contradiction in terms. This is because no true businessman can afford to depart from the norms of peace. Commerce, but it's very mature, makes one peaceable and willing to adjust. The same is true of Islam. Islam, by its very nature, is a wholly pacific and conciliatory faith. An atmosphere of strife and brutality is anathema to the performance of Islamic principles, which can produce results only in an atmosphere of peace. How then could Islam possibly approve of war and violence?

When Islam is, in truth, a peace-loving religion, how has it come to be portrayed as the very opposite? This is a complete misapprehension, which is traceable to two sources, one past and one present.

Let us first consider past contributory causes. It is a historical fact that certain battles against non-Muslims did take place during the Prophet's lifetime. These wars, however, were in no way related to the principles of Islam. They resulted rather from the external circumstances prevailing in the world of that time. These wars did not break out because Islam wanted to fight, but because others, by waging war against the Muslims had forced Islam to defend itself.

Islam came to the world one thousand four hundred years ago, in an age marked by religious persecution. It is a matter of historical record that, in those days, a man considered it his birth right to suppress by force all religions other than his own, or that of the state.

That is why in ancient times each religion experienced violent reactions from the adherents of other faiths. For instance, for about fifteen hundred years from the time of its inception, Christianity had been continuously subjected to persecution. Everywhere its followers met stiff opposition and were even subjected to torture or were killed outright, whereas today, the proponents of that time same Christianity are engaged in all-out missionary work without the slightest risk of victimisation.

If Christians were persecuted in ancient times, it was not because of their adherence to any militant ideology, the tenets of Christianity being the same in those days as they are today. The hostile reaction of the ancient world, as compared to the complaisance or even indifference of today, was conditioned rather by the age in which it took place – one in which religious persecution was the order of the day.

The modern age is totally different in that it is one of the religious freedoms. That is why proselytizers now meet, not with persecution, but with open-mindedness. All over the world, they are now presented with opportunities to carry on their religious work with complete impunity.

The same is true of Islamic history, in which all the incidents of armed conflict were due to the circumstances prevailing in that age, rather than to Islamic teachings. Islam had launched its missionary activities using completely peaceful means, but, it being an age of religious persecution, adherents of other religions opposed it tooth and nail. In this way, incidents of armed conflict became an unavoidable part of Islamic history. Nowadays, with this factor eliminated the possibility of such wars has also, in principle, come to an end.

Those who are unaware of this aspect of Islamic development tend to attribute early conflicts, quite wrongly, of course to tenets of Islam; they fail to appreciate that they resulted from external circumstances rather than from the internal features of Islam itself.

In modern times, Islam's aggressive image can be traced to the circumstances now prevailing in Muslim countries. In all Muslim countries, Muslims are divided into two broad categories, one called Islamists and the other secular or liberal.

With non-religious ideologies, dominating people's minds today all over the World, it often happens that when elections are held in Muslim countries, they are won by a secular or liberal group. Now if democratic relations are to be upheld, the Islamist group should bear with the liberals who have come into power until the expiry of their term in office. But Islamist groups in every country consider political power a right that they alone should enjoy. As such, whenever a liberal group is in control, the Islamist group assumes the role of aggressive opposition. Furthermore, whatever the activities of this Islamist group, they are all engaged in under the banner of Islam. As a result, its aggressive stance, whether ideological or practical, is attributed to Islam per se.

In actual fact, it is the self-styled Islamists who believe in militancy. And due to their misrepresentation of their own religion, others have come to think of Islam as a militant religion. This is simply a misunderstanding. The facts are quite the opposite.

There is a *hadith* to guide us on this subject. It says: "How you are, that is how your rulers will be."[23] That is to say that it is society which produces the type of people it wants as its rulers. This ruling class then represents society.

That is why Islam has very specifically given us this injunction that when the rot sets in the rulers or ruling class, we should not directly clash with them. We should rather devote all our efforts to change society in a constructive manner. The day society changes, the rulers will certainly change on their own. It is the society that determines what type of ruler it wants. That is why the actual problem lies in changing society rather than in launching militant campaigns directed towards the unseating of rulers.

The so-called Islamist group in Muslim countries has been engaged in ideological or practical campaigns directed against the rulers for the last fifty years. With no positive gain to date what has happened is that the image of Islam has been gravely distorted to that of a religion with violence as part of its creed.

A further error committed by the Islamist group is to suppose the whole world to be their enemies. Then, in order to counter these 'enemy' nations, they are continuously engaged in ideological and military warfare, depending upon circumstances. Indulgence in violence is thus to be found both on an internal plane against the Muslim liberals, and on an international plane, against non-Muslim nations.

This supposition that the whole world is the enemy of Islam is entirely without foundation. In the highly competitive world of today, one group or community is always trying to get ahead of the others. This is a state of affairs that has continued since man's advent on earth and it will continue until Doomsday. As such, it should be taken as a human challenge, rather than as a matter of enmity of opposition towards Muslims.

---

23. *Mishkat-al-Masabih.*

Conclusion

If we eliminate the erroneous impressions created by circumstances both in the past and the present, in particular by the Islamist politics, unguided as they are by the *Qur'an* and *Hadith*, the image of Islam that will emerge with be that of a religion based wholly on peace and mercy, which in reality is what it is. This is the real image as it evolves from Islamic teachings.

Al-Risala, August-September 1992

❒

48

Historiography

The starting point in Toynbee's philosophy of history was his contention that the proper unit of historical study must be acivilisation, rather than the traditional unit, the nation state.

Both these concepts, however, come to the same thing. That is, history should not be subordinated only to certain individuals but should rather be taken as the sum of all the activities of all groups of human beings. This approach, however, has come into existence only during the last few centuries. If we apply the term 'man-story' to the history, or historiography of today, we have to use the term 'king-story' to describe history before the modern era. It is only in modern times that history has come to mean the study of the academic, economic, social, political and cultural affairs of a given period. Ancient history amounted to a belittling of humanity in general; the common man was not worth mentioning. The only man worth mentioning was the one whose head was adorned by a crown.

This mentality of treating history as a 'story of king' was so confirmed that achievements relating to non-kings were not considered worthy of mention, however much they were marked by greatness. The most examples of these lacunae pertain to the great Prophets of the world. It is perhaps the strongest aspect of the story of man that it has omitted those very elements that should, in the writing of history, have been given top priority, namely, the lives of those pious men known as the Prophets, and all events relating to them. There corded history of humanity has elaborate descriptions of the kings. It records every single detail about them from the palaces they occupied to the generals they commanded. But the achievements of the Prophets are completely passed over.

People would find it very strange if a history of the freedom struggle of India did not mention the role of Gandhiji, or if a history of the USSR made no mention of Lenin. But a far stranger phenomenon is a recorded history of humanity, which is totally bereft of all mention of those pious souls, the Prophets. The final Prophet, that is, the Prophet of Islam, stands out as the sole exception. The reason is that he succeeded in changing those very factors in history that had been responsible for such tragic happenings in the past.

The serious gaps, which occurred in historical writings in the past resulted from the ancient historians belief that only the King were worthy of being recorded. Nothing else was of any importance to them.

The real events relating to non-kings were regarded as undeserving of any mention while even legendary tales and concocted stories about the kings were preserved in writings as if they were great realities. Take for instance the building of Alexandria, the renowned coastal city named after its founder, Alexander the great. Many strange stories are associated with the foundation of this story. One of them concerns sea genies who were said to have put obstacles in the path of building the city when the work was first started. Alexander, so the story goes, decided to see for himself what the genies were about. He gave orders for a large box of wood and glass to be made, and when it was ready, he had himself lowered in it to the bottom of the sea. There he drew pictures of the genies and then back on land, he had metal statues cast to look exactly like the drawings. These statues were then laid under the foundations of Alexandria. When the sea genies came there, and saw that genie: like themselves had been killed and buried in the foundation, they became frightened and ran away. The fact that this tale gained currency shows the credulous state in which the whole world lived before the advent of Islam.

In known human history, the Arab Ibn Khaldun (1332-1406) is the only historian to have changed the pattern of historiography. It was he who raised historiography from the level of mere king-story to the level of genuine mandatory. 'Kingology' was changed into sociology. The truth is that the science known today as sociology is the gift of Ibn Khaldun. He himself claimed that he was the founder of sociology, and there is no. reason to dispute his claim.

It was indeed Ibn Khaldun who gave to Europe the modern science of History. And it was Islam which bestowed this gift upon Ibn Khaldun. The Islamic revolution produced Ibn Khaldun and Ibn khaldun produced the modern science of history.

This change brought about in the concept of history by *Ibn Khaldun* has been described thus by the 20th century English historian, Arnold Toynbee: "A philosophy of history which is undoubtedly the greatest work of its kind that has ever yet been created in any time or place".[24] In much the same way, Robert Flint acknowledged his greatness: "As a theorist on history he had no equal in any age or country until Vico appeared, more than three hundred years later; Plato, Aristotle and Augustine were not his peers".[25]

Professor Philip K. Hitti writes:

The fame of Ibn-Khaldun rests on his *Muqaddimah* (Introduction to his book on history). In it he presented for the first time a theory of historical development, which takes due cognizance of the physical facts of climate and geography as well as of the moral and spiritual forces at work. As one who endeavored to formulate laws of national progress and decay, Ibn-Khaldun may be considered the discoverer—as he himself claimed - of the true scope and nature of history, or at least the real founder of the science of sociology. No Arab writer, indeed no European, had even taken a view of history at once so comprehensive and philosophic. By the consensus of critical opinion Ibn-Khaldun was the greatest historical philosopher Islam produced and one of the greatest of all time.

In Book I of the Muqaddimah, Ibn Khaldun sketches sociology, in Books 11 and III, sociology of politics; in Book IV sociology of urban life; in Book V, sociology of economics; and in Book VI, sociology of knowledge. The work is studied with brilliant observations on historiography, economics, politics, and education. It is held together by his concept of *asabiyah*, or social cohesion. Thus, he laid the foundation of a science of history which

24. Encyclopedia Britannica, 9/148.
25. Encyclopedia Britannica 9/148.

is not based just on .the description of kings, but which is, in a vaster sense, based on the economies, politics, education, religion, ethics, and culture of the whole nation.

Historians have generally acknowledged that the science of history had remained undeveloped before the emergence of Ibn Khaldun, and that he was the first person to develop the philosophy of history. The *Encyclopedia Britannica* says, "He developed one of the world's most significant philosophies of history."[26]

The question arises as to how it became possible for Ibn Khaldun to discover something which had remained undiscovered for centuries. The answer is that other historians were born before the Islamic revolution, while Ibn Khaldun was born after it. Ibn Khaldun was, in actual fact, a product of the Islamic revolution.

One belief which hampered the development of the science or art of history was what is known in religious terminology as polytheism. The whole world prior to Islam was one of divine kingship. Some kings set themselves up as gods without feeling any need to philosophise their claims while others claimed to be either the personification or representative of God in order that the public might accept without questioning their rights to absolute sovereignty. Even in the states of kings who made no claim to their power being derived from God, the same condition prevailed. That is, whether the kings claimed divinity or not, people everywhere associated divinity with kings. This was because whenever they came upon anything out of the ordinary, they took it to be a god, or amanifestation of a god. This mentality naturally was not discouraged by the kings. "The king has often stood between his people and their god, or as the god's representative."[27]

This state of affairs, which prevailed throughout the world, was radically altered by Islam. On the basis of monotheism, Islam brought about a revolution which eliminated the difference between king and commoner. All human beings, the offspring of Adam and Eve, were held to be equal. It was, uniquely, this great revolution of equality that paved the way for an Ibn Khaldun to lay the foundation of modern history in which the central position was held not by royal figures but by humanity itself.

26. Vol. 9, p. 147.
27. Encyclopedia Britannica, 1984 V/ 816.

Toward the End of the Prophet Muhammad's life, Maria Qibtiya bore him a beautiful and vivacious son in Medina. The Prophet named him Ibrahim, after the Prophet Abraham. Ibrahim was just one and a half years old when, in the tenth year of *Hijrah* (January 632 AD), he died. It so happened that the death of Ibrahim coincided with a' solar eclipse. From ancient times, one of the many superstitious notions in which people believed was that the solar and lunar eclipses were caused by the death of some king, or other important personage. They were to show, they thought, that the heavens mourned the death of the exalted in station. At that time, the Prophet of Islam was king of Arabia. For this reason, certain of the Medinans began attributing the eclipse to the death of the Prophet's son. As soon as the Prophet heard of this, he refuted it. There are several accounts of this incident in the books of hadith. One of these was recorded as follows:

"One day the Prophet came in great haste to the mosque. At that time the sun was in eclipse. The Prophet began to say his prayers and, by the time he had finished, the eclipse was over. Then addressing the congregation, he said that people imagined that the sun and moon went into eclipse at the death of some important person, but that this was not true. The eclipses of the sun and moon were not due to the death of any human being. Both the sun and the moon were just two of God's creations, with which He did as He willed. He told them that when they saw an eclipse, they should pray to God."[28]

The ancient rulers, on the contrary, encouraged such superstitious notions so that people would continue to regard them as superior beings. In known history, the Prophet of Islam was the first ruler who refuted such superstitious beliefs, showing them to be baseless. In this way, he led mankind along the path of enlightenment, eliminating the differences between men on an intellectual plane. He held as baseless all those suppositions and superstitions that had been responsible for creating and perpetuating to slave-mastermentality.

When the whole of Arabia came under the domination of Islam,the Prophet made a farewell *Hajj* pilgrimage in his last days, along with 125,000 companions. During this pilgrimage he

28. Sahih Al Bukhari Vol. 2, Book 18.

delivered hishistoric sermon on the plains of Arafat which is known as '*Khutba Hajjatul Wida*,' the sermon of the farewell pilgrimage.

This sermon was a declaration of human rights: "Hear' 0 people. All human beings are born of a man and a woman. All the apparent differences are only for the sake of introduction and identification. The most worthy before God is the one who is the most God-fearing. No Arab has any superiority over a non-Arab and vice versa. No black has any superiority over a white and vice versa. *Taqwa* (piety) is the only thing which will determine one's superiority over others."[29]

To this the Prophet added: "All things of the period of ignorance before Islam have been trampled down by my steps."[30] For the first time in ancient history, all sorts of inequality and discrimination were practically eliminated.

Only then did a new civilization come into being in which all human beings were equal. Speaking of the successors of the Prophet, Abu Bakr and Umar- Mahatma Gandhi said: "Though they were masters of a vast empire, they lived the life of paupers."[31]

This revolution was so powerful that even at a later period, when the rot had set in in the institutions of the government, and the caliphs had been replaced by 'emperors', the pressure of the Islamic civilization was so great that none of these 'emperors' could live in the style of the ancient monarchs. In Islamic history there are many such instances. The following incident, which took place during the reign of Sultan Abdur Rahman Assani, then powerful ruler of Muslim Spain, is an apt illustration.

Sultan Abdur Rahman ll (176-238 AD), a powerful ruler of Spain, built a palace, called al-Zahra, to the east of Cordoba, which was of such immensity that the word palace was not adequate to describe it. This magnificent residence came to be known as *Al-Madinah al-Zahirah* (the brilliant town). But, In spite of being so powerful and living in such magnificence, the Sultan did not regarded himself as being above the law.

It happened once that he missed one fast in the month of Ramadan without having any valid excuse which would

29. Sahih Muslim, Book 15, Hadith 159.
30. Sahih Muslim, Book 15, Hadith 159.
31. Harijan: Dated 27.07.1937.

be acceptable in terms of Islamic guidelines. He thereupon assembled the *Ulema* (religious scholars) of Cordoba, and told them of his lapse.

He asked them to pronounce a religious verdict, which would enable him to atone for it.

Al-Maqqari writes that one of the religious scholars present was the Imam Yahya, who promptly gave his religious verdict that the King would have to observe 60 continuous fasts in expiation. On leaving the palace he was asked by one of the *ulemas* why he had insisted on such a severe form of expiation when the *Shar'iah* also provided for the feeding of 60 poor people in atonement for one missed fast. Why had he not instructed the king to feed 60 poor people instead of fasting himself?

Angered by this question, Imam Yahya replied: "For a king to feed 60 poor people is no punishment." As we learn from the annals of *Andalussian* history, Sultan Abdur Rahmanll did accept the *fatwa* (verdict) of Imam Yahya, and did observe 60 continuous fasts. He showed no reaction whatsoever. He did not even dismiss Imam Yahya from his office.[32]

This can be explained in terms of the impact of the Islamic revolution, which had put an end to the difference between a subject and a ruler. It had created such an atmosphere of human equality that no one could regard himself as being superior to others. Not even a king dared to set himself apart from the commoners or to flout the law.

Before the Islamic revolution it was an accepted fact that the king was superior to a common man. For instance, the Roman emperor, Heraclius, a contemporary of the Prophet of Islam, in spite of being a Christian, had married his niece, Martina, thus offending the religious scruples of many of his subjects, who viewed his second marriage as incestuous.'[33]

It was known to the people that this marriage was illegal, yet there was no public outcry. This was because Heraclius was a king and, therefore, above any judgment by human standards. As a king, he had the right to do as he pleased.

---

32. Muslim Rulers, p. 415, with reference to Nafh Al Tib Part I, p. 362-368.
33. Encyclopedia Britannica, 1984, 8/782.

In ancient times, this extraordinary concept of the greatness of kings was so firmly implanted, as a matter of superstitious belief that ordinary citizens began to consider their monarchs to be innately superior creatures. The observance of special rites and rituals by kings was aimed at reinforcing this way of thinking.

The kings had thus, in their respective empires, achieved a temporal greatness, which was on a parallel with God's prerogative in the vastness of His Universe. It was but natural that historiography came under the influence of this concept of the 'divine right of kings' so that in practice, it became a chronicle or the lives of royal families with scant reference to the common man.

With the onset of the Islamic revolution in Arabia and neighboring countries, objects of nature like the sun and moon were dislodged from their divine pedestals. In like manner, kings were removed from the seat of extraordinary greatness. Now a king was just a human being like any other.

The influence of the Islamic revolution, which ultimately reached Asia, Africa and many European countries paved the way for a new atmosphere on a universal scale. With this new way of thinking the old king-centered mentality gave way to a man-centered ethos. Prominent expression has been given to a new approach to historiography in the writings of Abdur Rahman Ibn Khaldun, who in the foreword of *Kitab al-Jabar*, propounded his theory of how history should be written. This foreword, or *Muqaddimah* is considered so important that it has been published many times in several languages.

The most eminent' of *Mamluk* historians was Al Maqrizi, a disciple *of* Ibn Khaldun. It was through him in the 15th century *that Ibn Khaldun's* theories were introduced into Egypt. Later, other Muslim countries came under their influence.

Between l860 and 1870 a complete rendering of the *Muqaddimah* was published in French, thus introducing his historical theories into Europe. These thoughts took root in the soil of Europe and gained great popularity. Vico and other western historians developed this art, finally giving rise to the modern form of historiography.

Al-Risala, August-September 1992

❒

49

A Message

Some young Kashmiri asked me recently what my message was for Kashmir. I told them it was the same one that I had been repeating since 1967. It is 'simply that the solution to their problem lies in accepting the reality and not in emotional slogans or in the politics of confrontation.

From my study of the *Qur'an* and *Hadith* and my reading of history, I have found that this world is for those who have a grasp of reality and who devote themselves seriously to constructive work. Ignoring the reality and indulging in emotional outbursts will only compound the issue. Little else will be achieved.

When about to embark upon constructive work, one basic essential worth remembering is that action is not synonymous with steps taken of emotion. Action, in the best sense, means recognising opportunities and turning them to advantage. This necessarily entails starting with the possible in order to attain what, at first sight, seems the impossible. Starting with the impossible could mean losing even what is possible.

Another important fact is that whatever one achieves in this world is the result of personal worthiness. Nothing is ever achieved just by making demands and causing destruction. Any individual interested in making progress shall have to prove his capability through peaceful, constructive efforts. Only then will the desired goal be achieved. The same is true of community. In this world nothing is eternal – neither losing nor winning.

Here if one feels deprived, it is more often than not a case of self-deprivation. Such a situation and the feelings of resentment arising therefrom are often self-inflicted. The same is true of deceit. If one is deceived, it is very likely through one's own foolishness.

Failure is the result of unworthiness and ineptitude. Success is the result of having forged ahead and proved one's capability.

The correct steps to take in this world are those that allow you to proceed gradually, day by day. Steps that lead you in the reverse direction are no steps at all. They can, in fact be suicidal leaps.

Al-Risala, November 1991

❒

50

Tolerance: The Way of Nature

Tolerance is one of nature's universal principles. Without it, how could two mighty beasts as such the tiger and an elephant live side by side in the same jungle? It has been observed that when an elephant and a tiger cross each other's path, they quietly go their separate ways without showing any animosity. If, as a general rule, elephants and tigers did not display this mutual tolerance, then every chance meeting would mean a fight to the finish.

Just as nature has taught an elephant and a tiger to follow this principle of avoidance, so also has it endowed the human system with what is known in medical parlance as 'biological tolerance'.

"(Tolerance) in biology (is) the ability of an organism to endure contact with a substance, or its introduction into the body, without ill effect."[34]

This ability of the body to accept foreign elements is the bedrock of our entire system of medical treatment. Medicines administered during illness can be very harmful to the body as a whole. But the body accepts them, despite its susceptibilities, when correctly prescribed. It is thanks to the 'tolerance' of the body that medicine can enter it and effectively heal a diseased organ without there being any harmful side effects to other organs.

It is imperative that there should be the same show of tolerance in human society too. What the jungle beasts do as a matter of instinct and the human body does under nature's compulsion should be performed by man in full consciousness of its moral necessity. If an individual is to live peaceably with his

34. Encyclopedia Britannica, X/31.

fellow men, he must follow the path of tolerance as a matter of deliberate policy.

When people live together, there are bound to be differences, friction, complaints. This will happen in any family, society and country and, at the international level, such problems are often much more acute. But regardless of the level of contract, in any human interaction, there will always be unpleasant situations.

What is the remedy? The best answer is tolerance, on an individual as well as on a collective basis. That is the only practical method of living together if there is to be peace and progress. Without the spirit of tolerance, there can be no uplift or progress of the human race.

We should not make the mistake, however, of regarding tolerance as a state of passivity. It is rather a realistic approach engendered by a positive state of mind. It certainly does not mean opting for an inferior choice under duress when a better choice was possible. The truth is that there is no alternative to tolerance: it is a practical necessity and not a social weakness.

It frequently happens that when a man is faced with an unpleasant situation, his first impulse is to fight it out with the full belief that his struggle will really matters. But once he has imposed his will in this way on the situation, and it has been suitably adjusted in terms of his requirements, he sooner or later realises then the new state of affairs has aspects that are as bad as if not worse that the original situation, which -- since he had no sense of tolerance -- immediately drove him into an ugly confrontation.

The policy of tolerance gives us the time and opportunity to make correct decisions about what course of action to follow. It makes it possible for us to adjust to adverse circumstances and to seek out new avenues, by which to reach our goals. If, on the contrary, we reject tolerance as a correct attitude, and regard every untoward look, word or deed as a personal affront, we shall ultimately dismiss all human behavior towards ourselves as 'evil'. This 'evil' will really be of our own making, and if we finally become engulfed in it, we shall only have our own ill-judged attitude to thank for it.

If an elephant and a tiger did not tolerate each other, they would be inviting their own deaths. The very fact that they do tolerate each other gives them a new lease of life. One of the greatest advantages of tolerance is that it gives one freedom of action and the opportunity to shape one's life in a positive way. True success in life flows from the full utilisation of this opportunity to act. Any denial of this opportunity, through intolerance, can bring only destruction in its wake.

Al-Risala, November 1991

❐

51
Criticism

Why do people react so strongly to criticism? The reason is that criticism is taken as an insult. If they were to take criticism as a mere difference of opinion, their reaction would be less violent.

The strongest feeling in a man is the desire for respect. Under no circumstances would a man like to be insulted. When he encounters a critical attitude in others, he feels as though his honor and self-respect were under attack. This is why he is enraged by criticism and reacts strongly to his critics.

Criticism is, indeed, the bitterest pill for a man to swallow. And there is no difference in the reaction of the common man and the elite when it comes to this. There are only two types of men who can keep their balance when under critical fire.

The first is the one who fears God, and who has such a profound understanding of His glory that his own existence has no value in comparison. By accepting the greatness of God, he accepts his inferior station. Such a mental frame prevents him from reacting strongly to criticism. If the criticism is meant to belittle him, it does not matter to him, as he has already accepted his humble position.

The other type of man who does not react to criticism is the one with a scientific temperament. Science being the study of external reality, the scientist believes that reality is what manifests itself outwardly and not what exists in his own mind. The scientific temperament negates self-importance in a man and makes him a realist. It helps the scientist take a detached view of what is said by way of criticism. His attention becomes focused on the truth of the matter and not on hurtful comments.

A strong reaction to criticism only proves that a man is devoid of piety and has no true academic leanings. If such a man is criticised, he presumably deserves it.

Al-Risala, November 1991

❐

52

Rising Above the Psychology of Reaction

If a peaceful atmosphere is to be maintained in society while one goes about achieving one's ends, albeit in a peaceable manner, a great sacrifice is required. That is why he himself could set such a perfect example for the building of the life of the nation on the basis of non-violence.

One example of such a sacrifice can be seen in the Battle of Badr. In this battle, 70 Meccans had been taken as prisoners of war. All of them belonged to the nobility of Mecca and all were well educated by the standards of the time. Considering that in Medina, where the Prophet was staying, the people lacked such an education, the Prophet did not order the execution of the Meccans, but instead set a ransom for each of them. That is, each one had to teach ten children of the Ansar (Medinan inhabitants) how to read and write. After that they were to be set free.

At that time, one great risk was involved in setting these prisoners of war free. They being leaders of hostile tribes, there was the genuine fear that, once back in Mecca, they would use their freedom to incite the citizenry to prepare for another war. This fear became a reality when they succeeded in provoking their fellow Meccans to fight the Battle of Uhud.

Fully aware of the risk involved, the Prophet had, nevertheless, set these Meccans free. This instance not only demonstrates his love of peace, but also underlines the importance he attached to education. He felt that its importance was so great that it had to be acquired - even at the risk of a future war.

Conclusion

These few points, though in brief, show that Islam has a great role to play in countering the deadly challenges, namely violence and conflict, which are faced by the world of today. I would add that this scheme of Islam is not based on mere ideology, but has a genuine history of practical success to back it. The history of Islam shows that its message of peace is not just a dream of utopia, but is a fully practicable programme. It is a historical fact that the Prophet of Islam adopted such a well – considered strategy that all his successes were achieved with surprisingly little bloodshed. The toll of casualties in the revolution he brought about in Arabia amounted to only about a thousand on both the sides. This number is comparatively so low that this revolution can rightly be termed bloodless.

Islam, in short, is the science of strife-free living, supported by a factual history of peaceful co-existence.

Al-Risala, November 1991

❐

53

The Result of Reaction

Mr. G.D. Birla (1894-1983), besides being the topmost industrialist in the country, was also a very close associate of Mahatma Gandhi in the freedom struggle.

How the idea of national freedom took shape in the mind of Mr. Birla, is reproduced here in his own words: "When I was 16 years old, I started my independent business as a broker in Calcutta. During this period, I came in contact with many Englishmen, who were either my customers or my superior officers. I also saw their organisational capability and other qualities. But one thing I could not bear was their racial pride. I was not permitted to use the elevator to reach their offices. Neither was I allowed to sit on their benches, while waiting. This humiliation was very painful. As a result of this, I got interested in politics, which started in 1912 and continues till today."

The editor of *The Hindustan Times* (12 June, 1983) comments on this event:

"This was the beginning of his nationalism." Mr. Birla's nationalism was inspired by intense feelings of dislike. Similarly, the Islamism of the present-day Muslim leaders is born out of hatred for an opponent or enemy, whether real or imaginary. Both these sentiments are the results of reactionary forces, even though they speak in different languages. Neither of them could be termed a positive case.

To act on the strength of a positive incentive is one thing. But to be spurred on by a negative incentive is quite another thing. The former is 'action', the latter 'reaction'. A satisfactory result can flow only from right action. Reaction being negative in itself, no positive result can be expected from it.

Al-Risala, November 1991

❐

54

Islam: Creator of the Modern Age, Journey towards Progress

There were four centers of civilization before the advent of Christ - Persia, China, India and Greece. After the advent of the Prophet of Islam, the Abbasid Caliph, Al-Mansoor, built Baghdad in 762. He invited religious scholars and intellectuals to come from far and near, and encouraged the rendering of books in various languages into Arabic. This work started under the patronage of the state. In 830, Al-Mamun established in Baghdad his famous *Bayt al Hikmah* (house of wisdom), a combination of library, academy and translation bureau and an astronomical observatory. The work of translation continued with such speed and on such a vast scale that, within eighty years after the establishment of Baghdad, most of the books in Greek had already been rendered into Arabic.

During the Abbasid era, paper was being manufactured* on a large scale, so there was no dearth of paper for writing books. There were more than 400,000 books in the library of Cordoba (Spain) in the tenth century, whereas in Europe at that time, according to the Catholic Encyclopedia, the library of Canterbury was at the top of the list of Christian libraries for possessing 1800 books in the 13th century.

Al Mamun's astronomers used to performed one of the most delicate geodetic operations — the measuring of the length of a terrestrial degree. The object was to determine the size of the earth and its circumference on the assumption that the earth was round. The measurement, carried out on the plains of Sinjar, north of the Euphrates and near Palmyra, yielded 562/3 Arabic miles as the length of a degree of the meridian — a remarkably accurate result, exceeding the real length of the degree at that place by about 2877 feet. This would make the circumference of the earth 20,400 miles and its diameter 6500. Among those who took part in this Operation were the sons of Musa ibn Shakir and al-Khwarizmi, whose tables, revised a century and a half later by the Spanish astronomer Maslamah al Majriti and translated into Latin in 1126 by Adelard of Bath, it became the bases for other works both in the East and the West.

All these activities were going on in the world of Islam at a time when the whole of Europe believed in the earth being flat. In the 12th century, Al-Idrisi made a map of the world in which he even showed the source of the river Nile, which was not discovered by Europe till the 19th century. Muslims transferred to Europe the concept of the earth being round and the almost correct concept of the causes of the tide.

Ptolemy, the well-known Greek astronomer of the 2nd century, had presented the earth centered theory of the solar system, in his famous book, *Almagest*. This concept of Ptolemy dominated the minds of the people all over the world for about 1500 years, until, in the 16th century, Copernicus, Galileo and Kepler carried out researches which ultimately proved its falsity.

If a wrong concept about the revolution of the earth remained predominant for such a long period of time, it was due to the error of regarding something non-sacred as sacred. The Christians believed that the earth was a sacred sphere being the birthplace of the son of God (Christ). Because of this belief, they found the concept of the earth at the centre, around which the whole universe revolved, exactly accorded with their supposed concept. This concept of the earth's sacredness came in the way of Christians making any further investigation. They adhered to this theory until finally the naked reality forced them to reject it.

The *Encyclopedia Britannica* (1984 (4/522) says: "According to the old cosmology, the earth was the center of the universe, man was the highest creature of this earth, and his salvation was the central event in heaven and on the earth. The discovery that the Earth is the only planet among others that rotate around the sun, and that the sun is only an insignificant star among the innumerable galaxies of the cosmos, has shaken the old understanding of man. If the earth, compared to the huge expanses of the universe, was only a speck of dust in the structure of the macrocosm Newton and others began to explore the question of how man, the dust of dust, could continue to claim the holy privilege that he and his fame were the goal and culmination of God's actions."

The Christians held Christ to be a part of the holy trinity and developed the concept that the most important event of history ever to take place on the earth was the crucifixion of God's son for the atonement of man's sins. In this way, the earth came to hold a sacred position in their set of beliefs. They offered the stiffest opposition to any such thinking as could undermine the central position of the earth. It was this belief that came in the way of free investigation of the solar system.

In this way, holding the non-sacred to be sacred had locked the doors to all progress.

In those days, Muslims were so ahead of other nations that when they were extradited from Spain, the astrolabes they left behind, by means of which they had studied heavenly bodies, were turned into the clock tower of a church, as the Christians did not understand their use.

It is a fact that in ancient time polytheism and superstition held sway all over the world. And it is also true that it was this polytheism and superstition that were obstacles to all kinds of progress. The revolution based on monotheism which was brought about in the wake of Islam practically ended polytheism and superstition for the first time in history. Afterwards, as a natural result, human history took to the path of progress.

In ancient times, creative minds were born in certain countries. They could think independently of their environment. But due to the unfavorable atmosphere and hostile environment of the times their efforts could not be brought to fruition. The buds of their knowledge withered away before they could flower. However, when the Islamic revolution produced a favorable atmosphere, it unleashed a mighty flood of knowledge with had been kept pent up for thousands of years by the dam of superstition.

Al-Risala, November 1991

❐

55

Turn Your Disadvantage into an Advantage

Dr. Edward Livingston Trudeau was sent, as a young doctor, to the mountains where he expected to die of tuberculosis. But he did not die. As he lay in bed he had a vision of a great hospital where he could rebuild other sufferers. Flat on his back, he examined patients not as ill as himself. He raised money and laboured until his dream became the great sanatorium at Sarance, near New York, that helped thousands of tuberculosis patients. Trudeau's affliction turned an unknown doctor into a physician of worldwide fame.

Eugene O'Neill was an utter drifter with no plan of life until he was twenty-five. A serious breakdown gave him the requisite leisure, he says, "to evaluate the impressions of many years in which experiences had crowded one upon the other, with never a second's reflection". It was in the hospital that he first began to write the plays that revolutionised American drama.

Like any major experience, illness actually changes us. How? Well, for one thing we are temporarily relieved from the terrible pressure of meeting the world head-on. Responsibility melts away like snow on an April roof; we don't have to catch trains, look after babies, or wind the clock. We enter a realm of introspection and self-analysis. We think soberly, perhaps for the first time, about our past and future. Former values are seen to be fallacious; habitual courses of action appear weak, foolish or stubborn; illness, it seems gives us that rarest thing in the world — a second chance, not only of health but of life itself!

Illness knocks a lot of nonsense out of us; it induces humility, cuts us down to our own size. It enables us to throw a search light upon our inner selves and to discover how often we have rationalised our failures and weaknesses, dodged vital issues and run sulking away.

Al-Risala, October 1989

❐

56

Transplanting Fabianism in Indian Soil, the Non-Hitlerian Approach

Adolf Hitler, always used to keep a special pistol with him for his own protection. The .32 caliber gold-washed pistol with its ivory handle, floral engraving and Hitler's inscribed initials, it was taken from Hitler's Munich apartment by US soldiers at the end of World War II, and was recently auctioned for $ 114,000. This is the largest sum ever spent at a public auction on a military collector's item.'

Shortly before the World War II, Hitler achieved tremendous popularity in what was then an undivided Germany, and was soon to assume the powers of a dictator. His expansionist ("Lebensraum") policies found great favor with public, aimed at conquering Britain and pushing Germany's borders outward to the limits of Europe, and beyond, into the vast territories of the USSR. But in spite of all Germany's military might, and a powerful alliance with Italy and Japan, the final result was a humiliating defeat, which left Germany crushed and finally divided into two separate regions under the control of the USSR, Britain, France and the USA. Not only had Germany expanded its territory, but it had also lost its national identity in being divided into East and West Germany. At the bitter end, on April 30, 1945, Hitler shot himself dead with the very pistol he had kept with him for self-defense all throughout this period. Hitler had ruined himself along with his nation.

How Hitler Shot into Prominence

The Great Depression, that is, the economic slump in the US and Europe that began in 1929 lasted almost a decade. During this period, for a variety of reasons, industrial produce piled up in warehouses but failed to find consumers in the market. As a result, the factories were closed down. "A long decline in economic activity ensued, until in 1932 one out of every four US workers was unemployed. The Depression, at once, affected the European economy, rendering millions of workers jobless in Germany, Great Britain, and other industrial countries. By 1932, the total value of world trade had fallen by more than half, as country after country took measures against the importation of foreign goods. The great economic Depression had important consequences in the political sphere, strengthening extremist forces and lowering the prestige of liberal democracy.[35]

Whenever faced with any great calamity, the public attributes it more often than not to the misguided policies of the government. As a result, a pervasive atmosphere of mass unrest is generated against those in power. This being the way of public psychology, it is in no way surprising if those who rise in protest against government mismanagement are hailed by the people as their true saviors. The fierier the oratory, the more in earnest the orator is deemed to be. On the other hand, anyone who attempts to make a cool rationalisation of the problem in terms of the prevailing circumstances is regarded with suspicion, and seen as the agent of a callous and indifferent set of rulers. The general opinion about a quiet, sincere analyst is that he is only making insidious attempts to divert public attention from the true focus of activity.

It was just such set of circumstances which were exploited by Hitler during the Great Depression in Germany (1929-1939). He was vociferous in laying the blame for all of the country's afflictions upon the government of that period, and began making rabble-rousing speeches against it. In consequence, he soon became the most popular leader in the eyes of the German public. With the mass support he received—thanks to the economic Depression—he turned the Nazis into the largest party in the Reichstag (German Parliament). Hitler was appointed Chancellor in January, 1933, and soon proceeded to establish a dictatorship in Germany.

35. Encyclopedia Britannica, Vol. IV, p. 696.

A Different Example

British history, during the same period and under the same depressed economic conditions, took quite a different course. It was realised, of course, that a change of system was necessary if the lot of the common man was to improve, but the group that took it upon itself to investigate the prevailing conditions, and to decide upon and promote reform, was very different from Hitler's Nazi party in its style of thinking and functioning. Founded in London as far back as 1833, with the aim of ending the evils of the capitalist system, the Fabian Society was composed mainly of intellectuals. The composition of its membership might have made it too exclusively elitist in its activities had it not been for the efforts of one of the society's leading lights, George Bernard Shaw, (1856-1950) to attract large numbers of ordinary people to the movement by writing articles and making speeches, which were to the common man's taste. To further their cause, the young Shaw organised a procession consisting mostly of middle class people, but when it reached those parts of London where the prominent capitalist lived, some of the participants began to indulge in violence and stone throwing, breaking windows and injuring people.

This very first experiment, having taken the ugly turn that it did, turned the leaders of Fabian society against processions and demonstrations as methods of functioning. Since it was evidently extremely difficult to make public restrict themselves to peaceful demonstrations, they agreed that the Fabian should struggle to achieve their constructive aims without resorting to the ways of protest and demonstrations. Subsequently, the Fabian society adhered strictly to non-demonstration methods such as the use of the press, meetings, academic research, etc. Under the influence of the leading intellectuals of the Fabian society, they stressed the 'inevitableness of gradualism'.[36]

The deliberate renunciation of demonstrations as a method of achieving one's goal is a very difficult policy to adhere to in the world of today. It means being content with consolidation, where what is obviously desirable is extension. Then, where innumerable opportunities present themselves to court fame and popularity,

36. Encyclopaedia Britannia, Vol. IV, p. 20.

one has to subdue this urge and remain content with anonymity. The Fabian society seems to have been singularly successful in following such a policy. Although it played such a great role in British history, its leaders were consistent in foregoing any personal glory.

Because of its moderate way of thinking and avoidance of demonstrations, the Fabian society never became a popular movement in Britain. Even at its zenith in 1946, its members did not number more than 8,500. It was always looked upon as a movement of the intellectuals and it did, in fact, have profound influence upon the intellectual class of Britain. George Bernard Shaw, Sidney and Beatrice Webb (founders of the London School of Economics) and Clement Atlee were some of the more prominent intellectuals who came under its influence. An important stage was brought about in its development when its members joined the British Labour Party, quickly becoming its virtual brain. When the Labour Party came to power in 1945, fifty per cent of its members were Fabians, the most notable being Clement Atlee. This is quite remarkable considering that the membership of the Fabian society represented barely one per cent of British population.

Prior to 1945, the Conservative Party, headed by Sir Winston Churchill, had been in power, and it was during this period that freedom movements were gaining momentum in the British colonies. Churchill, known for his consummate oratory, has gone down in history as saying: "I have not become His Majesty's first minister to preside over the liquidation of His Majesty's empire."

His policy of opposition to colonial freedom was leading Britain in the same direction as Hitler's policy had lead Germany. Pursued to its logical conclusion, it would have led to armed confrontation with the far-flung British colonies, which would have been put through pitched battles and all the other horrors of war before gaining their freedom. In the final stages, they would ultimately have had to suffer even greater cruelty and oppression than hitherto. British losses would also have been very great in terms of manpower and the national budget, and whatever political and economic ties Britain had with its colonies would have been destroyed forever.

Fortunately, at the end of World War II, in 1945, the Labour Party came to power, and it began to rethink the whole colonial situation. Their realistic approach led them under the influence of its Fabian members, to the conclusion that under the prevailing conditions, it would be difficult for Britain to retain its hold over the colonies, which would sooner or later, demand to freedom. They saw that if Britain could grant them their one word without bloodshed. It was due to the Fabian brain that Britain made its historic decision in 1947 to give India (and subsequently other countries) its freedom.

As a result of this realistic decision, Britain gained enormously. On the one hand, it was able, to safeguard its international economic interests and, on the other, it was able to retain its international political prestige through the British Commonwealth of Nations.

A Lesson for India

Although post-Independence circumstances in India have not made it possible for anyone to become "Hitler," but most of our leaders have publicly espouse the cause of the sufferers and, blamed the government for the general malaise, and begin one word those in power. Not only do they get up and make fiery speeches against the authorities, they set in motion a whole terrain of processions, demonstrations, and rallies whose sole target is to abuse is the government.

The public, quickly whipped up to a state of mass hysteria by such leaders, crowd around them in frenzied hero-worship. Such movement gain such strength that they can even cause the government of the day to 'fall. But we should give careful thought to the notion that "a revolution is a successful effort to get rid of a bad government and set up a worse".

A recent example of just such a revolution in India was that launched by Jai Praksh Narain (1902-1979). In spite of the Janata Party's electoral success after the Emergency, this "total revolution" ended in total failure.

The Need of the Hour

The most pressing need of the hour is to launch movements in the country patterned on the Fabian Society's style of functioning, at both communal and national levels. Soon after India gained its Independence, Mahatma Gandhi (1869-1948) formulated a plan for setting up a party of this type, which he named the Jan Congress. He stressed our need for a purely non-political party, which would work towards the intellectual training of the public, and remain selflessly constructive in its functioning. For the Jan Congress to be successful, it would have meant the great leaders of the Congress voluntarily relinquishing the personal gains of power politics, and earnestly devoting themselves to this task in a quiet, unpublicised way. But no leader was willing to make a political sacrifice of this nature, thus after Gandhiji's death, his scheme, too, eventually died a natural death.

For the last twenty years, the writer has himself been the promoter of a quietly constructive, non-agitational movement and, by the grace of God, our mission is progressing satisfactorily. It is my sincere wish that all those, who are earnestly concerned about the future of our country, should adopt this selfsame approach. There is no better way of creating a new and brighter future for the nation.

Al-Risala, October 1989

❑

57

National Integration

National integration, one of the most widely discussed subjects today, is undeniably the greatest need of our country. Difficult of achievement, it is nevertheless a sine qua non of national progress.

No one who wishes his own country well would dispute the fact that national integration is a goal of supreme importance. But, when it comes to finding ways and means of accomplishing this, it becomes evident that there are many factions that are totally at variance with one another. One in particular would have it that the entire populace should have a common ideology and a uniform creed. But the creation of a mono-society of this kind would be an impossible task, because it would be such a strange divagation from, if not an actual perversion of the laws of nature. No scheme that runs counter to nature can ever succeed in this world.

It is an established fact that no two human beings have exactly the same physical structure. No two sets of finger prints are ever the same, and that is why individuals can be identified from them with one hundred per cent certainty. Science has even gone so far as to prove that every particle of the human body is different from its counterpart in another human body. This difference in particles exists not only in the body but also in the brain. It has been proved by biological studies that no two human brains are identical. The face being a reflection of the brain, it is seldom that two faces resemble each other in every particular. With all these physical and psychological divergences, how is it possible to rally all human beings around one system of belief? To have a single ideology is against the entire system of nature. When the creator has ordained diversity as a distinguishing feature of human beings, it cannot be arbitrarily abolished. The only way you can begin to solve the attendant problem is by frankly accepting the fact that this diversity exists and will continue to exist.

Hence our belief, the secret of national integration lies in intellectual adjustment rather than going for legislative impositions. To this end, we must explore the areas that could possibly provide us with a common basis for making reciprocal adjustments without the special identities of individuals and groups becoming lost or obscured.

Even without going into these niceties, we can state one clear-cut and fundamental principle, which should form the practical basis of national integration. It is simply that everyone should enjoy personal freedom, and that freedom should be curtailed only when it is likely to be harmful or infringe upon the rights of others. There is a story from the days of America's newly-won independence from foreign political domination, which admirably illustrates this point. It seems that a newly liberated American, out to celebrate his freedom in his own way, strutted exuberantly down the street, swinging his arms in a carefree manner with scant regard for the convenience of other pedestrians. Eventually, he hit a passer-by on the nose. The latter was enraged and shouted: "What kind of foolishness is this? Why are you walking in this frivolous manner and swinging your hands about in this way?" "America is free," replied the man. "I'm free to do as I want and walk as I wish." "Well," said the passer-by, "your freedom ends where my nose begins!"

It is quite possible for everyone to be free in his actions, but his freedom ends where his actions begin to encroach upon the lives of others. Enjoying freedom of action must also entail the honoring of other's freedom. In this lies the secret of successful national integration.

When knowledge is reduced to an avenue towards personal prestige, Ubayy ibn Ka'ab said: "Acquire knowledge, and practice it. Do not acquire it in order to beautify yourselves thereby, for there will come a time when learning will be used as an adornment, as people adorn themselves with clothes."

One who has successfully grown a tree from a sapling has also the capacity to grow a whole garden from seed. The case of national integration is on a clear parallel with this, for just as our whole garden full of flowers blossoms from a large number of individual seeds, so can our national integration blossom from a large numb something that we can already be said to be enjoying, for haven't all of us have at least one good friend from the opposite community? It is quite clear that the goal we seek at the society level, we all have already achieved at the individual level. Extend your personal experience to society as a whole and the result will be national integration.

Al-Risala, May 1987

❐

58

If we Gain why not

A short time ago, I met an Indian leader who publishes an Urdu weekly. For a long time, this paper had run at a loss, but later picked up and started making profits. The history of its phenomenal upswing was interesting to listen to. He told me that when he had launched this enterprise, there seemed to be no way that the circulation could be made to exceed 3000, and that this was a state of affairs, which continued for a long time in spite of his best efforts. Then, in 1985, came the controversy over the Ayodhya mosque (to the Muslims, Babri Masjid and, to the Hindus, the Ram Janmabhoomi). Exploiting this issue to the full, he brought out a spate of sensational articles — most of them sheer bombast — with deliberately provocative captions. As anticipated, his paper's circulation soared from a mere 3,000 to a spectacular 30,000. Congratulatory letters began to pour in from all sides.

While the Babri Masjid type of dispute is bad news for the Muslim community at large, it is, on the contrary, the best possible news for the leaders of that community, for that is the kind of news that is grist to every political and journalistic mill. It is no exaggeration to say that while, for the general Muslim public, it is a tragedy, for the leaders it is more of a comedy. It would be wrong to think that this applies only to a few stray cases; it applies to the entire Muslim leadership and the entire field of Muslim journalism.

The above success story reminded me of a certain Muslim villager who made a habit of visiting graves and *dargahs* (saints' shrines) to ask for favors, although, strictly speaking, a good Muslim should visit such sites only to pray for the departed souls, the granting of favors being the prerogative of the Almighty. A religious scholar, who lived in the vicinity, tried to make him see the error of his ways by pointing out that such an act was tantamount to polytheism (*Shirk*), but the villager's experience told him otherwise. It seems that whatever he had asked for at a graveside has been granted to him — even the birth of a male child. The advice of the scholar, therefore, made no sense to him, and he countered with: "If I benefit from going there, why should not I go?"

For the past twenty years, the writer has been advising Muslim leaders to eschew emotionalism in politics and to adopt a quiet constructive approach. To this end, I have had meetings with prominent Muslim leaders, entered into correspondence with them, and tried focusing attention on this issue through my writings and tried in every way possible to elucidate this point so fully that they would be left with no arguments against my point of view. Yet no Muslim leader is willing to accept this advice. It is because they are no different from the villager by the graveside. Each Muslim leader in his heart of heart thinks: "Why not dabble in emotional-ism? It is to my advantage."

It is a stark reality that what gives the greatest boost to both Muslim leadership and journalism is rioting. If communal riots were to cease in this country, we should see an end to their dominating influence.

According to Sajid Rashid, an Urdu journalist of considerable experience: "The most popular topic of the majority of Urdu newspapers is 'riots' and that, too, only Hindu-Muslim riots. The Urdu papers now find it inconceivable that a new issue should be published without some such sensational item. This is a matter of personal experience. The youthful editor of a weekly paper actually expressed such a desire to me. 'If only there could be a riot — the circulation of my paper would increase.'

"Most of the Urdu journalists are victims of this selfsame disease. Pick up any Muslim weekly and you will be confronted with such a picture of victimisation and persecution as would persuade you that there is no community more persecuted and more pitiable than the Muslims.

"There can be no two opinions about the fact that Muslims are fuel to the fire of communalism in this country. But the way this is presented by Muslim journalists it is having an adverse effect on Muslim morale, hence their sense of insecurity and persecution. A feeling of this kind undermines the spirit of self-reliance and power of decision-making that many in the Muslim world have begun to suffer from a kind of mental paralysis. We have to realise that, wittingly or unwittingly, most of the Urdu papers are engaged in the dangerous ploy of incapacitating the entire community." (*Urdu Times*, Bombay, 14 September, 1986).

Al-Risala, May 1987

❒

59

Good Character

Good character is the sum of personal virtues, which guarantees correct and agreeable behaviour in daily social interaction. A person of good character will invariably conform in his behaviour a strict code of ethics.

What should be the underlying principle of this code of ethics? According to a *hadith* it is simply this—you should like for others what you like for yourself, that is, you should treat others just as you want to be treated by others.

Everyone likes to be addressed with good manners and pleasing words. So everyone should speak gently to others. Everyone wants his existence to be problem-free, so he should avoid creating problems for others. Everyone wants others to deal with him in a sympathetic and cooperative manner. So what everyone ought to do while dealing with others is to give them his full sympathy and cooperation.

This standard of ethics is very simple and natural. It is so simple that anyone may easily learn it, be he literate or illiterate, able bodied or disabled, and regardless of his likes and dislikes. This *hadith* has given such a criterion for human ethics that no one can find difficult to understand. In this way, Islam has set forth, in the light of everyone's personal experience, what behaviour may be indulged in and what behaviour has to be refrained from.

According to another *hadith*, the best of us is one who is best in moral character. Accordingly, becoming a good human being has nothing ambiguous about it. Its simple formula is that of avoidance of double standards. One who lives his life by this formula is indubitably a person of the highest moral character.

Al-Risala, January-February 1999

❐

60

Faith and Reason

In its issue no. 134 (1992), the journal, *Faith and Reason*, published from Manchester College, Oxford (England), brought out an article titled, 'The Relationship between Faith and Reason', by Dr Paul Badham. Paul Badham is a Professor of Theology and Religious Studies at St. David's College, Lampeter, in the University of Wales. His paper in this issue had been presented at a Conference of the Institute of Philosophy of the Russian Academy of Science in Moscow in November 1991.

Professor Badham's paper can indeed be called thought-provoking, and as such, is worth reading, but he has made certain points I do not agree with. He states that philosophical certainty should not be confused with religious certitude. He writes: "As a philosopher of religion I feel compelled to acknowledge that faith could never be placed on the same level of certainty as scientific knowledge" (p. 6). On the contrary, I feel that faith and belief can be placed on the same level of certainty as scientific theory. At least, in the twentieth century there is no real difference between the two.

Knowledge is composed of two kinds of things, Bertrand Russell puts it, knowledge of things and knowledge of truths. This dichotomy exists in religion as well as in science. For instance, to the scientist who regards biological evolution as a scientific fact, there are two aspects to be considered. One is related to the organic part of species and the other relates to the law of evolution, which is inherently and covertly operative in the continuing process of change among the species.

When an evolutionist studies the outward physical appearance of species, he may be said to be studying 'things', whereas when he studies the law of evolution, he deals with that aspect of the subject, which is termed as the study or knowledge of truths.

Every evolutionist knows that a basic difference between the two aspects. As far as the study of things or the phenomena of evolution is concerned, direct evidence is available. For instance, because the study of fossils found in various layers of the earth's crust is possible at the level of observation, working hypothesis may be based thereon.

On the contrary, as far as facts about the law of evolution are concerned, due to the impossibility of objective observation, direct argument is not possible. For instance, the concept of sudden mutations in the organs is entirely based on assumptions rather than on direct observation. In the case of mutations, external changes are observable, but the cause, that is, the law of nature, it is totally unobservable. That is why all the evolutionists make use of indirect argument, which in logic is known as inferential argument.

The concept of mutation forms the basis of the theory of evolution. However, there are two aspects to the matter. One comes under observation, but the second part is totally unobservable. It is only by making use of the principle of inference that this second part of evolution may be included in the theory of evolution.

It is commonplace that all the offspring of men or animals are not uniform. Differences of one kind or another are to be found. In modem times, this biological phenomenon has been scientifically studied. These studies have revealed spontaneous changes suddenly produced in the fetus in the mother's womb. It is these changes that are responsible for the differences between children of the same parents.

These differences between off-springs are observable. But the philosophy of evolution subsequently formed on the basis of this observation is totally unobservable and is based only on an argument. That is to say that the 'things' of evolution are observable, while the 'truths' inferred from observation are unobservable.

Now, what the evolutionist does is put a goat at one end and a giraffe at the other. Then taking some middle specimens of the fossils he forms a theory that the neck of one of the offspring of the earlier generation of the goat was somewhat taller. Then when this particular offspring with the taller neck gave birth, this tallness for generations over millions of years ultimately converted the initial goat with a taller neck into a species like the giraffe in its advanced stage. Charles Darwin writes of this change in his book *The Origin of Species*: "...it seems to me almost certain that an ordinary hoofed quadruped might be converted into a giraffe" (pg. 169).

In this case, the existence of differences between the various offspring of a goat is itself a known fact. But the accumulation of this difference, generation after generation, over millions of years resulting in a new species known as 'giraffe' is wholly unobservable and unrepeatable. This conclusion has been inferred from observation only; the whole process of mutation developing into a new species has never come under our direct observation.

Exactly the same is true of the subject of religion. One aspect of the study of religion is the study of its history, its personalities, its injunctions, its rites and its rituals. The above division (knowledge of things and knowledge of truths) amounts to a study of the 'things' of religion. In respect of religion, objective information is likewise available. As such, the study of religion too can be done on the basis of direct observations exactly as is done in the study of biological evolution.

The second aspect of the study of religion is what is termed, in general, beliefs pertaining to the unseen world. These are the beliefs that are beyond our known sensory world. That is the existence of God and the angels, revelation, hell and heaven, etc. In this other aspect of religion, direct observations do not exist. The study of religion must, therefore, be done in the light of that logical principle called inference on the basis of observation, that is, the same logical principle the evolutionists employ in the second aspect of their theory.

When we look at it the light of this principle, then both religion and science are at a par. Both have two equally different parts. One part is based on such scientific certainty which permits direct argument. The other part is based on scientific inference, for which only the principle of indirect argument may be used. Keeping this logical division before us, we can find no actual difference between the two.

The unnecessary apologia for religious uncertainty, made by Professor Badham, is occasioned by his inability to consider this difference, and his confusing one area of study with another. Making the error of false analogy, he is comparing the first part of science to the second part of religion and looking at the second part of religion in the light of the first part of science. This meaningless comparison is responsible for the ill-considered conclusions he has arrived at in his article.

Had the worthy Professor compared the first part of science to the first part of religion and the second part of science to the second part of the religion, his inferiority complex (as a man of religion) would have ceased to exist. He would have felt that, purely as a matter of principle, the wrong parallels had been drawn. The argument used in the first part of science is equally applicable to the first part of religion. Similarly, the argument applied to the second part of science is equally applicable to the second part of religion.

This is a truth, which has been acknowledged even by a staunch and leading atheist like Bertrand Russell. At the beginning of his book '*Why I am not a Christian*' he has set forth what he considers a valid argument. He points out that in his view all the great religions of the world — Buddhism, Hinduism, Christianity, & Islam—were all untrue and harmful, and that it is not possible to prove their validity from the logical point of view. Those who have opted for one religion or the other have done so, according to Russell, under the influence of their traditions and environment, rather than on the strength of argument.

However, Bertrand Russell has admitted this fact when he says, "There is one of these arguments which is not purely logical. I mean the argument from design. This argument, however, was destroyed by Darwin."

He intends here to say that the existence of God is proved by the argument that in this world where there is design, there should be a designer. He admits that this method of argument in its nature is the same as that used to prove scientific concepts. However, even after this admission, he rejects this argument by saying that it has been destroyed by Darwinism.

This is, however, a wholly baseless point, as Darwin's theory is related to the Creator's process of creation rather than to the existence of Creator. To put it briefly, Darwinism states that the various species found in the world were not separate creations but had changed from one species into separate species over a prolonged period of evolution by a process of natural selection.

It is obvious that this theory is not related to the existence or non-existence of God. It deals with the process of creation instead of the creator. That is to say, if it was hitherto believed that God created each species separately, now after accepting the theory of evolution it has to be believed that God originally created an initial species which was invested with the capability of multiplying into numerous species. And then He set in motion a natural process in the universe favourable to such multiplication. In this way, over a long period of time this primary species fulfilled its potential by changing into innumerable species. To put it in another way, the theory of evolution is not a study of the existence of God, but simply of how God has displayed in the universe his power of creation. That is why Darwin himself has concluded his famous book *The Origin of Species* with these words:

There is grandeur in this view of life, that having been originally breathed by the Creator into a few forms or into one; and. that, whilst this planet has gone cycling on according to the fixed law of gravity, from so simple a beginning endless forms most beautiful and most wonderful have been, and are being evolved (pg. 408).

It is true that the new facts regarding the universe discovered in the twentieth century have revolutionized the world of logic. Now the difference between religious argument and scientific argument which had been erroneously conceived prior to the twentieth century has been eliminated. Now in respect of argument, the case of science too has reached exactly the same point as religion.

Newton (1642-1727) made a special study of the solar system, discovering laws governing the revolution of planets around the sun. His study was, however, confined to astronomical bodies, which can be called the macro-world. It is possible in the macro-world to weigh and measure things. As a result of the immediate impact of these discoveries, many began to think along the lines that reality was observable, and that proper and valid argument was one based on observation. It was under the influence of this concept that the philosophy generally known as positivism came into being.

However, the discoveries made in the first quarter of the century shook the very foundation of their preliminary theories. These later discoveries revealed that beyond this world of appearance, a whole world was hidden, which does not come under observation. It is only indirectly possible to understand this hidden world and present arguments in its favour. That is, by observing the effects of something, we arrive at an understanding which is an understanding of its existence.

This discovery altered the whole picture. When the access of human knowledge was limited to the macro-cosmic world, man was a prey to this misapprehension. But when human knowledge penetrated the micro-world, the academic situation changed on its own.

Now it was revealed that the field of direct argument was extremely limited. New facts that came to the knowledge of man were so abstruse that indirect or inferential argument alone was applicable. For instance, The German scientist, Wilhelm Rontgen found in 1895 during an experiment that on a glass before him some effects were observable, despite the fact that there was no known link between his experiment and the glass. He concluded that there was an invisible radiation, which was travelling at the speed of 186,000 miles per second. Due to the unknown nature of this radiation, Wilhelm Rontgen named it X-rays (*Encyclopedia Britannica*, 19/1058).

The twentieth century has seen the discoveries of a number of things like X-rays, which do not come under direct human observation. However, due to their effects having come to the knowledge of man, it was not possible to deny their existence. As a result of modern research, not only were different departments of science revolutionised but the science of logic too saw basic changes.

Now inferential reasoning was also accepted as a valid method of reasoning, for, without the discoveries like X-rays, the scientific structure of the atom, the existence of Dark Matter, etc., could not have been explained.

After the extension of this method of reasoning in modern times, argument on religious faith has become as valid as reasoning on scientific concepts. Exactly the same inferential logic that was employed to prove the newly discovered concepts of science was applicable to religious faiths to prove their veracity. Now differences in the criterion of logic have vanished.

Answer to Question

At the end of his article Professor Badham writes: And I have to acknowledge that the existence of so much evil and suffering in the world counts against any vision of an all-powerful and loving God (p.7)

Here I have to say that evil is a relative word. An evil is an evil so long as it cannot be explained. A doctor performs surgery on the patient's body, a judge sentences a criminal to be hanged. All this appears to be injustice, cruelty. But we do not call it so, simply because we have a proper explanation to give for the acts of the judge and the doctor. The same is true of the evil pointed out by the article writer.

The first point is that the evil existing in human society has not spread over the entire universe. Leaving aside the limited human world, the vast universe is perfect, par excellence. It is entirely free of any defect or evil.

Now the question arises: Why is there evil in the human world? To arrive at an understanding of this we shall have to understand the creation plan of the Creator. The creation plan of God provides the only criterion by which to judge the nature of the matter.

The creation plan of God as revealed to His Prophets is that this world is a testing ground, where man's virtue is placed on trial. It is in accordance with the records of this trial period that man's eternal fate will be decreed. It is for the purpose of this test that he has been granted freedom. In the absence of freedom, the question of life being a test would not arise.

The present evil is, in fact, a concomitant of this freedom. God desires to select those individuals who, in spite of being granted freedom, lead a disciplined and principled life. For individuals to prove their worth an atmosphere of freedom must be provided. Undoubtedly, due to such an atmosphere, some people will surely misuse this freedom and perpetrate injustice. But this is the inevitable price which has to be paid for such a creation plan to be brought to completion. No better creation plan can be envisaged for this world.

The present world appears meaningless when seen independently, that is, without joining the hereafter with it. But when we take this world and the hereafter together, the entire matter takes a new turn. Now this world becomes extremely meaningful and extremely valuable.

Al-Risala, January-February 1999

❐

61

The Making of the Indian Nation

Almost half a century has passed since India gained its Independence, but it is yet to join ranks of the developed countries. That is a dream still to be realised. And this is in spite of India being a large country with all kinds of potential.

One reason for this tragic failure is the Indian people's lack of national character. The majority of the deficiencies we find in the country today can be traced to this basic shortcoming. Bereft of this sterling quality, we have fallen short in taking the country towards progress and prosperity. Whenever a nation has made any progress, it has been due to this spirit of nationalism. Without such a spirit, no nation can advance itself either internally or externally.

Now the question arises as to why, during this period of just under 50 years, many countries have succeeded in fostering a strong, national spirit in their people, and now stand alongside developed countries like Singapore, Korea, Malaysia and Japan, etc., while India still lags far behind. There is one basic reason for this: attempting to achieve the possible by means that are impossible. Producing national spirit or character in India is certainly possible. It is just that we have set off on the wrong track, and once on it, it is difficult to retrace our steps and get on to the right track.

After Independence, an "Indian nation" had come into existence in the political and geographical sense. But, at the psychological level, the level of feelings and emotions, our position was still that of a nation in the making. For the desired national reconstruction to take place, our leaders proposed a recipe based on the concept of a common heritage with three main parts: religious unity, historical unity and cultural unity.

Religious unity implied that all religions were essentially one. It was believed that if this concept could take root in people's minds, it would produce a sense of unity all over the country. Historically, of course, this assumption was wrong; there is a long, sorry record of co-religionists fighting fiercely among themselves. For instance, in the war of *Mahabharat*, the warriors on both sides were from the Hindu religion. In the first and second world wars, the combatants on both sides were of the Christian faith. Babar had armed confrontations with his own co-religionists, finally inflicting decisive defeats on them. And so on.

The attempt to bring about religious unity in India has had active support right from the time of Akbar, who bolstered it politically, to present times, when intellectuals like Dr. Bhagwan Das (a contemporary of Jawaharlal Nehru) attempted to solve the problem with their encyclopedic knowledge of the subject. But this goal could never be achieved for the simple reason that the assumption that all religions are one and the same is incorrect; and no durable structure can be erected on false premises. It is an undeniable fact that there are differences between the various religions. Given these differences, it is difficult, if not impossible, for the adherents of one religion to reach the point of agreeing that the tenets and practices of another religion have an equal value. However, if the adherents of different religions see each other, first and foremost, as human beings, as members of the same human race, they can certainly accord each other equal respect. Through mutual respect, many social benefits can accrue, which would be rendered impossible in the wake of futile attempts at mutual recognition of religious beliefs.

Let us now look at how history comes into the picture. It is assumed that even where there are people of different persuasions, a common sense should of history will produce a common sense of nationhood. And where this is seen to be lacking, it is advocated that such a sense be inculcated. But this would again be an attempt to achieve the possible by means that are impossible. All countries, be they as small as Singapore, or as large as the USA, are inhabited by varied races and ethnic groups. In this respect, there are several different strands to their historical heritage. But in none of these countries has there been any attempt to bulldoze people into sharing a common sense of history. Instead, there has been an acknowledgment of each citizen's individuality. That is why, albeit imbued with different historical feelings, the various groups lead harmonious lives and are engaged in the common cause of nation building.

The third point concerns the acceptance of a common culture. This is wholly impracticable. Culture inevitably evolves a long historical process. It can never be imposed upon a group through any external agency.

After the World War II, a movement was launched in the USA to produce a common culture throughout the country by a process of Americanisation. A similar movement was launched in Canada, but in both countries, these initiatives were a failure. Ultimately, both had to abandon the idea of uni-culture and come to terms with multi-culture. In India, as elsewhere, this is the only possible solution.

The truth is that the only practicable basis of nationhood is patriotism. That is, the feeling on the part of the individual or group that their future is linked with one country and one country alone; that individual success is inextricably linked with the progress of the country; that the interests of the country must be held supreme, and that if sacrifices are required for the safety or advancement of the country, they must be willingly made. Without such feelings of patriotism, as are here defined, no country can be successfully run.

If the task of constructing the nation is to be successfully accomplished, we must rid ourselves of our obsession with such impracticable concepts as unity of religion, history and culture, and should forge ahead on the same lines as Singapore, Malaysia, Japan, Britain, France and America.

Our prime target should be the generation of patriotism in our country. And it should be a patriotism, which is based not on the past, but on the present and the future. The only way to do this is to instil in each and every individual a deep-rooted love of his country. Instead of wasting time on the impossible, we should concentrate on building the kind of national character to be found in developed countries. If we set ourselves sedulously to such tasks as these, we should, within the span of one generation, be able to create for ourselves the ideal nation.

Al-Risala, January-February 1999

❐

62

Man's Future

Gyani Zail Singh was born in Rajkot in Punjab in 1916. His father, a poor carpenter, could not give him a proper education. It was after joining politics that he acquired fame. Rising from the position of minister and chief minister, he ultimately came to hold the highest office in India—the President office. Having begun his life in a humble dwelling, he nevertheless managed to reach New Delhi's Rashtrapati Bhawan.

On November 29, 1994, he was badly injured in a car accident. He was immediately admitted to the Nehru Hospital at Chandigarh but he never recovered. Having begun his life with none of the trappings of greatness, he returned to that same state with his death on December 25, 1994.

A cartoon was published in the same newspaper, which brought the news of Gyani Zail Singh's demise. A fat man was shown perched on a chair, crippled with old age. These were his words:

"I have worked hard. And finally amassed all the money I'll never need. But I'm too old to enjoy it."

The same is true of all men. After great expenditure of physical and mental resources, man is able to achieve material progress. But when he reaches the height of success, the painful realisation dawns upon him, which is that this material progress is of no use to him. In spite of possessing everything, he is as helpless as the next person. How strange is man's destiny? He is in possession only of his past and present: he has no power over his future.

Here in this world wealth is as meaningless as poverty. Here, a royal life is as insignificant as a life in a lowly cottage.

Al-Risala, January-February 1999

❑

63

Peace in the Quran

At a three-day symposium held at the American University in Washington, on Feb 1998, I made a speech on Islam and Peace in one of its sessions. A part of this speech is given below:

"It is no exaggeration to say that Islam and violence are contradictory to each other. The concept of Islamic violence is so obviously unfounded that prima facie it stands rejected. The fact that violence is not sustainable in the present world is a sufficient indication that violence as a principle is quite alien to the scheme of things in Islam. Islam claims to be an eternal religion and, as such, could never afford to uphold any principle, which could not stand up to the test of time. Any attempt to bracket violence with Islam amounts, therefore, to casting doubt upon the very eternity of the Islamic religion. Islamic terrorism is a contradiction in terms, much like pacifist terrorism. And the truth of the matter is that, all the teachings of Islam are based directly or indirectly on the principle of peace."

The teachings of Islam in the *Qur'an* and *Hadith*:

The very word 'Islam' (from the Arabic *SLM*) connotes peace. According to a tradition of the Prophet, 'Peace is Islam.' (*Sahih Al Bukhari*) This means that peace is one of the prerequisites of Islam. Similarly, a *Hadith* states: A Muslim is one from whose tongue and hands people are safe. One of the attributes of God described in the *Quran* is *'As-Salam'*, which means peace and security. That is to say that God's Being itself is a manifestation of peace. 'Indeed, God is Peace'. (*Sahih Al Bukhari*) In the *Qur'an* divine guidance is likened to the paths of peace. (5:16)

According to Islam, Paradise is the ideal place for human abode, and is thus called the 'Home of Peace'. It is also said that the people of paradise will constantly utter the word 'peace'. It means that the social culture of the people of paradise will be based on peace.

The *Qur'an*, avers: "Reconciliation is best." (4:128), and judging by the consequences, the way of peace is far better than that of confrontation. By the law of Nature, God has decreed that success will be met with only on a reconciliatory path, and not on a confrontational or a violent course of action.

The wife of the Prophet of Islam, Aisha (daughter of Abu Bakr) said this of the general policy of the Prophet in social matters: 'Whenever the Prophet had an option between two courses of action, he always chose the easier (non-confrontational) one". (*Fath al-Bari*, 6/654)

This means that violent activism should not be indulged in if peaceful activism is an option. For, peace is the easier course as compared to violence.

For instance, trying to change the status quo in the very first stage of a movement is a hard option, while launching one's activities in the available sphere without doing so is an easier option.

Going to war in confrontational situations is a hard option while following conciliatory course in dealing with one's rival is easier. Countering aggression with aggression is a hard option, while countering aggression with patience and forbearance is an easier option. An agitational course of action is harder than employing quiet strategy. Adopting a radical method of reformation is harder than that of following a gradual method. Taking emotional extreme steps without a thought for their consequences creates difficulties. While a well-considered method, keeping an eye on the consequences, gives much better results. The policy of confrontation with a ruler is a harder option, while initiating one's action, by avoiding the ruler, in the sphere of education and learning is an easier option. These instances show us the easier and harder options, as demonstrated by the *Hadith*.

The truth is that peace in Islam is the 'rule', while war is the 'exception'. All the teachings of Islam and the practical life of the Prophet of Islam testify to this.

The Example of the Prophet of Islam

The Prophet of Islam received his first revelation in 610 A.D. in Mecca. God ordained that he carry out the mission of *Tawheed*. There arose a great problem in relation to this mission.

The house of the *Kabah*, which was built as the house of monotheism by the Prophet Ibrahim and his son Ismail, later on became a center of polytheism.. The first revelation might well have demanded the purification of the *Kabah*. But the first revelation made in the *Qur'an* was: Purify your vestments. (74:4) This means to purify one's moral character. If, in the first stage the Prophet had been commanded to purify the *Kabah* while Mecca was still under the domination of his foes, this would have surely precipitated clash and confrontation. Therefore, according to the command of the first revelation, the Prophet continued to perform his prayers peacefully in the *Kabah* for a period of 13 years.

Similarly, the Prophet and his companions circumambulated the *Kabah* on the occasion of *Umrah al-Hudaybiyah* in 629 A.D. During that time, the *Kabah* was still under the occupation of others.

The Prophet of Islam proceeded thus in order to avoid war and confrontation with the idolaters, and so that the atmosphere of peace should be maintained. The entire life of the Prophet is a practical demonstration of this peace-loving policy. At the time of migration from Mecca, the non-believers were all set to wage war, but the Prophet avoided this by quietly leaving his homeland for Medina.

On the occasion of the Hudaybiyah treaty in 628 A.D., a state of war prevailed. But the Prophet unilaterally accepted all the conditions of the idolaters and negotiated a peace treaty. On the occasion of the battle of *Khandaq* (trench), the 12,000 strong army of the *Qur'aysh* had camped at the borders of Medina in order to do battle. But the Prophet and his companions dug a long trench to set up a buffer between himself and his enemies, thus avoiding bloodshed.

The mission of Islam is based on monotheism. The goal of Islam is to make people realize the existence of the one and only God and to strive to bring about a revolution in their hearts and minds in order that they may love God as is His due. And the greatest concern of a man should be to remember and worship his Creator.

Such a peaceful mission cannot afford wars and violent confrontations. When a state of war and violence prevails, the normal atmosphere is vitiated and such circumstances as would foster intellectual movements and spiritual reformation cannot be effectively created. It cannot be denied that peaceful circumstances produce a propitious environment for Islam, while violent circumstances inevitably result in antagonism towards Islam.

War: A State Action

In Islam, war is not the prerogative of the individual but of an established government. Only an established government can declare war. In other words, individuals can pray on their own, but they cannot wage wars of their own. Only when a war is declared by the ruling government, can the public join in and support it, and not before that. Islam does not sanction individual actions on this issue.

As a general principle, the *Qur'an* tells us that, even where an external attack is feared, the common man should not act independently, but should take the matter to the ruler, and then under his guidance take proper counter measures.

The *Hadith* also states that 'the ruler is a shield, fighting is done under him, and security is attained through him'. This clearly shows that the decision to do battle and its planning are the tasks of an established government. The common man can play his role as need be under government orders, and not independently.

This Islamic principle shows that there is no room for non-state warfare, which is what we generally call guerilla war. A guerilla war is fought by individual organisations, not by the State. As far as the State is concerned, if it wants to wage a defensive war against any country it has first —in obedience to the *Qur'an*— to issue a proper declaration. Only then can it wage a lawful war. In Islam, there is only 'declared' war. Therefore, in accordance with this principle, no proxy war in Islam can be lawful.

Most Islamic actions are governed by certain conditions. The waging of war is also thus subject to certain principles, one being that, even when a defensive war has been declared by the State, it will be aimed only at the combatants. Targeting non-combatants will be unlawful. The *Qur'an* enjoins us not to do battle with those who are not at war. Such people have to be dealt with kindly and equitably. But you are free to do battle with those who are fighting against you.

If, for instance, a Muslim state is at war with a particular nation, and this war is in conformance with Islamic principles, it should still not permit any destructive activities against non-combatants (civilians), as was done on September 11, 2001, in New York and Washington. Similarly, in Islamic war, Muslims are not permitted to commit suicidal bombings in order to destroy the enemy. Strapping explosives on to oneself and hurling oneself upon the civilian settlements of even those with whom one is at war, for the purpose of destroying the enemy, and in the process killing oneself deliberately, is totally un-Islamic. This can, in no way, be termed *'Shahadah'* (martyrdom). According to Islam, we can get martyred, but we cannot court death (martyrdom) deliberately.

Al-Risala, September-October 2001

❐

Glossary

A

Abbasid	– A clan that came to power during 750-1258.
Abraham	– Prophet and the patriarch of the three Abrahamic religions—Christianity, Judaism and Islam
Abu Dawud	– was a Persian scholar of *Hadith* who compiled the third of the six "canonical" *Hadith* collections.
Akhirah	– An Islamic term referring to life hereafter.
Arafat	– Mount Arafat on the east of Mecca City.
Athar	– the sayings and deeds of the Prophet Muhammad's Companions
Ayodhya	– An ancient city of India, believed to be the birthplace of Hindu God, Lord Rama.

B

Babri Masjid	– A mosque in Ayodhya, which was built by Mir Baqi, one of the Generals of the Mughal Emperor, Babur.
Babri Masjid Action Committee	– A committee set up by the Government of India after the demolition of Babri Masjid.
Baital Maqdis	– Also known as Al Aqsa Mosque it is situated in Jerusalem and is third

holiest mosque in Islam.

Bhagavad Gita or Gita – A Hindu scripture in Sanskrit, which is also a part of the Hindu epic Mahabharata.

Bible – It is a collection of sacred texts that Jews and Christians consider to be a product of divine inspiration.

Bakkah – Name used for the city of Mecca in Qur'an.

C

Caliph – Also known as Khalifah, it is a Muslim civil and religious leader.

Cordoba – City in Ancient Spain, it is also known as Andalusia.

D

Dar Al Nadwa – Tribal Parliament of Mecca at the time of Prophet Muhammad.

Dargahs – A shrine built over the grave of a revered figure.

David – One of the Prophets in the three Abrahamic religions—Christianity, Judaism and Islam.

Dhikr (Zikr) – An Arabic term for remembrance of God.

F

Fasad – Violence

Fatwa – A non-binding legal opinion of a qualified jurist on issues pertaining to Islamic law.

G

Gabriel – According to the three Abrahamic faiths, He is an Archangel with the task of bringing the word of God to the Prophets.

Gaddis – Concept of self-styled centre of authority at shrines.

Ghulu	–	Extremism.

H

Hadith	–	Record of the traditions and sayings of the Prophet Muhammad.
Hajj	–	An Islamic pilgrimage to Mecca which every adult Muslim must make at least once in his lifetime.
Hanafi	–	One of the four schools of thoughts of religious (Islamic) jurisprudence.
Hanbali	–	One of the four schools of thoughts of religious (Islamic) jurisprudence.
Hijab	–	Veil.
Hijrah	–	It is an Arabic term for migration. This term is used to define the migration done by Prophet Muhammad and his companions from Mecca to Medina.
Hudaibiyah	–	A place on the outskirts of the City of Mecca, where the famous peace treaty between Prophet Muhammad and Qur'aysh took place.

I

Ibadah	–	Worship.
Ibn Majah	–	Collections of *Hadiths* by IbnMajah.
Iman	–	Faith
Imam Shaf'ii	–	He was an Arab Muslim theologian who founded Shaf'ii school of thought.

J

Jahiliyah	–	It is an Arabic term for period before Islam.
Jihad	–	It is an Arabic word for struggle.
Jilab	–	It is an Arabic word for long gown.

K

Kabah	–	Considered in Islam as the house of God, it is situated in the city of Mecca. It was built by Prophet Abraham and his son Prophet Ismail.

Kalima – It is the formal content of the declaration of faith.

Khandaq – Trench.

Khanqahs – A place meant for the gatherings of Sufi brotherhood.

Khatimiya – One of the Sufi spiritual order.

Kitab e Wahy – These are the Revealed Books, namely, Torah, Zabur, Gospel and Qur'an.

Khutba – Sermon.

M

Mahabharat – It is one of the two major Sanskrit epics of ancient India.

Maliki – One of the four schools of thoughts of religious (Islamic) jurisprudence.

Mishkat – One of the books of *Hadith*.

Mecca – A city in Saudi Arabia, where Hajj is performed also the birthplace of Prophet Muhammad.

Medina – City in Saudi Arabia, it is also the resting place of Prophet Muhammad.

Musnad Ahmad – Also known as Ahmad, it is a collection of sayings of Prophet Muhammad.

Murdiya – One of the Sufi spiritual orders.

N

NafsAmmara – Arabic term for ego.

NafsLawwama – It is an Arabic term for conscience.

Naqshbandiya – One of the Sufi orders.

P

Peepal – A fig tree considered religious by the followers of Hinduism.

Pir – A Sufi master or spiritual guide.

Q

Qadri – One of the Sufi spiritual order.

Qital – Violent activism

Qur'an – Central religious text of Islam.

Qur'aysh – An Arab tribe that historically

		inhabited and controlled the city of Mecca and Kabah. The Prophet Muhammad was born into the Banu Hashim clan of the Qur'aysh tribe.

R

Rabbaniyat	–	Spirituality
Rashtrapati Bhawan	–	Residence for the President of India.
RSS	–	It is known as Rashtriya Swayamsevak Sangh

S

Sabr	–	Patience
Sadqah	–	Giving Alms.
Sahaba	–	Arabic term used for Companions of Prophet Muhammad.
Sarsanghchalak	–	He is known as the Head of RSS.
Sahih Al Bukhari	–	Collection of *Hadiths*, it is recognized as the most authentic collections of Sunnah of Prophet Muhammad.
Sahih Al Muslim	–	Collection of *Hadiths*, it is recognized as the second most authentic collections of Sunnah of Prophet Muhammad.
Sahifatul Medina	–	It is also known as the Medina Charter.
Sah-Sarkaryawah	–	It is also known as Joint General Secretary of RSS.
Seerah	–	Biography of Prophet Muhammad.
Shankaracharya	–	He is a commonly used title for head of monasteries called Math as in the Advaita Vedanta (Hindu) tradition.
Shaf'ii	–	One of the four schools of thoughts of religious (Islamic) jurisprudence.
Shar'iah	–	Religious law, part of Islamic tradition.
Sulh al-Hudaybiyah	–	The famous peace treaty signed between Prophet Muhammad and Qur'aysh at Hudaibiyah.
Sunnah	–	Sayings, habits and practises of Prophet Muhammad.

Surah – Verse in the Qur'an.

T

Tabi'un – Companions of Prophet Muhammad

Tariqa – Sufi Order

Tasawwuf – Sufism

Tawheed – Oneness of God.

Tirmidhi – Collection of sayings of Prophet Muhammad.

U

Ulema – Islamic religious scholar.

Umayyad – Meccan Clan which came to power during 661–750 ce.

W

Wudu – Ablution or act of cleansing oneself with water before praying.

Z

Zinah – Arabic word for beauty

Zawiya – Western African term for Islamic (Sufi) religious school.

❒

Bibliography

1. *Qur'an*
2. *Islam and the Modern Age* (Urdu Edition), 1973
3. *Hijab al-Mar'ah al-Muslimah fil Kitab was-Sunnah*, 1914
4. At-Tafsir Al-Usmani with notes by Shaikh Mahmud ul Hasan, (Bijnore 1950)
5. *Abu Dawud Sunan* (book of Hadith)
6. *Sahih Al Bukhari* (book of Hadith)
7. *Sahih Al Muslim* (book of Hadith)
8. Muhammad 'Ali As Subuni, Rawai Al Bayan
9. *Encyclopaedia Britannica*
10. *The Book of Matthew*
11. *The Discovery of India*, 1946
12. *Verdict on India*, 1944
13. *The Influence of Islam on Indian Culture*
14. Fath al-Bari
15. Seerat ibn Hisham
16. Musnad Ahmad
17. *Organiser*, weekly, August, 1990
18. *Organiser*, weekly, December, 1993
19. *Organiser*, weekly, July, 1988
20. *Organiser*, weekly, April, 1993

21. *Organiser*, weekly, March, 1993
22. *Organiser*, weekly, April, 1994
23. *Organiser*, weekly, February, 1994
24. *Al-Risala*, January, 1989
25. *Al-Risala*, August-September, 1992
26. *Al-Risala*, November, 1991
27. *Al-Risala*, October, 1989
28. *Al-Risala*, May-June, 1998
29. *Al-Risala*, February, 1988
30. *Al-Risala*, May, 1987
31. *Al-Risala*, January-February, 1999
32. *Al-Risala*, August-September-October, 2001
33. *Origin of Species.*
34. *Why I am not a Christian.*
35. *Al-Risala*, January-March, 2015

□□□